FRENCH SAHIB

A NOVEL

Pierre Fréha

Translated from Original French
by Shonu Nangia

ROMAN Books
www.roman-books.co.uk

Copyright © 2011 Pierre Fréha

ISBN 978-93-80905-26-6

Typeset in Adobe Garamond Pro

First published in 2011
Paperback Edition 2012

1 3 5 7 9 8 6 4 2

British Library Cataloguing in Publication Data.
A catalogue record for this book is available from the British Library.

ROMAN *Books*
26 York Street, London W1U 6PZ, United Kingdom
2nd Floor, 38/3, Andul Road, Howrah 711109, WB, India
www.roman-books.co.uk | www.roman-books.co.in

Printed and bound in India by
Roman Printers Private Limited
www.romanprinters.com

FRENCH SAHIB

Family Tree

Radhika Rao (53) **+** Sushil (*defunct*)

Suneet (32) **+** Ammu (28) Abhi (31) Pradeep (30) Brinda (19)

Santosh (5) Amit (2)

Olivier Delcourt (72) **+** Bernadette (70)

Jean-Bernard (51) **+** Noémie (43) Christophe (49) **+** Béatrice (40)

Benjamin (9) Alice (12) Jean-Lou (8)

Olivier Delcourt ***** Domitille Surprenant (*defunct*)

Philippe (45) ❤ Pradeep

Olivier Delcourt ***** Laetitia Demasure (56)

Carole (34) ❤ Nadège (28)

Santz (2)

+ = marriage
* = affair
❤ = civil union

1

Rainbow in the Chennai Sky

Mrs. Rao made a face. *Her* face. It was a metamorphosis so rare and complete that only twice in their lives had her children seen it before.

She winced a few more times before letting her jaw relax.

They always made mockery of her problems. She would show them that she was in no mood for jokes.

Vexed is an ineffectual word, almost ridiculous. But what other word could she pull out of the bag? There was no point looking for a better substitute, one might as well stick to it. Anything else would be yet another word. She conjured up an adverb: *incredibly*. However, a pompous phrase such as "I am incredibly vexed" would cause some suspicion and would be just as unlikely to produce an effect on her blasé offspring. No, dramatic grandiloquence wouldn't do the trick. If she had simply said something like "children, you have no idea how serious this is!" the first one wouldn't have even looked up from the computer and the second one from the newspaper, while the third would have probably just walked away cheerfully, without even taking the trouble to ask what the matter was.

Each family has its special unspoken rules, monstrous and sublime. This is what the Rao family had turned into. Perhaps in the past Radhika had wantonly abused her histrionic abilities and now her battle-hardened children had learnt to take everything with a pinch of salt. It was something she would have to deal with now.

The last time that Mrs. Rao had put on such an expression was not so long ago. Dr. Panayappan had summoned her to his cramped office in Malar Hospital in Adyar and had informed her about her husband's hopeless state. He had not minced words. Mrs. Rao had returned home and broken into sobs in front of her bewildered children. But before doing so, she had contorted her face for an entire minute.

"What's going on? How is Daddy feeling?"

She had refused to reply. The grimace could not be traded for words so quickly. True emotions called for corporeal expression. Language impoverished feelings. Mrs. Rao could not bear the pressure of tragic news without deforming her proud face.

The first time that Mrs. Rao had contorted her face like that was some twenty years ago. Suneet, her oldest son, had seen it happen with his own eyes. Radhika had resigned herself to being separated from Pradeep, her baby, for a year. The doctors had insisted on a change of climate. One of her sisters-in-law lived in Darjeeling at that time. The journey had taken forever. She hadn't liked the atmosphere there and had almost brought the child back with her. But it had to be done. Neither Sushil nor the doctors would have pardoned her for such waywardness. A few minutes before the bus was to depart, Mrs. Rao had avenged herself and made her displeasure known by stiffening her jowl into a scowl hideous enough to make one weep. Suneet, that day, had barely recognized his mother.

What could the matter be today? What calamity were they about to face? With barely any make-up on, Radhika was staring ahead. It was a tactic. Abhi and Suneet, accustomed to their mother's excesses, exchanged meaning looks and decided to slink away from the room.

"Where are you going? Are you leaving right now?" cried out Mrs. Rao, feeling concerned that she was going to lose her audience.

"What's the matter, Mummy?"

"Sit down, please."

Brinda, pretending to be in the know, assumed a grave look of her own, not very unlike her mother's. For some time now, this youngest sibling had been trying to climb up the family ladder by ousting the older brothers. She had just turned nineteen, an age when she had begun aspiring to power within the family. Suneet, married and a father with two children, spent as much time at his mother's in Adyar (where they all met) as at his own house which was at a distance of less than ten minutes (whenever the auto-rickshaw skipped the red lights and made its way with determination, zigzagging between the potholes of Chennai).

"I must talk to you," Radhika declared to them.

"We also need to talk to you," responded in Suneet, jokingly. "Come on, don't always be so serious, Radha Rani."

"You never show me any importance," she muttered. "Which is fine. You are all so young, even you Suneet, even you! Look Bira, doesn't he still look like a little boy? It's a pity that he's such an ill-mannered little boy."

"Whose fault is it?"

Mrs. Rao shrugged with indifference.

"You also sit down, Abhi, please. I have enough problems on my plate already."

"Whatever!" mumbled Suneet.

"And if I remain standing, are you going to have any more?"

"Don't you start off now as well. I'm going to complain to Ammu. I don't get any respect from you at all."

"Okay, I'll sit down. In that case, Brinda, bring me some tea. I could really do with a nice cup."

"You think I'm your maidservant?" his sister retorted.

Mrs. Rao realized the danger: they were straying from the subject, the very serious subject that she wanted to talk about. The family summit she had called to order was turning into a bitter-sweet fiasco. They were incapable of being still. She felt tempted to blight them with one of her special looks.

"Go and bring him some tea, Bira. You can see he is acting like such a clown today."

"Oh, so I'm a clown now! Don't bother, Bira dear, my tea should be ready. I had already put the water on. I'll get it myself."

He got up and disappeared into the kitchen.

"And now we have to wait for him, that's what!" sighed Mrs. Rao. "We always have to wait for someone or the other, it's always like that. But at least you are all here today."

They all met together several times a week, but accidentally, according to Mrs. Rao. But whenever she wanted to have a meeting, poof, there was sure to be someone who would slip away.

"So where is Pradeep?" Suneet asked. You don't want to talk to him? We are four of us. Why isn't he here?"

Somewhere from the back of her throat Mrs. Rao produced a hoarse sound, and the anguished look that she had had on her face earlier reappeared faintly. Suneet and Brinda exchanged glances. It was Dipu this time who was in the hot seat. Mrs. Rao's pained look had just unmasked the culprit.

Feeling shaken all of a sudden, both Suneet and Brinda waited silently for Abhi to return with his tea. No longer were they in a mood to fool around. A powerful oppressive feeling had overcome Suneet, as if he had understood. Good Lord, anything but that! So that's what the grimace meant! It had better not be that! For the longest time, their lives had revolved around Pradeep's sickness. For the past eight years his leukemia had not been mentioned, his remission had been total! Total, according to the results of the blood test, he repeated to himself.

His eyes filled with tears. Together again at home, without Daddy, confronted with the same sorrow. Oh Dipu, don't do this, don't do this to us, said the older brother to himself. Your brother has been miraculously cured! He could still hear the words of the doctor who had prescribed the chemotherapy.

"You can cry, my dear," Radhika emphasized with a yawn. "Bad news is bad news! And God, when he sees your tears, will surely help us," she added without much reflexion, only half convinced herself, for her devotion seldom went beyond such invocations. "What is Abhi doing? Brinda dear, please, go and see. He hardly enters the kitchen, he is probably still looking for a cup."

Brinda got up and went to find her brother. She found him sitting on a stool.

"Ma is waiting. What are you doing?"

"I don't like it when she makes that face."

"She just did it again."

"I don't like it. She had that look when she announced Daddy was dying."

"Maybe so. But whose death could she possibly announce now?" the pragmatic Bira asked, too young to remember the days when Dipu would spend as much time at the hospital as at home. "Don't stay here like that, come on. It's going to be no use."

Abhi improvised a plan.

"I'm leaving. I have things to do. You can tell me everything later. I have to go to a game. I need the exercise."

"You said you don't like it when she scowls like that, aren't you interested in finding out?" she persisted.

"Nope!"

Abhi sneaked off. Just one minute with Mummy and sometimes it took up to a week to recover. Torture caused by a simple random remark, or something said over the phone. Sometimes she would not say it but think it so loud that it hit the ears like a burst of thunder. Her silence, all the things she left unsaid, acted like poison. One felt like just running away, being out of reach, safe from the deafening din of family life.

Mrs. Rao had grievances of her own: Abhi was so hard to understand. There was a certain gentleness about him that she found suspect. It rendered him, well, out of reach. Suneet, at least, didn't have that aura of mystery. He was accessible and well-settled (married). Locked up in his social armor, the glinting metal of his soul was enough to put an observer off balance: he had his act together and everything about him was so clear and dazzling.

What she found so striking about them, was how they could all so quickly disappear. Why were they all prone to disappearing so fast? They fled from conversations, real conversations. What were they afraid of? What had she done to them?

As she waited with a sense of foreboding, Radhika sipped the tea that Abhi had abandoned. Since he was no longer there and would probably not be returning anytime during the day, she decided to postpone the Summit. There was going to be no use talking to Suneet or to that cheeky Brinda if the energy that she derived from the presence of all of her children was going to be missing. There was a subtle interplay of influences within the family that lent itself to the formation of the most surprising alliances. Perhaps it was mere caprice, or perhaps it was because that inscrutable Abhi had ditched them without the least consideration for his mother that she announced the end of the official meeting. They were free to spend some more time together if they wanted to, but they were no longer liable to be called to order by the force of a grimace.

Abhi walked over the bridge without looking at the hospital on his right where his father had breathed his last. He made a left turn and walked for half an hour before he got to Elliot's Beach. This was his favorite beach, his most preferred spot in Adyar. He liked Besant Nagar. There were fewer dilapidated buildings, fewer broken pavements, and fewer garbage dumps. And more greenery, sometimes hidden behind the compound-walls. The history of the place was very palpable. The interwoven paradoxes of the southern part of the city lent it that impression. Abhi was very attached to Chennai. It was no longer called Madras, at least not officially (it was a little hard to get used to the new name, but it wasn't as bad as getting used to Mumbai). And even though in the wide world beyond, tourists recounted horror stories about the condition of the proud Tamil capital, Abhi knew all about its treasures. He was not a son of the soil (the Rao family was originally from Bombay), but he just felt a strong and inexplicable love for the city. Chaotic, overcrowded, or dilapidated, it didn't matter to him. Adyar irradiated with an almost invisible charm that gave it a force which neither foreign nor Indian tourists took the time to discover.

He arrived at the mouth of the Adyar River. The bridge between the two banks was broken in the middle. He had always remembered it being that way. Every particle, every inch of space, including the shanties along the bank, which looked miserable but nevertheless sported satellite dishes on their roofs, seemed to bathe in an atmosphere half profane, half divine. The redundant bridge itself was of both the worlds: the last pillar of a temple as well as the victim of an administrative decision halting its construction. Elliot's Beach had witnessed a certain Leadbeater inaugurate a new chapter in the eventful history of the Theosophical Society with its high walls enclosing an immense, almost terrifying, dwelling. It was on this beach that he had spotted the young Krishnamurti who would later acquire a house in the early 1930's. Located on Greenways Road, the house happened to be next door to the Rao residence.

Not too far away from there, in Alwarpet, Pradeep, Radhika Rao's youngest son, had begun to make Philippe Delcourt feel uneasy about the whole thing. Pradeep had come at nine o'clock sharp to pick up Philippe Delcourt. Their destination: the Rao residence in Adyar; their objective: an introduction with the family! The Frenchman didn't know what to expect, he hadn't even recovered from his jet lag. A time difference of four hours and thirty minutes.

"You've told her, right?"

Pradeep's face turned red like a beetroot. He was standing in front of the mirror in the bathroom with the door half open. Philippe was looking for something in his suitcase.

"No."

"Why not? Why haven't you?"

"Do you think it's that easy? Do you realize where we are? In India! You are in India. I . . . I need time. It's not the right time to say anything, don't push it."

His tone was firm. The young Indian brushed back his thick black hair with confidence. It was obvious. Tell his family? Why not just show up at home inebriated? It would be the same thing.

"You are making such a big deal out of it. I'm sure that . . . "

A big deal? He absolutely had no idea!

"You don't understand this at all. There's no use insisting."

Dipu felt as if he was already humiliated, rejected by his family, and even threatened by Krishna himself. Well, not Krishna. No one could manipulate Krishna, no one. But his mother, how would she react? Philippe was mistaken – even if he were to say it, even if he were to tell her, she would somehow find a way of remaining in denial. The words were unutterable. And she had acted surprisingly cold the last few days, as if she

16

had guessed something. So had she guessed? On the other hand, Dipu remembered with some resentment the contradictory promises he had made in Europe. What about them now? The buttons of the Frenchman, who had just arrived in Chennai a few days before, were definitely getting pushed.

He checked himself out in the mirror again. Fear really had a funny effect on you. His hair looked so bad. She would definitely comment on it. Even his mustache, unevenly trimmed, was not pleasing to him.

Here they were, about to meet his mother and Philippe was bringing up all these annoying issues that had relevance only in the West, not here, especially not in the South. Although the North, he reflected, hardly fared better in this regard. Bombay or Delhi, maybe, and Bangalore too perhaps, but in any case, even the relative freedoms that existed in some cities couldn't undermine the importance of family. His heart began to beat faster. How would she react? In Paris, he had enjoyed complete freedom . . .

Morale does impact physical appearance. The mass of hair on Dipu's head had begun to resemble a jungle ever since Philippe had set foot in India. It was bizarre but true. The chaos had spread to new territory.

He took his comb and dipped it into the jar of brilliantine.

"You've been here less than a week and already you are reminding me about a promise that you claim I made, in Paris. I think we only talked about it, when we were in Florida, do you remember?"

It sounded like, well, bad faith, an involuntary act maybe. "Now we're really going to be late, and she'll blight me with her looks."

Don't look at me like that, Radha Rani. Why are you so uncompromising?

I'm like India.

No, don't say that, Mummy, India isn't like that.

You don't know India very well then.

In the other corner of the room, Philippe was struggling with a long piece of fabric.

"You promised me that . . . "

"What promise?"

"We were at Chouchou's," he continued, as he tried to adjust his new white dhoti that Dipu had given him.

Chez Chouchou was a French restaurant with bright neon signs at the intersection of Fruitville Street and Orange Avenue in the heart of Sarasota in Florida.

"No no no! Not like this!" exclaimed Pradeep. "Not like this. You have to start all over again. I told you yesterday you have to tighten it and tuck it in from the left. It's quite simple. And then you fold it a couple of times on the other side so that the golden edge is visible.Like this."

"I'll never get it. It's a real hassle," he lashed out, overcome with panic as well. "I would like to put my jeans back on again, there's no need to complicate things the first time."

Dipu looked on as his French friend struggled with the five meter long piece of fabric.

"Try once again."

Blue skies accompany the rains in November in Chennai as the monsoons begin to come to an end.The locals are indifferent to the rain. While the heavy downpour thrills the urchins in the streets, it does bother the tourists. Adhering to the advice proffered by their travel guides, most tourists spend less time in the capital of Tamil Nadu and instead opt for the idyllic beaches of Mahabalipuram, a low-key heritage village with thousands of years of history that lies not too far on the highway to Pondicherry.

"Impossible!"announced Philippe after yet another failed

attempt. "It keeps falling off. Where are my jeans?"

Pradeep turned around.

"Please wear the dhoti. She'll be very happy. It'll create a much less tense atmosphere," he added, feeling his moustache with his tongue. "We will need that!"

"I feel like such an idiot."

"And you don't have to walk like you are wearing a straitjacket."

"Can I roll it up?"

"Absolutely not."

"Why not?"

"Not at my mother's. Besides it's not that hot. Relax your body. Try feeling more casual."

Unconvinced, Philippe launched his attack. "How can people wear such things?"

"It's comfortable. And anyways, it's the traditional outfit."

"Are you sure the dhoti is indispensable for this meeting?"

"Indispensable, no."

Pradeep stood in front of the mirror feeling anxious. There had to be a common ground, a compromise, between a promise made in Florida (after the leek fondue, just before the tray with the pasteurized cheeses) and the reality of family in India. He picked up his hairbrush. He was no chicken.

"I feel hurt, very well, just wear your jeans," he uttered, without really meaning what he said. "Let's not argue anymore about it. No, not like this, I've already explained. You've got to raise it from the waist so that it doesn't touch the floor. It's not a wedding gown."

"Like this?"

"Just wear your jeans."

"No, this is fine. I think I can manage. It's not falling off. It's properly tied."

Dipu whistled softly.

"You think so? Wear the jeans."

"That's not what you wanted."

"It's less risky."

"I'm pretty sure it won't fall off."

Dipu emitted another soft whistle.

"It could. You never know. Where are your jeans?"

"You think so?"

He nodded his head, or rather shook it from right to left, a gesture that the Frenchman had learnt to identify, if not imitate, correctly. In India one said yes, or almost yes, by appearing to say no. This spectacular gesture by itself would have been enough for him to fall in love with the country he was visiting for the second time in his life.

While the *Foreign Sahib*, as Leela—the maid who came to do the dishes and clothes—called him, was slipping into his comfortable jeans, Pradeep concluded his hair brushing session. It was high time they left.

Tall and broad shouldered, the sahib from Paris greeted Leela as she arrived at that very moment. Though he didn't know any Hindi, nor a word of Tamil, he had overheard a conversation between Attik, the male servant from Uttar Pradesh, and the young migrant washerwoman from Bombay. He had no idea what they were saying about him as he stood right there between the sink and the terrace door, but Leela had pronounced the words *foreign sahib* twice. When Philippe checked with him later, Pradeep confirmed that the foreign sahib was indeed him.

"I'm the foreign sahib?"

"It's you. A gentleman from another country."

Leela, dressed in a yellow sari, addressed Pradeep in Hindi.

"She says she will not wash anything today. She will do it all tomorrow."

"Namaste, Leela," said Philippe with a smile.

"Namaste," she responded reluctantly, without looking at him.

She had from the very first day rebuffed the Frenchman's friendly overtures. Ostensibly because of the language barrier, she avoided him without the least embarrassment, as if she was within her rights to do so.Her avoidance was only too obvious. She had however not reckoned with the conciliatory nature of her new employer who had one morning even gone to the extent of inviting her to have tea with him. She had refused. The foreign sahib may very well have had impeccable democratic manners, but as far as she was concerned he could take his democratic manners elsewhere!She had no desire to sip tea with the sahib.

"And with me," went one step further Attik, who slept on the floor in the living room, "he didn't want me to stand behind his chair when he was having dinner."

"Why?"

"I didn't budge, and I served him," he continued, indifferent to the question posed. "The sahib doesn't sleep well," he randomly added. "He got up and went to the bathroom to piss five times last night."

The young Muslim spoke a little bit of English and could occasionally communicate with Philippe.

"Ready to go?"

"One sec!"

"Always one sec. Ah, that's right, I had forgotten . . . "

"What?"

"You are functioning on IST, Indian Standard Time."

Pradeep responded with a shrug. Naturally! In Europe, one was always doing things, always being punctual, on top of things. One was always running, doing this, doing that, which took its toll. Even in Bombay, the supreme reference point, one didn't rush about so much. True, you had to rush to catch the crowded local trains, but you could slow down your pace once you got off onto the platform. He was now back home in Chennai, among his people, and he was rediscovering the sweet pleasure of the languorous pace that is characteristic of the Indian way of life. No foreign sahib was going to dictate to him how much time he could have to prepare himself for a family reunion that promised to be as significant an event as his own birth or the Independence of India. It was delicious to live life in the mode of lateness with the energy of an entire nation behind one. And besides, how could Philippe, with his ignorance of India, understand the soothing rhythms of IST. A child of GMT, he needed to learn new lessons about the flow of time. India would see to that!

The slower of the two was not the one you might believe. Philippe pretended to be efficient when confronted with delay, which wasn't necessarily the best strategy.

"Mummy must've prepared only some light snacks," he announced by way of vengeance. "She seems to be feeling tired ever since I got here."

"What kind of snacks? If only you knew how excited I am about meeting your family."

He could hardly believe what he had just said. What kind of snacks? It would take many centuries of globalization before the thin slices of chewy meat that Europeans were so crazy about appeared on Indian plates. During the six years and seven months (he knew this figure by heart) that he had been in the West, mainly France, Dipu had successfully stayed away from such food. The Brahmin in him had accomplished the feat of adhering to the diet of his caste.

"I don't know," he replied, and as Attik and Leela were having a conversation on the terrace (actually she was shaking the rug with her arms wide open while he watched), he also added, "my Krishna."

"Hare Krishna."

"I am ready."

"Great! You have shaved your mustache! This is what I call

marking the occasion."

"I don't know what came over me. I saw it in the mirror and I decided it needed to go before I introduced you to them. Everything will go well, won't it?"

"Yes, Anon. Don't worry."

"Don't call me that in front of my brothers, please. They might wonder what's going on."

Some months earlier, Pradeep Rao, in the final stages of his Master's in French had told him: "I'll come to see you anon."

"Anon? Anon!" exclaimed Philippe. Do you even know the meaning of that word?

"Of course I do," Dipu retorted with his inimitable accent. Philippe continued his teasing.

"It's very old fashioned. Where did you learn this kind of French?"

"I learnt it," he replied dryly, swallowing half his sentence. "It's obsolete."

"I'll come anon," had insisted the Indian, who didn't quite understand this whole obsolete business. He was only repeating the word his old Parisian landlady used sometimes when she made him do some of her errands.

"And I'm going to call you Anon," threatened the Frenchman, "so that you learn correct French."

"You don't know anything, this IS proper French," said Dipu as the face of the old lady flashed in front of his eyes.

Thus, for some months now (and even after they had reached India) Philippe had been calling Dipu Anon. It was a nickname, something of a secret code, and although not entirely devoid of the intent to harass, it evoked a certain magic. Infusing sparkle and mischief in the atmosphere, it evoked memories of anticipated events. Whenever feelings became too strong, they needed to be expressed without words. It was then that Philippe called him Anon. The beauty of the early days would come alive.

The moment of a very serious and dangerous meeting was drawing near. They were about to meet the Raos. The sky suddenly became dark as they climbed into the rickshaw. As they reached Adyar, the rain stopped and a rainbow appeared in the sky.

2

The Missing Mustache

To acquaint oneself with an ideal *foreign sahib*, the authentic one, one would have had to go to Suresnes, the chic Parisian satellite town where our own sahib's daddy lived. With his impeccable blue and gray suits, Delcourt Senior, Senator-Mayor, could easily have passed of as the head honcho of the East India Company, dutifully putting up with the tropical heat as he whiled away his time, or as the Governor of an overseas French territory, living in the colonial luxury of a winter residence, delegating the essential of his duties to his loyal subordinates. That was the stuff he was made up of.

The Senator had succumbed recently, albeit without much enthusiasm, to the allure of the Internet by accepting to reach out to voters through a website that had been created at the behest of the Office of the President just after the Fourteenth of July. The referendum campaign in favor of a Yes promised to be grueling. Urgent preparations had to be made. Whoever fired the first shot would win. The ex-minister made Philippe and Pradeep responsible for launching a website as quickly as possible. The job had to be done, he declared, in less than eight days, before the vacations would start in August.

"It could easily wait till September, I think," quibbled Philippe, who had been hastily placed under one of his father's staff members, Dolorès Lassuspigat. There were rumors, albeit false, that she was Delcourt's mistress as well.

"You are wasting precious time," rebuked the father.

In only a few clicks, practically unassisted by Philippe, Dipu, the brilliant programmer that he was, designed a sober and informative website devoted to the proposed Constitution for a valiant new Europe, a Europe already jaded from so many previous treaties. The timing of this new treaty seemed appropriate inasmuch as Dipu and Philippe were also moving in the direction of a civil union. Thanks to Dipu, Delcourt, six months ahead of the actual referendum, was in control of a website that exhorted *internautes*, France's cyber-savvy citizens, to vote in great numbers and support the Constitution. They also quickly posted an online quiz for the benefit of the visitors checking out the site. "There are many myths surrounding the European Constitution: It was drafted by a small group of bald technocrats who kept citizens in the dark about the details of the project. True or false?" There were twenty-odd similar and rather ridiculous questions designed to educate the public by way of a game.

"We are the Constitution's Indo-European couple, *n'est-ce pas*? The voting will be in May?"

"Yeah!"

"Which day of the week?"

"Sunday. What did you expect?"

"The English will be casting their ballots on a Thursday."

"Here, they prefer Sundays. It's more practical."

"Hmm. Do you think you could help me a little today??"

Philippe could only think about their upcoming trip to India. He already knew the map of Chennai by heart. He was finally going to meet the Raos. He let Pradeep do the final check of all the details of the website on the eve of the launch of the website.

"Don't worry, I'm sure it's perfect."

"Why are they voting on a Sunday?"

"No idea! It doesn't make any sense because each time the politicians panic about the voters in their district being away on a Sunday. It definitely adds to the excitement. It would make more sense to catch people during the week. So when are we going to Florida?"

The dissonance grew around mid-August. The first discordant note was sounded by Lassuspigat, the Senator-Mayor's second in command. In an interview with a local newspaper she announced that she would vote Yes even though she wanted to vote No. Inadvertently, she was expressing the general tendency. "Since the party supports the proposal, I will vote in favor of it on the day of the referendum. We had discussions, my colleagues prevailed. I am not personally in favor of the idea." Delcourt put up with it. The referendums in their country were beyond all logic. Toys that could be manipulated! It was the latest fashion now to settle scores on the back of Europe. There was speculation in the tabloids that the "couple from Suresnes" was breaking up.

The legitimate Madame Delcourt was voting Yes without any ulterior motives. The success of *Voteyes.com*, the website created by Dipu, inspired many cyber-adversaries (*Voteno.com* had already been preemptively reserved by the partisans of Yes to thwart their opponents. A lawsuit had been filed, but nobody had been able to prove who was behind the manipulation, the owners of the site were headquartered on a Pacific island!). The most virulent amongst these adversarial sites always popped up at the top of the page on all search engines whenever anyone carried out a keyword search under *patriot*, *France*, *Clovis*, etc. Pradeep was entrusted with the task of hacking into this site in order to block its access by the public. It was reminiscent of the operation carried out against Al-Jazeera Television during the first Gulf War. A piece of cake for the Indian! He executed an attack that brought down the site completely, forcing the *patriot* webmasters to go back to their manuals. Delcourt triumphed, but not for long. *Keepfrance.com*, a new website with a flamboyant blue, white and red color scheme, surfaced. The scoundrels! They had more resources than the Senator-Mayor who was acting clandestinely, without the permission of his party.

The success of the piracy operation had an unexpected positive spin-off. The Senator began seeing in Dipu a worthy and useful future son-in-law. His only daughter, Carole, was already officially in a civil union, so why not Philippe? He had gotten wind of their desire for a civil union. He announced to them at the end of August that he was completely fine with it and that it would be preferable if they made it official before the Referendum. Similar to the treaty for Europe, it would be a union between two men this time, two men who didn't have much common: neither age, nor culture—just like the partners of a unified Europe. Getting free publicity on the back on his son seemed to him a very natural thing.

Twenty years ago it would have been a different story. There would have been lots of drama. And pain. He would have used an iron fist to discipline any child of his who dared to be in a relationship that was the least bit out of the norm. Mere suspicion would have been enough for a family court marshal which would have been followed by exemplary rejection measures. He would have literally declared war on any of his offspring defying his authority. He would have spied on this individual, subjected him or her to intense interrogation, and threatened to cut them off from their inheritance. He would probably have preferred to see them dead rather than put up with the sneering looks of his colleagues in the Senate. All this were things of the past.

The Senator-Mayor had changed his colors totally. Smoking his cigar, he keenly followed the debates over the issue of same-sex union and decided that the lobbyists pressing for all kinds of rights were doing the right thing. His rival, the Deputy-Mayor Brillard had after all declared that he was against the movement. Hence . . . For once, here was an issue that allowed them to take sides. He got passionately involved with the whole question and made appearances on television shows where he acquitted himself impressively for someone who himself had had multiple illicit affairs (but only one marriage, no question of a divorce). If they banned divorce, he wouldn't have minded it at all. With foresight he chose the right camp. Family history had forced him to change his perceptions on society and sexuality. He even went on record stating he was in favor of gay marriage. There had been a new addition to the family - his daughter had only recently adopted Santz, a child from a village in northern Sumatra.

The rickshaw entered Greenways and dropped off Philippe and Pradeep at the entrance to the house, which was just off a small road that led to the Adyar river. Dipu greeted the tailor on the footpath outside working on his sewing machine (Mrs. Rao no longer found him trustworthy because he had botched an outfit that she had ordered for her grandson). Further ahead, on the corner of the street, a barber ran an open air hair salon. His tiny mirror hung on the boundary wall of the Rao's home.

They entered the garden. Philippe was dazzled by the sight. Two huge banyan trees veiled the entrance to the house. He stopped in his tracks, lost in contemplation. Dipu proceeded towards the steps to the porch and greeted the servant.

"Here we are!"

"I forgot the rangoli," Satish greeted Dipu with a sniff.

"Bad omen," thought Pradeep to himself. Hopefully his mother hadn't noticed. It was the same timeless ritual. Every morning, after he woke, the servant took his stencil and traced a design on the threshold with yellow chalk. He replicated the same design in front of Mrs. Rao's closed bedroom door. The day could then begin. Anyhow, it had already begun but it was safe to bet that during the course of the day there would be one or two flare ups, superficial reconciliations, and then some more clashes. The tradition of drawing geometric designs on the floor was prevalent in non Hindu families as well. Satish had made rangoli patterns with white chalk for a Parsi family in Bombay before entering into service with the Raos.

The design materialized in a few seconds just as Mrs. Rao made an appearance to welcome her son.

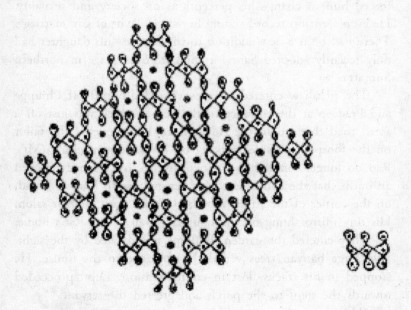

"Hello Dipu dear," said Mrs. Rao embracing her son on the porch.

"Are we late?"

"You are not late, you are fine," she corrected him, ignoring the shadow tailing him. "Not too late."

Philippe edged closer and observed Mrs. Rao's silhouette in the shadowy light. He brought his hands to the level of the chest and put his palms together to do a namaste, emulating the disciplined practitioners he had seen in Buddhist meditation circles in France. He had encountered this gesture much less frequently in India than he expected. He remained in the position as she took her time to shift her gaze towards him. Dipu had never described his mother. He had been evasive even about her age, as if it were a religious taboo. Just as Delcourt Junior came within a meter of her, he intuitively realized that great difficulties lay ahead. He felt a knot forming in his stomach. She resembled an icon, a legendary character straight out of an old Bollywood classic. Her overall appearance conveyed unarguable youth. She reminded him of the fourteen year old lolitas who made themselves look twenty by applying make-up and imitating adults. Her expression, despite the dim light around them, was noticeably severe. She seemed much more mature than her physical age. Sixty-five years at least, he thought, though logically she couldn't be more than fifty or so. Philippe wondered if she was younger than him. He did some quick calculations: she belonged to his older brother Jean-Bernard's generation. Radhika, with her medium height and her hair tied into a neat bun, showed a smooth face that, to him, seemed formidable. Attractive features, toned down by an inquisitorial look. "She's an actress," he thought to himself as he waited for her to acknowledge his greeting. Mrs. Rao's presumable youth, albeit belied by her heavy family responsibilities, was a very intimidating discovery. It didn't augur well.

She finally inclined her head, and then turned around to lead them into the living room. Philippe made acquaintance with Tommy, the Labrador of the house. Tommy was the only dog allowed inside. Radhika allowed four other dogs into the garden. They were stray dogs, the lucky chosen ones. She fed

31

them, looked after them, and even had them vaccinated. They had the same status as Satish, the servant who had been in her service for seventeen years. Tommy's status was on a par with that of her children. She wouldn't have tolerated a stray dog sleeping inside the house any more than she would have tolerated Satish occupying a part of the house other than his pigeonhole next to the laundry room in the western wing of the house.

Tommy came up to Philippe to claim the customary caresses he expected from visitors and leapt up all around Pradeep.

Mrs. Rao would have been at a loss to explain the sense of unease she was feeling after being introduced to the person whom she would have never dreamed of calling a *foreign sahib* like a vulgar servant. Radhika was not in a very good mood. She had not had enough time, since she had woken up, to digest the idea that her youngest son wished to impose upon her the visit of a foreigner about whom she knew nothing. She too had slept poorly. The morning had brought with it annoyances and botherations all too typical of such mornings.

She suddenly noticed an ant crawling near her feet. It was the height of horror.

"Satish!" she shrieked.

"Memsaab called?" he asked, running in from the kitchen.

"The ants have come back!"

"Oh!"

"I just saw one," she exclaimed, glad that she could blame insects for her lousy mood.

Satish bent over. He could see nothing but stomped heavily on the floor in a gesture of victory over the stray ant.

Mrs. Rao sighed and assumed an apologetic look. For the very first time she turned and looked steadily at the one she couldn't have ever imagined as her future son-in-law. "I don't care much for ants," she explained gracefully.

"Is it some kind of phobia?"

"They wouldn't come if Satish stopped dropping chapati crumbs all over the place. They would just stay outside. Satish! Make some tea! I have to do everything myself in this house," she added smilingly, without budging from the sofa. "That's how it is nowadays."

The word *tea* produced a calming effect immediately, even before it could be prepared. The atmosphere became less tense. Dipu collected himself somewhat. His eyes kept shifting between his mother and Philippe before they settled on Satish and then finally on good old Tommy. He was perspiring. The ceiling fan turned slowly. Why hadn't he done what he had done with the others, why hadn't he hidden this one too? He rubbed his forehead. He wanted to kick himself for making such a dumb decision. He looked to see if he could find the ant somewhere on the big blue and green ceramic floor tiles in order to keep himself occupied. He hadn't believed even for a second that the sensitive Satish had really killed it. He also couldn't remember his mother ever having had such a strong aversion to insects. The return of the ants was not a good omen.

Even in his wildest dreams, he wouldn't have been able to visualize what he was experiencing now: in the family living room, pressing against the back of his armchair, he was watching his mother stare at Philippe, with a sense of panic hitherto unknown. He had met guys at Marina Beach before but nobody had ever passed muster to appear for the ultimate test: a meeting with Mrs. Rao. Just like the stray dogs, nobody had ever crossed the threshold.

This was the first time he was breaking the rules. Just as a dog on the streets of Adyar that was graceful and less emaciated had better chances than the others of gaining admission into the hallowed interiors of the Rao residence, a Westerner could, with some luck, be liked by the lady who exterminated ants. At twenty-eight years of age, Pradeep had decided to let go. The

Indian version of the coming-out-of-the-closet adventure could begin. The years he had spent in France had given him exceptional strength, the kind of strength one gains by hiking in the mountains, and even though he found himself wiping his brow, he conserved within him the precious treasure of inviolable freedom.

Mrs. Rao couldn't understand at all why she was entertaining this elderly sahib in her living room. He had graying hair on his temples and seemed to be the same age as her beloved husband at the time his illness had snatched him away. Who exactly was this man? Who could explain? The ant incident was over and it was time to attend to this question. She was intrigued by a detail. Why didn't he dye his eyebrows? His hair were black, but his sideburns were white like the snow in the country from where he had come. Radhika only had a sketchy idea of the geography of the countries that were far from India, and she instinctively associated Europe with snow. She was fascinated by snow. Observing that he didn't have a mustache, she sensed a red flag. In Madras, it was seldom that one came across men who did not sport a trim and elegant line of hair above the upper lip.

"Oh, you've shaved off your mustache, Dipu! Why did you do such a thing? You had it till yesterday," she said, and if she could have added, "Put it back on immediately!" she wouldn't have hesitated. "When did you shave it off? What made you do it?"

"Just like that. I don't know, you know, I . . . I'm going to let it grow again," he stammered in response to his mother's firmness.

"Why would you do such a thing? It's unbelievable how horrible it makes you look. It's just unbelievable."

"No. Really? It was just a sudden impulse," replied Dipu, with consternation.

"It'll come back," commented Radhika in an unconvinced tone. "And you also don't have a mustache," she added, inviting their guest into the debate.

"I've never had a mustache my whole life," Philippe exclaimed, suddenly feeling more comfortable. "I don't like it."

"Here, we keep them," Mrs. Rao replied dryly in a voice that was soft and accusatory. "My husband always had a mustache. Didn't he, Pradeep?"

"Yes, Mummy!"

Satish returned at last with their tea. Preoccupied with the absence of a mustache on the faces of the two men in front of her, Radhika was slow to react. Philippe discreetly glanced at his friend. He had never seen such a woebegone look on his face.

3

A Gem in the Family

Mrs. Rao felt perturbed, unsettled; her heart was drier than Udaipur's Lake Pichola. She had not anticipated it. That strange announcement of his after the previous night's dinner had been so sudden. With that wimpy drawl of his he had declared that he wanted her to meet a friend. Something was not quite right.

At three o'clock that morning she had thought she heard him leave. The most disturbing ideas began to fill her mind. Mrs. Rao was a widow, the mother of four children, three of whom were still not married. Suddenly, this shattering intuition: he wanted to marry a French girl. What did she know about his life in Paris after all? Though he had been calling her every week, she really didn't know much. And now here was the proof: the mustache. He had to have shaved it off this morning, inside the apartment belonging to this elderly gentleman, this forty year old sahib. Maybe he was the fiancée's brother? But why had he done it there? Ah, these rich European sahibs owned sophisticated instruments that were not easily available in India, and they flaunted them in front of Indians.

While she had woken up with a headache, the hammering she had felt inside her head at that time was nothing compared to what she was feeling now. A migraine would have been more desirable than the apparent good health she was feigning in front of them, and it was all because of the paracetamol; it thinned one's blood without giving one the tools to confront one's fears. As usual, her children had not been any great comfort, except for Suneet, maybe. He had not walked off, she had just had enough time, as she stood between the doors, to ask him about his opinion of Dipu. He had looked her straight in the eye with his new "head of the family" attitude, and had murmured some platitudes before standing up and leaving. She did not admire his detachment at all, this serenity that this thirty-one year old son of hers exuded. Serenity? Where did he get it from? Sometimes her eldest son was as intimidating as the huge diamond she wore on her finger.

Who would support her? She had immediately rushed to find her paracetamol like one rushes to chant one's mantra early in the morning. Abhi had fled the house even before she could have begun talking, and Brinda had made fun of her before leaving for college. Did they know something? Her daughter-in-law Ammu, ah, she was the only one she would be able to open her heart to, her dearest Ammu. However, not only did Ammu remain extremely busy with her two little darling sons, Santosh and Amit, but her indiscretion and her fondness for gossip made her an unreliable ally. The ideal daughter-in-law, super smart, always dressed in new and trendy *salwar kameez* oufits that she picked in Spencer Plaza in Anna Salai. Filled with energy, she always knew how to allay her mother-in-law's worst fears. The catch? Her intelligence came with a price: the satisfaction of her deep rooted curiosity. What a gossip she was! Mrs. Rao remembered. In her wilderness, Mrs. Rao could only count on the support of Tommy - at her feet, and Satish - in the kitchen. He was busy making chapatis, and had already destroyed her by giving her such bad news. Instinct, a calamity exclusive to anxious mothers was whispering devastating rumors.

"Dipu, you aren't going to believe this, but just guess what Satish did this time," continued Mrs. Rao, reluctant to let the conversation get bogged down because of their missing mustaches.

"He is raising ants?"

"I don't understand why you all love to make fun of me. Perhaps I should ask Ammu what she thinks about this."

"Ask her!"

"As a matter of fact, she recently got hired as a psychologist in one of the hospitals. What was I saying?"

"Satish."

"Ah yes! Mind you, she only works part time, which gives her time to look after the kids, and also to deprive me of their company sometimes," she added with a cough.

"So what did Satish do?"

"It's unheard of, Dipu, completely shocking. How long has he been with us? I don't know what do with him. He threw one of my diamonds into the toilet."

"No!"

"I had misplaced it yesterday after I cleaned it with some gin like I always do, I had put it somewhere, God knows where. On the dresser in my bedroom, I think. This morning while I was having a terrible headache, I asked him if he had seen it, and he informs me that he thought it was a hard boiled sweet and had had thrown it away."

"No way!"

"It wasn't exactly my favorite, but nevertheless... Your father bought it for me in Trivandrum as a gift when you were born."

"Oh."

Mrs. Rao looked at him keenly.

"I'm not very attached to jewelry," she said untruthfully. "He's a simpleton. He should have asked me before throwing it away. One does not throw away a diamond just like that," she continued, ignoring Philippe who was watching her.

The Frenchman thought it opportune to express sympathy. He tried to contort his jowl into a mini grimace without much success.

"Last month, I entrusted him with my eyeglasses, just imagine, he managed to break them before they could be sent to my optician in Delhi. I will never know what actually happened. He brought them back to me with broken lens. What should I do, Dipu? Sometimes he does everything perfectly, and then I trust him with a new job. And sometimes he does it all wrong, as if he were doing it on purpose. He manages to bungle everything. He is so enthusiastic, he tells me everything will be done properly, and I believe him!"

"That's very unfortunate," commented Philippe.

"Yes, very."

Mrs. Rao felt much better after airing the problems she was having with Satish. After the death of her husband, the servant had become indispensable. He was entrusted with all the jobs that Radhika's children avoided. They had turned him into a nanny and a housekeeper without consulting him. They sent him to the other end of Chennai to pick up a piece of silk, to get the television repaired, to get the digital camera fixed (the one that Pradeep had brought from a trip to Dubai) . . . It could be taken for granted that with Satish in charge, one out of two missions was doomed to fail. Radhika would then become furious which would leave Satish flabbergasted.He would turn all red as if his mistress had shamed him, would hang his head and excuse himself. However, even if he were to commit all the mistakes, all the blunders in the world, she wouldn't have replaced him. She had decided that she was going to keep him forever.

"He is a fool," she would tell Suneet "but what to do, we are too attached to each other; what would I do without him? He tries his best."

"Could it be that you need to spell things out more clearly to him, perhaps?"

"It's possible. I always think he'll understand what I mean, but no. I tell him, "Satish, go to the opticians, they will remove the lens, that's all, you bring them back." Guess what, he manages to find a cheap store selling soft drinks and sachets of aspirin on the ground floor, and funny looking old-fashioned sunglasses upstairs, you see, and he brings them back broken. The incompetent people there did not know what they were doing. If I understood correctly, they used very big pliers. That's our Satish."

"And why didn't you take it yourself to your optician in Adyar?"

Mrs. Rao made a pouting face.

"I thought he would remember where he needed to go. God knows why he went to that place three kilometers away. He must have wanted a cold drink, and they must have offered to remove the lens. Isn't that pathetic, Suneet?"

She had nevertheless decided not to dispense with his services and continued sending him on perilous missions.

"Satish!"

"Memsaab?"

"Don't forget to drop off my blouse at the dry cleaners, do you understand? It is to be dry cleaned only, do you understand?

"Like the last time?" he stammered.

"Exactly! This time, everything will go smoothly," she said, calling upon Philippe Delcourt as her witness.

The sahib was watching with attentiveness. All these servant stories which seemed to be at the heart of Mrs. Rao existence were making the atmosphere heavy without making it unpleasant. He still didn't know for sure if he liked her or not. Happy days lay ahead for family egocentrism, he thought to himself, be it Indian or European.

Her kids had all become adults. Influenced by her daughter-in-law, Radhika had begun taking an interest in psychology in order to forge a tighter bond with them. She swallowed the hotchpotch of analytical theories and Hindu spirituality that

Ammu dished up. The catastrophic incident involving her eyeglasses had triggered a major therapeutic operation that had been going on in full swing for the past month.

"It is your guilt that makes Satish act so confused. That's why he breaks everything."

"What do you mean? I don't think I understand. What does my guilt have anything to do with it, even if I were guilty?"

"He is very intuitive, like you. He doesn't need to know the details. He can feel it. Deep inside, he knows you want to see your glasses broken."

Mrs. Rao groaned and adjusted her sari.

"How can you say such a thing? I'm wasting my time listening to you. I had them especially made in Delhi, and by the way, they told me that the frame would be titanium, can you imagine, and I believed them, an ordinary five hundred rupee frame . . . Really, Ammu, you say such unbelievable things, I'd rather not listen. I called them and told them I was sending them back for replacement, they promised to send me a genuine titanium frame this time, so finally I had to tell them that the lens broke because that fool was wrestling with the frame, and now I have to pay to get the lens replaced. And you say it's my guilt that caused it!"

Ammu straightened the front of the chic *salwar kameez* that she was wearing.

"Satish is like you, he is your mirror. He hates chaos, but he attracts it. He is lost without it."

Radhika dropped the matter and declared that she would take yoga, astrology and ayurveda classes, like Abhi.

"All three?"

"He does it on the weekends. I'll start with astrology," she decided prudently.

Mrs. Rao did not translate her plans into action and forgot the silly story about guilt which she hadn't even understood to begin with. Her *bahu* was a brilliant girl, a bit much, perhaps. The psychology she had studied had done something to her head. She'd be better off wearing more traditional clothes. God only knew what Ammu would come up with if she talked to her about things more pressing than a pair of glasses! It was a perfect example of her bizarre streak of mind. However, that very evening, once she had returned home, after Satish had opened the door and brought her a cup of tea five minutes later, she couldn't keep herself from observing him as he shuffled out of the living room and telling herself, with a pinch in her heart, "here is my guilt serving me tea." Unable to resist as he returned with the three biscuits that she liked having with her tea - it was a ritual, the biscuits were something she couldn't do without - and feeling all muddled, she asked him if he believed himself guilty.

"Guilty of what, Memsaab? I do everything as I am told."

Satish's little outburst of dishonesty produced a reassuring effect on her.

"That's not what I'm saying. You . . . Well, yes, you are not guilty."

"No."

"Well . . . I must not have correctly understood what Ammu was saying. But you don't know what she said, anyway."

Satish prepared to leave.

"So, wait, it's me who is filled with guilt, and you assume it on my behalf. You understand, don't you?"

He nodded his head imperceptibly. Discussing topics that were so deep didn't seem necessary to him. "Are we still sending the broken spectacles to Delhi?" he asked.

"Yes, my optician here cannot change the lens. He finally gave me a definite answer. Something about going through the same supplier. The shade has to match. The next time you'll be careful to not just go anywhere, right? You promise?"

"That will depend on your guilt," he replied, much to Mrs. Rao's astonishment.

"Oh Satish! Ammu is the one who will be content to hear that."

"He is intelligent," she told herself, putting down her cup. "A fool would never say something like that." Comforted in her decision never to get rid of him, she reckoned that he demonstrated as much proof of his stupidity as of his intelligence.

"But first of all, tell me, why did you order your spectacles from Delhi in the first place?" Ammu asked in surprise. "Wasn't that strange to begin with?"

"I didn't have a choice! Satish broke the only pair that I had with me by sitting on it, yes, it's crazy, I know."

"He sat on your glasses?"

The incident, still fresh, had not yet been exploited by Mrs. Rao. She hadn't breathed even a word of it up till now. Satish had cried instead of apologizing and it had touched Radhika's heart. She had been quick to interpret the incident as a favorable stroke of fate and had decided to take advantage of the opportunity to go in for a new titanium frame.

"We will get one here, it will be cheaper here than in Adyar. Let's go! How can we possibly go back home without eyeglasses?"

Two days later, the optician had the pair that she had chosen sent to her hotel in South Delhi. "It's made of titanium, right?"

"The highest quality titanium, Madam!"

Ammu was shocked to hear the story.

"He sat on your eyeglasses? I hope you understand what that means."

Radhika braced herself for the worst. "I think so. It means that he is absentminded, what else! That's how I see it. Mind you, it's the first time this has happened," she said defensively.

"He sat on your power, he is challenging your authority, and that is what you subconsciously want him to do."

43

It was very hot, and Mrs. Rao, exasperated, got up and turned the knob to increase the speed of the fan.

"We both struggled for four hours deciding which pair I should get. Your theories don't make any sense to me. Believe me, poor Satish, he was so upset at what he had done. If you had seen his tears you wouldn't be saying such things. He's a clumsy fool, but good at heart. I should never have left those reading glasses on a chair, in a way it's my fault. How could he have known that they were lying there? Sometimes you come up with the weirdest things, Ammu dear."

The optician in Delhi acknowledged a misunderstanding over the titanium frame and agreed to a discount on the price of the glasses. Mrs. Rao, unaccustomed to such complex transactions between Madras and Delhi, had to put up with the sarcasm of her children. Satish kept pace with the whole affair with more and more aloofness, without appearing bothered, which in Radhika's credulous mind confirmed her *bahu's* idea that he felt all the less guilty since it was she who was responsible for him with respect to all the details of their common domestic life. She came to the conclusion that with each passing day, as he committed more and more gaffes, he turned more and more into a member of their family.

The telephone rang just as Dipu was wondering why his mother was not offering his friend Philippe anything other than tea.

"Ammu! How are you? Fine, thanks . . . Pradeep is here . . . Yes, with one of his friends. You already know that? Of course! *How could you not know?* French, yes. Yes, French. From France, I suppose. *How complicated she makes everything! Maybe she knows something I'm not being told?* Isn't it? From where else do you think? Yes, from France. You don't know what happened? Suneet didn't tell you? I thought he must have told you . . . Well, you are my only *bahu*. You should be, because Satish threw away one of my diamond rings . . . one less . . . "

"He threw away a diamond ring? Don't you think it's possible he may have stolen it?"

Mrs. Rao cried out in shock.

"That's just crazy! You are too much, Ammu! I wouldn't even dare to repeat what you just said out loud," she exclaimed for Dipu's benefit. She sometimes liked making him feel jealous of his sister-in-law.

"What is she saying?" he asked, falling into the trap.

"Poor Satish! He thought it was one of those fake diamonds you gave me," she explained, using Satish's error to torment her daughter-in-law. "Yes, poor fellow, we would have all done the same. Where did I get it from? My Sushil had bought it for me after Dipu was born . . . Yes, Dipu. Oh! What are you saying, Ammu?"

"You doubt it? I have a feeling it didn't happen by chance. I'm convinced, believe me, that it was Dipu that Satish tried to throw into the commode. It's very symbolic."

"I'll call you later, I'm a little busy right now, Ammu dear," she answered, wishing she didn't have to end the conversation. "By the way, how are things with you? And my Santosh, how is he?" she asked, ignoring her other two year old grandson who was less favored because he still couldn't have a conversation with her.

"Everyone is fine. I find the coincidence astounding," added the *bahu*. "The day Pradeep brings home one of his friends for you to meet, and not just any friend, Satish throws away, without your permission, the object you were given at his birth. Quite interesting."

"Very interesting. I must go now, Ammu dear. We'll talk later, won't we?"

Mrs. Rao could not get over it! That Ammu! Her tongue spread poison and moved faster than even the monsoon clouds

45

when they retreated! It was ridiculous! First of all, Satish had not even known about the visit. So there! Unless, unless of course . . . he listened behind closed doors. *What am I thinking? What difference does it make? There is absolutely no connection between the diamond which was accidently thrown away and the coming of this Sahib who has brought with him all this bad luck. It's all his fault*, Mrs. Rao logically concluded, satisfied that she had discovered the culprit.

"What did she say, what did she say about me?" Dipu wished to know. He did not trust his sister-in-law.

"What do you think she can say about you? She loves you like a son," replied Mrs. Rao, knowing very well that this was not true.

She disappeared into the kitchen.

"Satish, tell me something."

He was sitting on the floor, eating rice and *dal*.

"You knew, didn't you, that . . . Pradeep's friend was supposed to come today?"

"People are always coming and going all the time around here," he replied after a moment.

"Who comes here all the time? Don't exaggerate!"

Satish began enumerating: Brinda's friends, Abhi's friends, Suneet's old friends who showed up at the most odd hours, the driver, it was like a non-stop revolving door, and who opened the door to let them in?

"Okay, I know that, you open the door; I'm talking about him. Have you seen him before? By the way, offer them some snacks, they look like they are expecting something. The Frenchman might be feeling hungry."

She left the kitchen without getting an answer, convinced that Satish had not known. Therefore not guilty, as usual! Satish was so jealous of his prerogatives; he never let anybody intimidate him. The way he had answered denoted real force of character

46

(something exhibited by her children as well), but it was associated with his servant mind. He hadn't had an education, his universe was so limited, but Mrs. Rao had never been more satisfied with him, despite the disappearance of her diamond.

She had made up her mind. There was nothing going on between these two. After all, for an Indian and a European to be friends these days was no longer such an unusual thing— it was a natural expression of the solid education Dipu had received. There seemed nothing wrong in it. But why had Dipu seemed just a little uncomfortable? She would have to talk to him as soon as possible. Did he really intend marrying Philippe's younger sister? Of course, it could be discussed, she was ready to discuss anything. But what if the matter involved . . . whatever it was, the situation called for another meeting. The one this morning had unexpectedly turned into such a joke. But that had been her original idea. Obviously, something was cooking, but what? The Frenchman's good looks were kind of reassuring. Yes, Philippe wanted to see his sister's new family up close! In any case, she would summon them all for a new Summit. It had to be done.

4

Family Matters

The opening scene of a chapter devoted to the *bhabis* (*belles-sœurs* in the French language, which literally means "beautiful sister") could take place in Madras and just as easily in Paris. It makes no difference. Conspiracies transcend frontiers. Treachery knows how to thread its way through the various acts in the drama of life. The thirst for vengeance is tenacious, at times, especially since it has to be quenched oneself. Brothers-in-law are a convenient prey. Dropping down from the sky for you, they are the ultimate angels who descend to serve you.

Incapable of unity, the Delcourt family had been through its share of hidden intrigues. In this complex game of chess, the external pieces had influenced natural trajectories and subverted all possibility of a durable unity. As a general rule, just like concubines, they stayed in the shadows, adopting discretion as a tactic, refusing to officially get involved in conspiracies. They delegated, as far as possible, the hard hits. Ammu had no peer in the Delcourt family. If one had to look for the French version of the brilliant psychologist *bahu*, Noémie would have raised her hand and taken the floor. There was no real resemblance between the two *bhabis*. The French *bahu* had not been able to impress anybody with her style, let alone impose her status as a daughter-in-law of the family. She was the second "non civil-union *bahu*" of the Delcourt family. She had met Nadège only once, at the town-hall, on a summer day, when they had celebrated the civil union between Carole (the Senator-Mayor's only daughter) and Nadège with triumph.

Philippe Delcourt's *sortie du placard* (the intrepid Gallic answer to the Anglo-Saxon "coming out") four years earlier had made it abundantly clear how much solidarity and loyalty there was within the Delcourt family. It had turned into a real drama. All kinds of hidden passions had suddenly gotten unleashed. Like a tidal wave engulfing the idyllic beaches of senatordom, flattening its scenic but flimsy beach huts, it had taken the entire clan by surprise. The great Delcourt cathedral lay demolished, moribund, its stained glass windows its only remnants, its only source of light from the sky. Everything had been lost because of a confession!

It had been a hot and oppressive June afternoon, not quite conducive to the revelation of personal secrets by sons summoned by their fathers. Fathers with whom they could discuss private matters, except that such matters are not just private matters, but attachments - sometimes because they give one a sense of importance, sometimes because they are things that are best not revealed since they seem to tell everything there is to tell about one. And they do tell everything, just like a blossoming flower. While the son was speaking, the father was calculating the repercussions on his public life. For Philippe though, it was the experience of a new birth.

At that particular moment, Delcourt Senior handled it well. He gazed at his son and even appeared understanding. *What the heck, that's the way he is, what harm can it do, I'm different too in a way, I understand, it's all right, unless, unless . . . oh damn!*

A symphony of gossipy voices soon caused the atmosphere to change. A shower of missiles was launched from behind a first line of defense named Noémie Delcourt. She became – and nobody really understood exactly why she was poking her nose into this whole business – the queen of a conspiracy against her brother in law. She laid the foundation of a plot by attacking the decision of her perverted relative to come out of the closet. Why did he want to come out of the closet? Since he hadn't ever done it so far, why did he have to do it now? The *bhabi's* shenanigans were successful. There was general unanimity. Out of bourgeois habit, people in the family took the side of the one who was stronger! Cousin Alexandra, who was of a somewhat spiritual temperament, was one of the rare ones who detected hidden jealousy behind Noémie's persecution of the Sahib. She filed this information in her mental drawer by classifying it under the label of "insoluble family entanglements."

That which had been a secret for 20 some years could not, on a mere whim, change family status so suddenly. Nobody had given him permission, and if he transgressed conventions, he would pay the price that they would impose! After initial hesitation, Madame Delcourt declared herself in favor of a reprobation targeting the stepson against whom she had always battled (without really hating him, it must be said) ever since he had been a little boy. Motivated by a dark desire for revenge, Noémie carried out maneuvers designed to finish off the brother in law who she believed had received undue favorable treatment in Olivier Delcourt's will. A year earlier, bypassing the other contenders, the generous Olivier named Philippe the inheritor of a five bedroom apartment in Paris. She tried to instigate her father-in-law (who had been decorated with the *Légion d'Honneur*) against Philippe by evoking the way the latter had chosen to behave. Her complaints found natural echo in a family that outwardly claimed to be in favor of a more liberal way of life. It was an opportunity for this rich and respectable daughter-in-law to make it known to her father in law what an error he had made by giving away the apartment. This is what he was getting in return: an ignoble and shameful confession! What was the bastard thinking? That he might get a bigger share of the property by exposing his soul? But they were not interested in knowing anything about him! May he have a wretched life in that apartment! It shouldn't have gone to him! They would have never treated the senator like that! Why hadn't he given it to the right people? The plot succeeded, family relations exploded like an atom bomb that everyone for years had been hoping to see explode. Noémie had belatedly realized that the muck she had become stuck in was too deep. She had slipped into depression and had just recently started coming out of it.

What they couldn't tolerate was Philippe's march towards his freedom – it somehow compromised the prison in which they all lived. Noémie and Jean Bernard, both surgeons, had no desire to be spectators to somebody else's freedom, especially that of a member of their own clan, born out of a union that hadn't lasted even two years.

Noémie had been born in Algeria to a modest family. Her father had had the dubious distinction of being nicknamed the Brutal Colonel Valera (in a recent article of the *Nouvel Observateur!*). What a flattering title! He had joined the ranks of the OAS, the *Organisation Armée Secrète*, at the time of the Coup and had earned notoriety, along with his commandos, for his torture of the Algerians. Did his daughter derive some sort of inspiration from these infamous events? Excess had become a daily affair with her, like a favorite beverage that she could not do without. The Algerian war, at the end of which she had returned to France (returned isn't the most accurate word since the Valera family, of Maltese-Spanish descent, had no ties with the metropolitan France of the colonizers), had turned the young girl that she was into an almost crazed woman. Violence had been her companion all these years: on the outside it was the civil war in the heart of Algiers, the fear of terrorist attacks on the way to school, and then the extreme winters of Paris; on the inside it was the hysteria of a repatriated family, unwelcome, vengeful, living in a house in Suresnes with inadequate heating that had been lent to them by a perpetually traveling uncle.

It was monkey business but the facts were all there. Noémie, with her Pied-Noir[1] brand of hysteria, got the upper hand over Philippe whose own background was so far removed from hers. His mother was a Canadian. Playing an incomprehensible double game within the family, Olivier Delcourt suddenly announced that he couldn't accept his son's avowal and that he was going to take measures against him. The measure that was the most spectacular was also the most ridiculous. It was July and he forbade Philippe to wear shorts. He also demanded to know how many times he had prostituted himself, since he had to have done that, he couldn't expect them to think otherwise, they had proof, and if that wasn't the case, why was he making all this fuss? The brilliant senator, before his scheduled appearance on television, went berserk for a few months as Noémie increased his psychological woes by fanning the flames opportunely like one of those professional Algerian mourners who get summoned by bereaved families. He began complaining of terrible aches and announced melodramatically, which was something new for him, that he was "afraid" for his health.

The breach had been made. What a miracle! Noémie lunged without hesitating. Adding fuel to the fire of her father-in-law's anger, she became more audacious. "If anything were to happen to you, rest assured, I will kill him." Although accustomed to the extravagance of his political adversaries, the Senator-Mayor, the chameleon that he was, secretly felt that his daughter-in-law was going too far. Despite the jealousy and hate that he could sense in her, he couldn't but embrace and thank her. She at least wasn't in the habit of making twisted confessions; she

---

[1] A term that appeared after the Second World War to designate the European inhabitants of Algeria during the colonial era.

knew how to control herself!

"A Pied-Noir *fatwa*, I couldn't have ever imagined it!" he confided to Dipu in Florida one evening. "I could never have imagined that I would become a victim of such a hysterical money making beast. She's a witch, she's ageing well with all that primrose oil she puts on her face."

"She makes a lot of money?" Dipu was curious.

"Lots of it! Like a whore!"

In India, wealth is synonymous with good fortune and duty and Pradeep couldn't understand what the connection was between the *bhabi's* enormous income and family intrigues. How could someone so wealthy act so mean and wicked, and deliver such hard blows?

Philippe explained, "Okay, good point, but you see, in France, people of the same social status don't all do the same horrible things. Each class, each clan, each caste as you would say, has its own style of ugliness, but the level of the ugliness is the same, it's the nature of the ugliness that changes with the amount of money people have in the bank."

"Really?" a surprised Pradeep interjected as he greedily tucked into his crème brûlée. "It's not like that in our country. My family is very nice. I love them very much. They give me all the love I need. I would do anything for them."

"Me too," insisted Philippe, not wanting to be left behind. "My father is cool now, at least officially he is. And you see, he likes you too, everything has worked out."

"In my family, there are no problems!"

Well well well! For what it was worth, such a claim called for close scrutiny. A trip to India to meet such a family was in order. A tropical expedition that could not be missed at any cost.

Age accomplished its task as amnesia began to overcome the Senator-Mayor. He forgot that he had participated in a plot against his own son, in a "murder" that revealed his strong will to survive, to fight, to combat, to stay till the end! His faculty of forgetfulness was flawless. What was there to be gained by remembering the thorny issues that only created so disturbance with their unnecessary details and caused so much turmoil that one went crazy? It seemed almost as if Father Delcourt had always, from the depths of his heart, encouraged his third son to lead a wanton life. *Travels, insouciance, gaiety, indiscipline, defiance of conventions . . . and whatever else in the world you want, dearest son. It's all on me!* Noémie remained on her guard. No amnesia for her. She didn't need to remember that her machinations had failed only so that she could fall harder. The apartment was a lost cause. She avenged herself by milking her father in law of money she didn't really need and acquired a country villa. He also let her have a hundred thousand euros from an account in Switzerland.

It must be said that Olivier Delcourt had become an expert in circumventing laws, laws that require a father to love his offspring (and not just count on them), a mayor the public he governs, and a citizen his country! How had such a deep transformation taken place over the course of a life? Age sometimes prevails against all logic and brings about profound changes - just like sagging cheeks!

That distant era had left a tell-tale whisper, a bitterness that prefigured everything: their words, their steps, their smiles. Forgotten, yet unforgotten, as if an imprint had been left on their hearts. The past had touched them the way time's sublime gift touches social norms. Imagine a slow descent into a somber family catacomb. A besieged fortress, an endless labyrinth with passages linked to each other. A sudden lit candle appearing in the toxic air to guide you. An overwhelming feeling of gratitude. Hope reborn. The feeling that nothing is lost. Some kind words uttered in a dark corridor, and it all starts again. Oh, now all is solved, we are friends again, isn't that wonderful?

Call it illusion if you will, but then it would be denying that illusions are necessary to existence just like the most vital pleasures in life, like the relish of a tasty meal, or torrid intimacy in the bedroom (if one feels that intimacy should be torrid, that is).

Although it really served no purpose, at regular intervals and even in India, Philippe, disconnected from the present, would experience flashbacks and see scenes from the unpleasant movie that was his childhood. He always felt he had been despised during his childhood, as if despise had been a subject matter taught in elementary school. Cacophonous background music. His stepbrothers picking up (or maybe they intuited the procedure on the school playground by themselves) methods of excluding him, keeping him at a distance, as if he were some sort of a monster with one ear, four arms and one eye instead of feet. He had landed up one morning straight from Canada. Delcourt Senior used to smoke cigar after cigar in those days. Tortured by his public responsibilities, he was imperturbable then when it came to his children. He had accumulated an overdose of political mistakes and family problems that kept him preoccupied. Jean-Bernard and Christophe took charge of their new younger brother and showered such contempt upon him that he believed for a good thirty odd years that was how the love of brothers was meant to be: saturated with disdain and condescension. Until it became real love, with some chance. The two apprentice-sorcerers succeeded in their destructive mission. It was an education that gave hangovers. Who was there to protect afterwards? The liquor of contempt destroys your dreams and crushes them. You try to stand up again but the fear of falling down again, of attracting contempt, returns like a permanent hangover which drags on morning after morning.

It's funny, thought Philippe, funny in a sense, to wake up

after forty years with a hangover as long as life itself and to realize that one had become intoxicated so early on as a child - an intoxication so deep that one didn't even suspect that it was there. To realize that one had been duped, or rather induced into a comatose state, almost invisible to the naked eye. *He is the most rude child I've ever seen.* Ensconced on her pedestal of principles and good manners, Bernadette Delcourt criticized him relentlessly for the explosive insolence she read in his eyes, the permanent look of defiance that had become his trademark. She had decided to fight, irrespective of the age difference. She hated being opposed. It wasn't long before she reached that state of perpetual emotional overflow which poisons existence. *He dared to talk to me like that! He didn't speak to me! I almost slapped him! Why didn't I throw him out?* Whenever one entered a room, the other would prepare to leave, or get ready for a confrontation. The two never ever reached the ecstatic state of an *entente*, an understanding. What they had between them were relations, tortured, composed of silence, attraction and hate. They were obsessed with each other to the point of dreaming of total deliverance from each other.

Plenty of memories were coming back to him now that he has woken up and was in India, as if traveling serves yet another purpose: reminding one where one comes from. And yet, this wasn't really the case, since, from the moment of his arrival, he had been caught in the maelstrom of India. The first few days, Paris interfered in his experience of Chennai. It was in the form of strange flashbacks that invaded and merged with the images of India. One morning in Anna Salai as he was looking at this huge billboard advertising a new generation of cell phones (an obsession that is just as widely shared in Asia), he remembered that on the eve of his departure, while he was going down inside the metro station in Paris, he had caught sight of an offensive new advertisement. The slogan said: *This summer come to your nearest Albert restaurant to see mussels ride on the surfboard.* Hm mm! It was on the wall to the right just before one reached the platform. Perhaps because he was in a bad mood, heading for his big trip, that Philippe almost ripped off the poster. They were making fun of mussels! How strange. They were being insulted underground in Paris. Sometimes he also insulted - in his heart - human beings, his family mostly, not mussels. It wasn't enough that people ate them. People also had to make fun of them to make the operation more legitimate. He stopped to contemplate. The image made him feel sick, nauseous. He hated this kind of humor, at the expense of a species. The West was all this too, the darned West that had rationalized the art of selling. This was how in Paris people reveled in the ideology of good taste. Having arrived in India, Dipu's warm welcome hadn't erased the past.

In the rickshaw as they were returning from Alwarpet, Philippe wondered about Dipu's silence. He observed once more that everybody in Chennai was wearing dhotis, except for him. "So?"

Pradeep spoke. "How did you like her?" There was a hint of excitement in his voice, as if they had just witnessed a spectacle susceptible of eliciting mixed opinions from the public. "Why is the driver taking this route? Again a detour! How do you like her, tell me."

The rain had been violent. Their vehicle swerved several times as the driver tried to avoid some potholes.

"Let's see. She was a little surprising to me. One gets the impression that as she is talking about one thing she is already thinking about the next thing."

"Hm mm."

"I'm not even going to wonder if she likes me or not. Who knows!"

"Hm mm."

"Some rain this was! It's too early to say anything."

"She is quite impossible!" Dipu burst out all of a sudden. "She'll never leave us in peace. I saw it in her eyes. Why did you have to say all those things?"

"I was just preparing her for what she will hear one day from your mouth."

"She is so difficult!" he repeated. "You think you have prepared her! She is impossible, always has been. I know her."

Mrs Rao had retired to her bedroom after their departure, avoiding Satish who was lingering in the hallway. She could barely contain her anger. She had tried seeing it from many different angles (as best as she could of course), but the result was the same: she felt furious. Completely consumed. However much she tried to ignore the things she had heard, and digest the lively and rather agreeable pleasantries she had exchanged with him, the fact remained that the sahib had said some weird and incomprehensible things. He had talked about a strange European concept of marriage between people of the same sex. At first she had laughed, after all how else could one react? *He's telling us all this to make us laugh, and we ought to laugh cheerfully, oh these Europeans, they're so fascinating, just like the serials we love to watch on TV.* But the insistence had been a little strong, and the heaviness of the joke ended up making her more alert. The Frenchman's seemed to be of somewhat limited intelligence, really, why did Dipu need to have a friend of this sort? How could such a marriage story possibly be of interest to her? Besides, she hadn't read about this in any newspaper, which wasn't surprising because it was really just a joke. Only one out of her four children was married. In the next few years there were going to be three wonderful weddings for which she would gladly make all the necessary sacrifices. She had promised this to herself when Sushil was dying. Abhi was next on the list but Pradeep spent so much overseas, it was a pity his search had been delayed. She had no one in mind for him. For Abhi, there was no dearth of choices. "I only have one *bahu*," she lamented to herself. "Why do other mothers have as many *bahus* as sons, and not me? It's not Satish's fault, anyways."

It was her *idée fixe*, her obsession. Her comments were directed less towards Abhi who was the right age for marriage than towards Pradeep who she believed was resisting. "I am the *saas* of only Ammu. I want to be the *saas* of three others as quickly as possible," she decreed, forgetting that given her age (nineteen years) and her personality, it was going to be a long time before Brinda embarked on the chaotic and exciting journey called marriage.

"Don't worry," Philippe assured him as he paid the driver. "Everything will work out by itself."

"I doubt it."

"It will, trust me!"

"Nope."

"I'm still your Krishna, that's what matters."

From inside the rickshaw, Pradeep looked out at the water streaming on the road. "You aren't exactly Prince William, but you'll do."

"Prince William?"

"I've always dreamt of meeting a handsome prince, a young European prince."

Philippe burst out laughing. "Sorry to disappoint you. I've never really been compared this way before.

"What do you mean?"

"Nothing."

Philippe repeated "Prince William" several times as he ran towards the apartment. Too bad Mrs. Rao had missed it. She would have loved it!

Seriously, a European prince to take care of her son? Why not? This time the joke was a good one, one could laugh. She would have convulsed with laughter. Pradeep of Chennai walking arm in arm with a prince descended from Queen Victoria and Emperor William. With Satish as their buffoon!

Back at the Rao's, the harder she tried, the more incomprehensible the Frenchman's humor seemed to her. She decided she would ask Abhi what he thought. She however didn't need to go tell such stories that afternoon itself with the monsoon bothering everyone. *Poor Dipu must've gotten all wet while accompanying, what was his name, Philippe, back to his apartment. Well, not his apartment!* He had rented a kind of apartment somewhere and she didn't even have the address! Hearing Abhi, who had just returned from his long walk on the beach, she went to meet him.

"Did you have had a nice walk?"

"How did it go?"

"I don't know what to make of it. I don't how I should take it. It's fine, I guess."

"That's good."

"Let's all sit down. It's quite serious."

5

Cats are Bad Luck

Mrs. Rao decided to recount the details of their visit by stressing on the jokes. She had never laughed this much in her life! *What an incredible story it was, Abhi, that our friend regaled us with!* Attempting to convince herself, she made an effort to be humorous.

"And you see, in any case," she exclaimed, still shaking with mirth, "this fellow, Philippe, he's a Catholic and we are Hindus. Even if I tried, I would not be able to imagine you marrying a Catholic. He mentioned . . . I can't remember the name, a . . . silly custom that they have, it's like a marriage except that it's not a real marriage."

"What is it called?"

"I don't remember."

"If he were a Hindu, would it make it better?"

Mrs. Rao reflected intently. "No. Our religion does not allow it. At least, I don't think it *would* allow it, right? Well, it makes no difference, Abhi. Let's see, why do you even ask? It would probably just make me feel better, I suppose. He would be from here, he would be like us."

Jokes aside, this wasn't really the real problem. If he were from here, if this French sahib were a Hindu, he would not have this twisted sense of humor that made one shudder. Only the Europeans could invent such things, that too not all of them, surely. Sitting on the edge of a chair that Satish had opportunely slid towards her from the anteroom, Mrs. Rao began critiquing the French. She did not have much knowledge of Europe, except for England. She was from a rich family that had lived in Colaba, Bombay, which was, in her mind, a perfect replica of Chelsea, London. The same kind of chic boutiques, the same pastries, and hordes of tourists with backpacks who these days no longer looked like real hippies and who crashed there for the night on their way to Goa. Where else can one sleep in Bombay if not in Colaba if one came from Europe? Ancestral memories of the colonial period that had been passed on to her by her parents surfaced in her mind to convince her that the English would have never invented this . . . what had he called it . . . this *pax*.[2] Yes, that was the word! Her Majesty's subjects doing such a thing . . . absolutely ridiculous! Abhi had already disappeared. Intrigued, she asked Brinda, who was camped in front of the computer, to do a search on Google. They got their results and were very soon reading up on Pax Romana which left Radha even more confused.

"It means peace? Are you sure?"

Brinda nodded.

"Let me sit on the chair, will you, I want to see with my own eyes, all this rubbish!"

Encumbered by her apple green sari, she settled down in front of the monitor on Brinda's desk and pronounced the suspect word aloud: *pax*.

"Peace? How is it possible? You tell me, Brinda. How can peace come about from such a deterioration of our values?"

"I may not have looked it up correctly. You did say *pax*, correct?"

"That is what I heard him say."

They finally gave up searching, feeling discouraged.

---

[2] Pacte civil de solidarité (pacs): French civil-union

Satish chose that very moment to make an agitated entry into the room.

"What's the matter? What is it now?" Mrs. Rao exclaimed.

"Bad news, Memsaab."

Memsaab was not in a mood to listen. She got up somewhat unsteadily and started making her way to her own room.

"You can tell Brinda. I've had enough of bad news for now. What's the problem? You forgot to go to the cleaners to pick up the clothes? Well, just call them, what's the place called? *Precious Dry-Cleaners*? Tell them that you will come on Monday. We ought to switch to another dry-cleaner. What they do to my linen is anything but precious. Anyway, it's not the end of the world," she added, and a sound that may have been a sob escaped from her throat.

"No big problem with the cleaners, Memsaab. It's something else."

Mrs. Rao shrugged with indifference and went inside her room.

"So Satish, what's the bad news?" Brinda demanded to know in her capacity as Mrs. Rao's worthy heiress. She slid back into the seat in front of her desk. "Oh, Vanessa is online!"

"Well, I only wanted to . . . "

"Hi Vanessa," Brinda began typing in Yahoo chat. *"What's up! Here, the news isn't too good. My brother Pradeep just landed up with a real strange fellow. My mother suspects he's gay. She hasn't said it but that's what she thinks. Well, at least that's what I think she thinks."*

"I just . . . " continued Satish, "I was just making a pile of all the clothes for laundry . . . "

"Yes, yes, it's serious, quite serious. More serious than you can possibly imagine. What could we do? It was completely unexpected, of course ☺"

"It was doing just as usual. I pick up all the clothes that are put on top of the washing machine and on the rack, and sometimes I sort them and sometimes I don't . . . "

"We won't be able to hold out. It's too confusing for my mother. He made us put up with him the whole day. I haven't met him yet, but I found out everything . . . "

"So this time I did not separate the clothes because I saw that they were all bright colors, there was no risk, they were all cotton, mostly towels . . . "

"Vaness', do understand! Our society does not allow such things, I won't say it's a terrible thing like my mother does, u know her, u know how she talks, but anyway she's kind of right, it's not something that's allowed. He must get married, and hopefully not to this guy ☺"

"There was no need for me to do things differently. There were towels mostly. So I take this whole heap together and I put it inside the drum, the washing machine . . . "

"So what's the problem with that, Satish?" interrupted Brinda, who was preoccupied with the chat she was having with her American friend. *"It seems that this guy, the Frenchman, he talked about the feelings that men like him have, who want to marry other men. And that we supposedly don't notice them, that our society doesn't notice them, that it was all very sad, I can't tell you all the things he said. My mother thinks it was all a joke, that's what she says she thinks . . . "*

"I started the washing machine as usual, the short cycle, because the clothes were not very dirty. And the water was not hot . . . "

"Okay," responded Brinda abstractedly as she continued working the keyboard. *"My mother is definitely getting worried."*

"Fortunately . . . "

"He should run away, he should go and settle down somewhere else, she was devastated, he'll probably go abroad because here it's just not possible, he doesn't have enough money, so he may go there and

settle down there, with . . . with him . . . They joked about it, I wasn't there ☹"

"The washing machine went through the full program, I wasn't paying attention . . . "

"That's fine," Brinda assured him. "*He jokingly told my mother that gay life was not accepted in India, that it was such a problem. Can you imagine he dared to say that to us as if it's our fault that people are like that. What does Dipu do when he's with him? It's a real mystery. Maybe he'll spend his whole life with him as if he was his guru!* ☺ *Do u understand? Life here is a waste of time, Dipu is so brilliant, he'll never make that much money here, too much corruption, and on top of that people here accept only one kind of marriage* ☺"

"Until . . . oh I don't know how to say all this, Memsaab will be . . . !"

"You forgot to remove the clothes from the machine? So just remove them *na*! *What a funny fellow, this French guy, it's the most surprising that's happened this year . . . My mother isn't coming out of her room. It doesn't change anything because when he sees her, he still embraces her affectionately, and she hugs him too. But all the same, they r avoiding each other.*"

Tears welled up in Satish's eyes all of a sudden.

"Lalli . . . " he said finally.

"You forgot to give her milk? Then go give it to her *na*. What are you waiting for? And what does this have to do with the washing machine? How old is she now? Ten weeks? Twelve? I don't quite remember. Small kittens need milk, Satish! *So you see, the whole atmosphere has been affected here . . .* "

"It's not a milk problem. She had her milk."

He patiently waited for Bira to finish sending a new round of replies to her correspondent. She could type very fast. In the amount of time that Satish needed to pronounce three words she could type three lines!

"She had her milk. Oh, Lord Krishna, pardon me."

"What's wrong with you today? You are too much! *Abhi is the only one taking all this calmly. It seems he suspected it. In my opinion, mummy also had her suspicions. But for me it was a complete surprise, Vaness' I can tell you that much. She had a strange look this morning, he had not said anything to her, only that he wanted to introduce a friend. I think she doesn't know anything officially, or they wouldn't be making jokes. We don't really know. That's what she claims. He didn't tell her much, something about a peace contract, that's how they do it in France, if I'm not mistaken. He . . . Oh! Wait.* What's wrong, Satish? For heaven's sake, stop crying."

"It could have been much worse." Satish muttered, imitating Mrs. Rao's frown, "It could have been a real catastrophe."

"*There, they have this thing which is like a marriage. Can you imagine the look on my mother's face? Marriage! She refuses to even hear how it works. She says it's not possible, it cannot be true. I agree with her.*"

"I didn't realize when I picked up the clothes that Lalli was there in the pile. I didn't see her and I put her also inside the machine . . . "

"*She's become obsessed with that funny word which I've forgotten, she talks about that only. She thinks she didn't understand correctly and wonders why he talked about all that, which is true, why did he? So you see, that's what happened. She told me again just now that it was all a misunderstanding . . .* What! What did you say? You must have gone mad! Mummy, Mummy! I'm calling the police!"

Radhika came running. Seeing her, Satish stopped frowning.

"What happened? What happened? What's going on?"

"Satish killed my Lalli," Brinda yelled, sobbing. "Where have you put her, you beast?"

"I've taken her out of the machine."

Mrs. Rao didn't seem bothered at all by the news.

66

"I've always believed that a cat in the house is a bad omen," she commented as she adjusted the gold bangles on her wrist. "Somebody must have cast a spell on us with that kitten."

"How can you even say such a thing, Mummy!"

Feigning indifference, Satish looked away towards the window.

Finally he said, "She is fine. She is sleeping now."

"She is fine? She is dead, of course! She is sleeping! Mummy, call the police, I beg of you! Satish has killed my Lalli!"

"Satish, I don't understand this at all. She is sleeping? You say that she is sleeping. How did she die? What happened?"

The servant gave her an abridged account. Mrs. Rao lightly wiped her wet eyes with the end of her sari.

"My God, it's . . . it's . . . I don't know what to say. Nobody's going to believe this. Nobody!" she repeated as if the word was of utmost importance. "You put the kitten in the washing machine?"

"Memsaab, it was sleeping," he defended himself, suddenly fearful of being fired.

"And you, you idiot, don't you sleep?" exploded Brinda. "She was sleeping, of course she was sleeping. On a pile of clothes, naturally, it's soft, it's comfortable. You should've made sure, you fool. Where do you expect her to go and sleep?" fumed Brinda, as if there was only one obvious place in the whole house for a cat to sleep comfortably: on the top of the clothes for laundry.

Satish was determined to blame the animal.

"She doesn't sleep there normally. She climbs into her little box."

"So?" responded Brinda with greater fury. "She doesn't need your permission, you fool. She can do whatever she wants. This is her house, not yours! You are just a stupid idiot and a big fat liar."

Mrs. Rao observed the debate with much interest, without even a sign of anger towards Satish. This time he had not thrown away her jewelry. He had not even tried to get rid of the kitten for which the only emotion she ever felt was not affection but impatience (whenever she saw it jumping about on her furniture).

"Calm down, dear. Everything is all right, isn't it? What is her name again? Lalli?"

"You are cruel and mean," Brinda continued. "You did it on purpose, Satish."

"My dear, you are feeling overwhelmed. Satish didn't do anything wrong," Mrs. Rao gave her assessment. "He's a little slow to learn, that's all."

She felt satisfied knowing that for once that it was not her jewelry, or glasses, or dry-cleaning that had met with misfortune at the servant's hands. No, this time it was not she who was the victim of Satish's foolishness. If it were not for the poor cat she would have sent him right back to the kitchen without even giving him a light scolding.

"Darling, don't be upset. If I understood correctly, she was not hurt. Where is she now?"

"She went back to the same place, she is all shaken, but she is okay, I think. I felt her all over to make sure."

Brinda looked as if she would faint and slumped into her chair in front of the computer.

"Mummy, please! Go away. I can't take it anymore. I can't bear it."

"She is breathing, she is all right," insisted Satish. "I had selected the short wash cycle," he reminded them. "She stayed on top of the wet clothes. I rarely remove the clothes immediately after washing them, it depends on what I have to do."

"Oh . . . "

Brinda stood up crying and ran out of the house. Mrs. Rao went over to the laundry room thinking about the incident. It was a known fact that cat hair attracted vibrations of poverty. Sad thing to say, but it would be so much better if the cat disappeared from the house, she thought to herself. And besides, Brinda was so emotional. She still read Enid Blyton. At her age! She had read too much of that Blyton stuff, those five idiots with their stupid dog had influenced her so dramatically. She'd be better off reading Harry Potter. That would definitely be an improvement!

Satish followed her. "You should have been more careful," she admonished him, as she thought about Dipu.

"I can say this now, Memsaab. It's a very strange cat."

"Why do you say that?" she asked him interestedly as he trailed her up the stairs.

"She is different from the other cats. She causes problems."

Mrs. Rao immediately thought of her son. He also had a knack of causing problems.

Lalli was sleeping soundly, knocked out by her ride in the washing machine.

"I'll reprimand Brinda. She shouldn't have spoken to you like that."

Satish returned to the kitchen and Radhika picked up the telephone. Ammu listened, incredulous. Her prediction had been correct – nobody could have believed what Satish had done!

"It's amazing how agile these kittens are. God only knows how she managed to survive inside the washing machine . . . she probably managed to cling to the sides of the drum, on the top. Satish had programmed a short cycle, it was only half full. She was destined to survive, wouldn't you say?" Mrs. Rao concluded.

The palpable silence at the other end was an indication that her daughter-in-law was preparing a preliminary series of remarks.

"Satish unconsciously wanted to kill Brinda's cat, no doubt about that."

"Why do you say that? It was an accident. How was the poor fellow to know that she would be hiding inside a pile of laundry? Really Ammu, for once I see no reason for finding fault with him. It could have happened to anyone, even to me."

"Hm mm," Ammu responded. She sounded unconvinced. "The murder of this kitten stems from the insurrectional and unhealthy atmosphere inside the house . . . "

"Oh! Ammu! Ammu! You also think that cats are an inauspicious omen? I've always thought so."

"That's not what I was saying. Satish has unusual psychic powers."

"Satish? Are you sure? If you had only heard how Brinda spoke to him! Speaking of powers, what to make of a kitten that can survive a wash in a machine? I have noticed," she said suddenly as the evening darkness started descending on the house, "that everything has been going wrong since the arrival of the Frenchman."

At nine o'clock that night Mrs. Rao called her eldest son on his cell phone. Brinda had still not returned home.

"I'm quite worried. Bira left the house, after you know what . . . that unfortunate washing incident, I have no idea where she is, she got such a big shock . . . "

"I know."

"At the same time," she added, as she tried to smooth a crease in her sari with her free hand, "it's not such a big deal compared to you know what. If you could only see how well the kitten has recovered. It's acting more energetic than all of us combined."

A little later she knelt down in her little puja room. She decided to wait there till her daughter returned home. She looked at Krishna's statue.

"Bira, my darling, come back," she began praying. "Your brother is causing us so much worry, so please come back. I will not criticize you for reading, even at your age, Enid Blyton. Lord Krishna, listen to my prayers, please send her back, her cat is fine and Satish was absent-minded as usual."

She then prayed to Ganesh, and finally to his father, Shiva.

When she was done with her prayers she had an idea. "I'll make an appointment with the doctor," she decided.

6

Any Cure for Dipu?

She was determined. She would convince him. Panayappan had
treated Sushil, and had done a fairly good job; he would know
how to cure Dipu. It was important that Dipu's sickness be
tackled as quickly as possible. This is what had complicated
everything during her husband's illness: they had wasted too
much time. Acknowledging to herself that the disease this time
was *very* different, she decided to make use of leukemia, which
he had once suffered from, as a polite pretext. She felt hesitation,
especially since she thought it impossible to seek Ammu's
opinion, god knew what her psychologist *bahu* would say. An
horrible memory resurfaced to torture her, and she almost
canceled her appointment. On the eve of his death, she had
absented herself for a just few hours to get some rest at home,
and the poor Sushil, on seeing Panayappan had lost his mind
and had deliriously told him (in a feeble but brave tone): "You
will finish your days in prison!" The nurse who was present had
quickly reported this to Mrs. Rao when she had returned. "Why
did you say that?" she had asked him, intrigued.

"He tried to kill me, he will spend his life in jail."

"Oh Sushil!"

And she could have added: "Not him, dear." Believing that
the hospital was keeping him against his will, shortly before
lapsing into a coma, he had repeated his prediction thrice to
the doctor. It was the last symptom of his degenerated mental

state.Radhika had not fully forgotten the incident. The idea of renewing contact with someone whose professionalism had been insulted by her late husband was not a very pleasing prospect. She couldn't refrain from mentioning the anecdote when she talked to him on the phone. Dr. Panayappan expressed his astonishment.

"Dear Mrs. Rao, I assure you, I don't have the faintest recollection. You are sure?"

"Alas yes, Doctor. One of the nurses was present."

"Well, I'm still here in my office to serve you, and I don't see any iron bars blocking the view from my windows. Do you know any judges? You can petition them to free me."

His humor was reassuring. He definitely would not be as jolly when she told him what was wrong with her son, and the steps that had to be taken . . . before it became too late.

She took a long time to get ready and chose her jewelry carefully. On her way out she crossed Satish who looked her in the eye several times and then turned around and followed her. She remembered what Ammu had said. Psychic powers? The art of making chapatis led to all sorts of things.

"What is the matter? Why are you staring like that?"

He defended himself by shrugging off her question and continued making his way to the garden.

"Satish!" she persisted. "Have you done everything I told you to do? How many chapatis did you make?"

It was a ritual question that she used every time she wanted to bring him to heel. As always, he gave her a surprised look.

"About twenty. A little more."

"That's good. Make me some pomegranate juice. I'm going to be late. Call a rickshaw in fifteen minutes."

"To where, Memsaab?"

"Malar Hospital."

"Memsaab is feeling sick?"

"I'm feeling fine. You are really inquisitive. What do you wish to know?" she asked, feeling inclined to tell him everything - whatever he didn't already know thanks to his habit of eavesdropping behind doors.

"That you are not feeling sick," he cleverly replied.

"Then stay calm. There is someone in this house who is sick, I think, but it's not me."

"Brinda?"

"Hm mm. No."

"I'll make the juice and then I'll find you a rickshaw," exclaimed Satish without budging from his spot.

But Mrs. Rao had changed her mind.

"No. There's no need, I'll walk. It will do me good. I should walk a little. It's very close."

The sun had come out again. It was the first of December. A little earlier that morning, she had had a conversation with Suneet. They had taken stock of the state of NRIs: non-resident Indians, Indians who lived away from India, like Pradeep had done for seven years. Mrs. Rao had been frank with her opinion:

"It's so absurd that he wants to go and live in Europe again. If I have understood correctly, outsourcing is bringing jobs here, the brain-drain has stopped, and all these multinational companies are hiring young people."

"They don't pay the same salaries."

"What more does he want to achieve by getting his ridiculous Green Card?"

"The Green Card is for the US, Mummy, not for France."

"Maybe it's a different color, but it's the same thing. What do you say, my dear . . . Ammu was telling me that more and more foreigners are coming to Chennai; they all want to work here! Having something to do with India on your resume is considered a very good thing. And here's our Pradeep, going against the tide! Instead of taking advantage of the boom, the

74

wonderful arrival of all these companies looking for brilliant youngsters like him, his majesty prefers to live in exile in an old country, where he will never be accepted, where he will only be just one more Indian among them, out of the billion plus that we are."

"So, are we not an old country?" Suneet asked in puzzlement.

Radhika had very carefully read the entire article in the Times of India.

"Of course not! We were born, we took rebirth if you will, in 1947. We are therefore a very young. As for them," she added with a scowl of disgust, "they are old from everywhere. They are not making babies, they are raised ill-mannered and . . . "

"And . . . "

"And . . . they solemnize despicable marriages," she exploded. "And that's the truth! I don't want my pure and innocent son to be influenced by such boorish people, in a country where boys and girls are told to marry each other like they were being sent to a movie theatre to watch a good movie. No! You understand, Suneet? It's out of the question," she added, implicitly admitting that the question was now a relevant one. "Though, of course, the issue has nothing to do with our Dipu."

"Of course not."

"Definitely not," she continued, feeling comforted. "Satish!"

The servant came running from the yard where he had been washing some dishes from the previous night.

"Yes."

"Bring it," she simply said.

He gave her a meaningful look, a look of acquiescence, and then scampered back to the kitchen. She wanted her bowl of hot water.

"What was I saying? Yes! No, it does not concern him, but you see, as Ammu would say, one never knows."

Suneet felt sure that she was putting words in the mouth of

75

the absent *bahu* to suit her own interests. Verbal manipulation was one of her fortes. Denial always played an important role when she planned a strategy.

"I'm not running after dowry," Mrs. Rao clucked. It was an indirect reference to her neighbor, Mrs. Menon who, according to Mrs. Rao, had no intention of letting go of her son Gopal, with his fair complexion and muscular legs, without getting adequate compensation in return. "But if it comes to that, we will cross the bridge when we get there. Love or no love, everyone needs money."

Suneet listened in silence to his mother's incoherent words.

"Don't worry, Radha, you've been making a mountain out of a molehill ever since Dipu returned."

"First of all, you know very well I don't like it at all when you call me Radha," she rebuked him, distracted from her bigger worry. It was annoying the way they were all prone to treating her like a child by shortening her name. "A mountain out of a molehill? Can you clarify what you mean, instead of blaming me? You don't even know what I'm talking about," she lashed out.

"Pradeep's marriage."

Mrs. Rao shrugged.

"What marriage? Who is talking about marriage?"

"You are!"

"Thank you, Satish. Two ants," she added, giving him a look that was reproachful and conniving at the same time.

"Two?"

"What was I saying? Yes, I've seen two ants since this morning. It's no big deal. The question is not if he will marry. He is not that old, we still have time. What I do not want is for him to go back to France. Who will look after him over there?"

"He's got good friends," Suneet suggested with uncertainty.

Mrs. Rao looked at her bowl of hot water intently.

"I know only one and . . . "

"And?"

She let the suspense hang in the air as she made herself more comfortable in her armchair.

"He's actually quite nice, mind you, he makes me laugh; I find him quite funny . . . "

"Really? That's good news."

"Not really," she protested. "He is totally devoid of substance. All he can do is tell jokes, that's not enough. By the way, do we know what the parents do?"

"The father . . . the sahib is a minister in their government, or a senator, something like that. I don't know what term exactly they use."

"Well, well, well" she uttered deploringly, feeling impressed in spite of herself. "He's in the government . . . "

"Actually, he's retired, he's quite old."

"I suppose you found out from Ammu. I really wonder how she manages to stay so well-informed in spite of being so busy and not even having enough time to come here. It's an art, I guess. He's very old? The son isn't young either," she thundered. "A former minister. That doesn't change the basic fact. If he is no longer in the government, it is not of much use. Is that good or bad?" she anxiously asked all of a sudden.

Suneet was not sure, and was in a hurry to leave. He had his own family, equally demanding, if not more, as the family that he came from. Dipu's overseas adventures, and their current repercussions did not merit these long discussions. Family, at times, was nothing but an enterprise, a war-making or peace-making machine. Each family had a boss, employees, and a culture. In the most extreme cases, a cancer that ravaged, became bigger. Or a complete farce, with actors and dialogues. And always, the roles. Roles distributed with utmost regard for hierarchy, with all the extras, the décor, and the malaise, thrown in for good measure. Everybody played a role, which was assigned, before it got snatched. And ultimately everyone ended up identifying the role they played with themselves.

"Both!"

"No. It's good," she decided. "It means that in spite of everything he comes from a respectable background."

Dr. Panayappan stood up as she approached him, and invited her to sit down. He was also fair, like Mrs. Menon's son. He was wearing a small pair of eyeglasses with rectangular lenses. His mustache was perfectly trimmed. The knot of his green polka dot tie was visible behind the lab coat that he was wearing.

"I think I have already mentioned this to you, Mrs. Rao. The suddenness of your husband's death remains, for me, very surprising. I'm of course speaking from a strictly medical point of view. He was responding to his treatment quite well and then suddenly . . . What happened?"

Radhika had not crossed Adyar River to reminisce over her dear husband's death. She patiently waited for him to finish his litany before stating her opinion in a flat tone: "It was time for him to go."

"Remind me again, what was it that he said, just before he died?"

Radhika felt like her blood was starting to boil.

"You will be spending your life in prison."

"Interesting. Very interesting. Why did he say such a thing? Whom was he addressing?"

"You."

"Yes, I know. But to whom was it addressed? You don't have an idea? He didn't say anything else? Anyway, how may I help you, Mrs. Rao? What's the matter?"

Finally, she could bring up her reason for being there. His office had a bird's eye view of the Adyar and its banks lined with slums where she could see children playing. Their sounds however did not come till the windows of the office. A woman with a pot of water on her head walked slowly in the distance.

She came to the point immediately. She suspected, there was no real proof, that, how to say this, her youngest son was attracted by . . . you know what doctor, gay, as they said these days, how could medicine help him? Dr. Panayappan did not smile or show any emotion. He had total self-mastery. He suspected a ruse.

"You mean how medical science views it?"

"Yes, you understand what I'm trying to say."

He acquiesced with a look on his face which, in other circumstances, might have indicated the opposite.

"You have never thought of remarrying?" he suddenly asked, as he fidgeted with his pen.

The bomb had its effect. His voice was glacial. This wasn't the first time someone had come to him for such purposes. He was not a psychiatrist, she knew that well, but here she was, knocking the doors of medical science over something which was not at all related.

"Remarrying? How is that related to my question? If there is a connection, I don't see it, I'm sorry," said Mrs. Rao, sitting up very straight.

"Please don't apologize. There is no direct link. I was just wondering."

His gamble had paid off. Radhika's face had become red.

"How do you spend your time, Mrs. Rao? I suppose your husband left you well provided for."

"We had investments, and he also had life insurance," she heard herself say, as if he had a right to all her private information. "Once again, I don't know why you are asking me all these questions."

He gave her another diplomatic smile which made her even

79

more uncomfortable.

"No particular reason. I was just trying to understand."

"I'm here to talk about my son, not about myself. How does what I do with my time have anything to do with the problem my son is having?"

"I could be mistaken but I think it is you who might be having a problem, not your son."

"And all these questions help you convince yourself?" she retaliated with a hint of anger in her voice.

Panayappan seemed to be having fun at her expense.

"How old is your son?"

"He is twenty-eight. But he's still a baby."

"Of course. And you are this baby's mother."

Covered with lots of heavy jewelry, Radhika was becoming more and more disconcerted by the way the meeting was unfolding. He was not behaving as she had imagined; he wasn't asking her any questions about Pradeep, he was delving into *her*. She made another attempt.

"He has lived away from India for seven years, he has just come back. I have really been affected by what I'm guessing, you know. It's possible though that I may be wrong . . . "

"Ask him about it."

"For the time being, I cannot. He would lie in any case. And I don't wish to hear it."

"Well, in that case, there is nothing to be done! Take some deep breaths, do some yoga, and let your son be in peace."

"That's not what I was expecting from you."

"We don't expect a lot of things that happen to us, but they happen all the same."

Mrs. Rao stood up.

"Indeed," she said indignantly. "I obviously have not knocked on the right door."

"Yes, you have. Because you have reminded me of your

husband's death, and believe me, the medical aspect of the circumstances would be of greater concern to me. I wonder why he said those words. He envisaged prison for someone in his entourage, who could that be?"

It was too much. On the verge of tears, she made her way to the door, opened it and halted. The shocking and monstrous words that she had just heard, plus the memory of the time just before Sushil's death overwhelmed her and she almost collapsed to the floor. Dr. Panayappan rushed forward and caught her just in time.

"Keep your cool, don't let it affect you so much, Mrs. Rao. Accept your son the way he is, not the way you want him to be. Even at your age, taking things calmly in one's stride helps one grow," he chided.

"Thank you very much," she managed to mumble when she shook his hand.

She did not wait till she was inside the elevator before she began crying. The hospital lobby was packed with people and she cut her way through the crowd towards the exit.

She had forgotten to talk to him about the leukemia. Her tears doubled as she walked towards the bridge in search of a rickshaw. He had not cared to listen to her. Why?

"Oh my darling, there you are!"

She was overwhelmed by a new flood of tears when she saw her little Santosh run towards her, followed by Satish who was trying to catch up. The child seemed happy at having escaped from him.

"Come here, come here, I want to kiss you, let me give you a kiss. I love you my angel, you know, Daadi loves you so much, sooo much, soooo much . . . "

Santosh jumped into his grandmother's arms.

"What time did Ammu drop him off?"

"After you left, Memsaab."

"My darling, Daadi will have to put you down, because you know I'm an old lady. I'm not that strong. Did he have his milk?"

"He refused," explained Satish, who seemed to have as much difficulty with the child as he had had with the kitten a few days earlier.

"Why were you crying, Daadi?" asked Santosh as he drew his finger across Radhika's cheek.

"Crying? I wasn't crying. Oh, you can tell that I've been crying, how can I cry when I have my little angel here with me? Daadi wants you to eat something."

"You cried," insisted the child categorically as he tested her tears with his tongue.

Mrs. Rao gave up.

"Yes, yes, I cried. Because I was so happy to see you, honey."

"No, you were crying before," he insisted. And then you cried again."

"Oh my god, Santosh. Now you have to taste something else besides my tears. You don't find them nice, all these tears, right?"

She put him down when they reached the verandah.

"I'm not hungry," protested the five year old.

"Okay, you don't have to eat."

"I'll tell Mommy that I tasted your tears, I'm not hungry any more."

"Oh my little darling! Dipu is here?"

"No, Memsaab. Only Brinda is here."

The telephone rang. Santosh charged at the instrument. "Mommy, Mommy!" he yelled. "Daadi was crying, Daadi was crying."

"Oh, what are you saying, dear? Let me talk to Ammu, will you."

Once again she was unable to hold back her tears. She took leave of Ammu and hung up.

"Yes, I'm crying, my dear," she said, finding comfort in Santosh. "I'm crying a lot! Daadi has a lot of worries; she is sad. You are not upset with her, are you, because she is crying?"

Santosh needed an explanation.

"Are you about to die?"

"No, I'm not going to die."

"I am not afraid of dying, Daadi . . . "

"No my dear," she said absent-mindedly, putting him on her lap and kissing him on the cheek.

"No."

"I know."

Santosh opened his little hand and counted till three.

"After we die, we wait for three years and then we are born again."

"Oh! Goodness gracious! You are teaching me something new. Drink just a little milk, to make me happy. Who told you about this, honey?"

Santosh remained silent and snuggled up against his grandmother. He had no intention of revealing his sources.

"Three years? You know, it takes so many lives to come out of all this," preached Daadi, thinking especially about Pradeep. "I am saying this to you; I must be crazy, you are not old enough to understand, although you are so wise."

He immediately pulled out his tongue at her.

"Do you want a biscuit?"

"Eeew!"

Satish heard him and gave a small cough. He has been at the receiving end of a whole series of eeews since the arrival of the child, eeews of disgust, but not just those, eeews of annoyance, of boredom, eeews that were multipurpose . . .

"Tell me, my dear," she called out, spotting Brinda who had

just emerged from a long chat on Yahoo with Lalli in her arms. "Pradeep's friend . . . "

"Oooh, he's so tall and handsome," Brinda gushed.

"Handsome? You really think so? I've been meaning to ask you, although it's just a minor detail, mind you. I felt surprised, you know by what?"

"That he doesn't have a mustache."

"No."

"That he speaks better Hindi than you?"

"Oh Brinda. I'm not trying to be funny, I'm serious."

"I'm listening. I'm not trying to be funny either. Wait a sec. Let me put Lalli down before she scratches me any more."

Satish was no longer allowed to come near the animal.

"This will astonish you, my dear. I thought he looked less fair-complexioned than most French people."

"You think he is dark?"

Mrs. Rao remonstrated.

"No. Not dark. Not dark like us, but not fair either."

"Fascinating!" mocked Brinda. "Fascinating! Am I the only one you are revealing this secret to?"

"Santosh, go outside and play in the garden with Lalli and Tommy. Satish, keep an eye on him, don't let him out of your sight, understand?"

"Yes, Memsaab. I will sleep well, tonight."

"He does not have a very white complexion," confirmed Brinda after a moment's reflexion. "I bet he uses something. He must use some kind of tanning lotion, tons of it."

"Ah, so you see. I wasn't wrong. It's not like I have known a lot of French people in my life, but I have eyes. Tanning lotion, did you say?"

"One cannot really say that he does not have a light complexion either," said Brinda complicating matters. "He is somewhere in between."

"Hm mm. Please can you keep an eye on Santosh from the window? Even though Satish looks after him perfectly well, I'm never at ease."

"Don't worry. I'll watch over him."

7

Kuchu's Game

"What do you mean, a mantra?"

Abhi's eyes looked as if they were going to pop out of his head. A mantra? He was not sure if he understood. One was supposed to receive a mantra from one's master; it belonged to you because it was given to you, one could not make it up all by oneself like a *dosa* or a *chapati*. And this Philippe Delcourt was telling him just the opposite! Since the moment he had landed in India he had been repeating three words that he had himself invented, and he called it a mantra . . . It was an appropriation of the spiritual kind. Abhi found it very surprising, if not too upsetting. He preferred to adhere to the original principle, which was quite simple:

"You did not receive it from a guru, so it's not a mantra! Is it something religious?"

"No."

"Ok."

One could repeat, shout from the rooftops of all the houses in Madras whatever one wanted.Linking the words to god was not a necessity. One was free to buy inner peace in the bazaar of spiritual propaganda if one so desired. There was no law against it.

"I received it from the sky all the same," the Frenchman protested. "From heaven."

Dipu's brother began to laugh. This French fellow from Paris was so funny, so entertaining.

"Ah, so it's come from heaven! And what is it?"

"It's a little like . . . it's three powerful phrases that I repeat. Hold on, do you know NAM MYOHO RENGUE KYO?"

"I confess I don't!" Abhi replied as they set foot inside the gardens of the Theosophical Society in Adyar, opposite Malar Hospital where Mrs. Rao had just been dealt the most crushing defeat of her maternal career. How could one possibly know everything, spirituality had become such an open-air bazaar...

"Last week, you see" Philippe Delcourt began, "all of a sudden, it was worse than having the blues - I wasn't depressed in the technical sense - much worse, I can't explain. When it's not going well, when one emphatically says right after waking up that it has to stop, that life has to stop . . . "

"Oh," exclaimed Abhi, taken by surprise by the avalanche of personal revelations, but since they were coming from someone who was "almost" a brother-in-law, it was okay. Here was an extraordinary *jeeja* who prepared his spiritual meals himself! How intriguing, not to mention the rest . . . "Have you been to the Theosophical Society before?"

"No, this is the first time. Beautiful building!"

"Sorry for interrupting you," murmured Abhi.

It would have taken a lot more to disrupt his train of thoughts.

He was experiencing so much passion, so much intensity. "Incredible India," was what one read in the huge advertisements. "Incredible India" was being sold from the highest levels of the nation, which made it seem a little less so. It was inevitable that the Tourism Ministry would meddle one day. There were times when he felt he was on a whole different planet, except that he had never felt that much at home anywhere else: it was the most unexotic place, the least exceptional, just "home," a kind of Europe revisited after the Middle Ages where one could use a cell phone to make a call, a place where events were no less or more extraordinary than where one came from. One simply felt at home, finally, in everything one did, whether it was cry, laugh, hope, fear, or live. He felt freedom from the meaningless roles that caused one to fragment into a thousand pieces back home. It was just him, and the joy of being. The embrace of existence.

Everything seemed to be coming together. He had all the time. The sand, the mud, the monsoon were all like a slate on which he could read his innermost thoughts. It was all coming together, everything would fall into place . . . in this life, or the next. He had the feeling that it could only be all good. Healing was the ultimate goal.

His mantra was about family. The lack of love that he had endured since childhood.Roles had substituted for the lack. Like at the theatre, roles had been distributed in the great family drama. He had the impression of being liberated from them, though without being healed.

He was discovering a new connotation of love in India. He could glimpse it through his "foreign" eyes. It was discernable even through the deforming prism which was the Rao family. The prism rendered absolute certitude impossible. Could a country, because it was called India, claim to diffuse more love, more joy, and more truth than any other? It did not seem possible, and yet... What was the source of his sensation of being so alive, of belonging to the world at last, of not being the prisoner of a country hemmed in by its narrow frontiers, its delusions of grandeur, its acts of war and its subjugating violence? Once you transcended the expected complications, just because you had reached there, India took you by the hand and accepted you as you were. Out of a thousand year old habit India knew you, understood where you were coming from, what you had passed through, your journeys, your failures, your follies; it let you keep it all, had fun with it, gave you second chances, encouraged you to do it again, differently, believing in you.

Pradeep had an afternoon appointment in the French Department at the University of Madras. He assigned Abhi the job of keeping the sahib company; they were not going to abandon this complex sahib just like that, even for a day. They were going to let him manage all alone. Tightening the family net around him was part of the pleasures that Dipu, now on his home turf, sought as a kind of test for his suitor to pass in order to qualify as his ideal companion.

They entered an immense hall inside the main building of the Theosophical Society. It was solemn—it felt like an unadorned church or a government ministry. "Elegant and unbreathable," Philippe thought to himself. "As unbreathable as theosophy." Philippe had a problem with the word itself. The atmosphere was charged with what seemed to be a decades old blend of spiritual fusion and confusion, enthusiasm, certitude, and fraudery. An elderly gentleman speaking the Queen's English came up to them. He introduced himself as William Smith and told them he was from southern England, spending his retirement years in Chennai, inside the Society's walls. He and his wife had been members of the T.S. since the early forties.

"Leadbeater? You want to know when he died? Let's see. It's funny that you ask. I must say, I don't know. Unless . . . Laura!" he called out turning towards the big hall with the impressive columns like those of a Roman church. "Laura!"

A petite woman wearing pants and a white tunic appeared at the top of the stairs that lead to the mezzanine. The room served as a library.

"In which year, do you remember, did Leadbeater die? It was before we came here for the very first time, isn't it?"

She nodded.

Philippe had one more question which was burning on his lips and he wasn't going to miss the chance.

"They say, unfortunately I don't remember where I read this, that Leadbeater was . . . was gay, as they say these days," he added to clarify the anachronism.

"Oh, definitely," Abhi exclaimed to himself in silence. "Definitely!"

William Smith did not show any more embarrassment than as if he had been asked to turn on the fan.

"I cannot shed light on the subject. He was a bishop, but I suppose that does not mean that he could not have been one. It would be easier for me to tell you when he died," he added with a smile.

Philippe felt sure that he knew the answer but was not inclined to reveal that kind of information.

"1934!" exclaimed Laura.

"Hmm. Did you know that he was French in spite of a name like that? He was a Le Bâtre, a builder whose name got anglicized. Well, my friend," continued William Smith, "he invited, on the third of November 1884, people from his parish to come and have tea and cake, and then, that very evening, he disappeared! Two days later he was in Port Said, boarding English steamboat that was coming to Madras. And he came to this place. That was the beginning of his association with the Society."

"Fascinating!"

"It certainly is."

Philippe realized it was time to leave. Mr. Smith would not have hesitated to recount the whole life of Charles Webster Leadbeater along with all the minute details for which even one full day would not have been enough. Harpooning visitors from his armchair was an art that the retired gentleman had mastered; the retired Englishman knew the technique well. Pleasant *salon* style conversation skills in conjunction with theosophical matters seemed to be his cup of tea.

"Thank you for sharing your knowledge," added Philippe as

he shook his hand. "Can we go that way?"

"Please, by all means."

They made their way along a path bordered by small houses. It resembled English countryside, with tropical trees added. Endowed with a school and a hospital, T.S. felt like a veritable city inside the city.

"Extraordinary, don't you think?"

"What is it that is extraordinary? I come here for walks all the time," clarified Abhi who had never had a conversation with a member of the Society, let alone a foreigner.

"I was referring to the old gentleman. And before that I was saying . . . Yes, last week. I went through a critical phase.

"Ah yes, you were depressed."

"Er... no. Actually, yes. Just a sudden impression that I had failed in life. Failure isn't quite the right word; it's too mild."

"Oh, sorry!" sympathized Abhi, as if Philippe had just complained about some gigantic traffic jam on the roads of Madras. "Sorry to hear about that!"

Philippe thought it best to quickly close the tap of personal confessions and refrain from making any further disclosures. He did not want any more "sorrys" to rain down on him. Not that he sensed any coldness; it was just a cultural expression that bothered him. He felt he would not be able to survive another "sorry" if Abhi continued to force himself to seem at ease. As if they had mutually understood, they walked in silence.

Had Leadbeater, mischievous in his time, quietly bestowed clairvoyance on them via the elderly Smith? As they walked along the main path inside the T.S., they were both thinking about the family figure: their fathers. For Abhi, it was lack and absence, the pain of having lost him so early. For Philippe, it was rage and impotence - because he was still there. Opposite emotions. Abhi often missed his father; Philippe often resented that his was alive. One suffered from his absence, the other from his

91

presence. Harsh towards his own, he was wonderful, attentive, towards his constituents. Philippe had found himself pushed into a state where he had formulated his own mantra. Crossing the oceans was so worth it!

The only filial tenderness that Father Delcourt had ever been capable of showing, according to his third son, was the tenderness of money which he knew how to dispense at the right moment, not so much to seek pardon as to compensate for his inability to express himself in any other manner.

Philippe suddenly began reciting his new mantra:

"I do not have a brother named Jean-Bernard, I do not have a brother named Jean-Bernard, I do not have a brother named Christophe, I do not have a brother named Christophe, I do not have a sister named Carole, I do not have a sister named Carole, I do not have a father named Oliver, I do not have a father named Oliver."

"What does that mean?" asked Abhi, who didn't know French.

Philippe translated his mantra for him into English.

"How strange!"

"That's right."

"Very very strange! Does it also work the other way round?"

"What do you mean?"

"Oliver does not have a son named Philippe, for example."

They came to a tree. It was one of the most spectacular trees the sahib had ever seen. A banyan that had a circumference of at least twenty meters. Its vertical hanging roots seemed to be forming more trunks which in turn formed what seemed a private enclosure within the bosom of the tree. To the sahib, the confused mass of hanging roots seemed as entangled as the anthroposophic theories of Rudolph Steiner with their almost similar benign madness.

"I don't know. You would have to ask him."

"So this means that you are both very detached from each other," hazarded Abhi.

"We will be detached when the mantra will have been repeated enough number of times. We will be neither at peace nor at war; we will just be detached. I'm sure the mantra is useful, phony as it may be. Sometimes one believes one is working towards ones detachment but actually one is doing the exact opposite, one just reassures oneself like that. Detachment seems so unbearable, so dry, the word detachment. So, one works towards ones attachment by creating the opposite impression for oneself."

Abhi seemed quite fascinated, dumbstruck, in fact. He had not imagined this person, whom his mother had taken delight in calling a depraved monster—without any faith or conscience or a good family name (in the days preceding his arrival) to be so deep! Olivier Delcourt's various marriages had caused Mrs. Rao's head to spin. How many brothers did he have in all? And the sister, was she married? Much as they teased her, or refused to listen to her, they did pay attention to what she said. Her point of view, if she had one, always dominated. The only thing that shocked him about what Philippe had said was the kind of relations, the chaotic ties that seemed to prevail in this French family. How could one be so convinced that one did not have a brother or a sister anymore while they were all alive, ready to support you in the face of the slightest adversity. *I don't have a brother named* . . . The mantra was absolutely unthinkable in India. Not only for him, but also for all the people he knew, from north to south, from Delhi to Madras, and from Mumbai to Kolkata. He had never heard anybody talk about their family like this before. How could one reach such a stage, this state of "detachment" towards those who had done everything for you, given you everything, given you life itself?

"I created this mantra because I needed it, because I'm in

India, and especially because we have reached a point where neither peace nor war will work. War brings about destruction, bitterness, and more wars. And peace doesn't bring about anything better, just illusions. So neither war nor peace. Detachment!" he concluded, resting against the huge truck of the banyan tree like an old maharaja resigned to surrendering his province to the Union.

"And all this in India!" remarked Abhi, unsure of what he wanted to say.

"All this for the sake of ending up in India," Philippe lamented, jokingly, "alongside the handsome Pradeep whom I will take back with me to France."

"I certainly hope not!"

He could picture Mrs. Rao's frowning face. It was accompanied by visions of calls for help, fainting bouts, threats, financial blackmail, hunger strikes. Who would pay the price? They all would, including the poor Satish. He was sure to bear the brunt. And he would become even more muddled, mixing up cats and bundles of laundry. Not to mention the risk of a heart attack.

"He's shaved off his mustache. It suits him well," said Abhi.

The official theory about Pradeep's mustache prevailing in the Rao household stated the exact opposite, but Abhi felt obliged to make amends for his heartfelt outburst a minute ago.

Detachment . . . Abhi often went to Sri Ravi Ranganath's ashram in Mylapore. He had even dragged Radhika there once. She had all but fallen asleep with boredom while there! The master gave talks three times a week, except when he traveled within the country or went overseas. He enquired from Philippe if he would be interested in accompanying him there in the near future. "Oh, I forgot, Sri Sri has gone to Europe, but the ashram will be open."

"I would like that very much. I don't know him. Is he one

of those export gurus?"

"Not at all! He has devotees all over the world, so he visits them from time to time. We can't keep him here all the time just for us."

Philippe nodded.

Satish was beside himself. One of the dogs that Mrs. Rao absolutely did not tolerate inside the house was compensating for it by going berserk in the garden. Kuchu was the subject of a very serious row between Radhika and the servant. She suspected that he had inculcated in the beast a very strong liking for ball-games. The size of the garden did not help either. She often lectured to him that the dogs that roamed the streets or the ones she saw in her friends' homes were much calmer. And often more starved. So who excited him? She failed to understand how this stray dog had managed to pick up football all by itself. She had even taken pictures. In the beginning, the fascinating spectacle had amused her, the children too. The dog pushed the ball with such energy that it seemed that he was dribbling it. After a few weeks, Mrs. Rao, terrified that he might knock her down, turned on Satish whom she accused.

"I'm fed up with this dog playing football by itself in my garden. It's such a bizarre sight. I will not put up with it."

"I will not play with him," announced Satish.

"But I'm not asking you to play with him, you idiot," Radhika flared up. "What have I done to deserve such a fool? That's not what I meant. Oh God! To whom should I pray to make you intelligent?"

"Yes, Memsaab."

"What I mean is stop giving him the ball. If he didn't have it, he wouldn't play like the devil."

"But he wants the ball," Satish reasoned.

Mrs. Rao was at the end of her rope. She was convinced

that Satish encouraged Kuchu instead of taking the big ball away and controlling him.

"You will not give him the ball, that's it! You have no control at all over this stray animal. You can't let him have his way with everything."

"I notice that exercise has been good for him. He looks like he is in much better health than when we found him. Memsaab remembers how thin and scared he was?"

"Have you ever seen Tommy run like this after a ball? No. So hide that ball, and no more discussion. Oh God, all the things I have to take care of. And one day, do you realize, what if he knocks down Santosh, this crazy . . . what do you call him? Kalu . . . "

"I keep an eye so that it doesn't happen," emphasized Satish.

Mrs. Rao did not believe that.

"DO ME THE FAVOR OF NOT GIVING THE BALL TO THAT DOG WHEN SANTOSH IS HERE," she thundered furiously.

"Yes Memsaab."

It was of no use. A fortnight later, from the window, Bira and Radhika once again caught sight of the dog dribbling like Zidane and chasing after the ball that Satish had replaced with a smaller one.

"If Santosh were in the garden, the monster would make him fall," snapped Mrs. Rao.

The phone rang.

"Oh Ammu! Yes, fine dear . . . thank you. Please, Brinda, stop him, I can't take it anymore."

"What's the matter? Satish?"

"No. Well, yes. The new dog."

"The one that plays with the ball? Santosh talks only about that. I wanted to talk to you about something else," Ammu said in a rather mysterious voice. "How was your meeting with Panayappan?"

Mrs. Rao almost dropped the phone in surprise.

"You knew?"

"What, what?" Brinda exclaimed in excitement, turning back immediately instead of going out to the garden.

"Nothing! Go, please. Take care of the dog for me."

"You don't want me to hear you."

"Dear, how can you say such things," lied Radhika, still feeling perplexed. How did Ammu know that she had visited that rude man in whose office she was never going to set foot again?

Brinda was not the one to give up.

"What did she know?"

Radhika pretended to be in pain, and in a calculated move let the receiver drop. She then replaced it on the phone.

"I'm not feeling well at all. And this dog won't stop barking. Do you hear the racket? Satish should either take the ball away from him or get rid of him. He should take him back to the beach where he picked him up, it's so tiresome!"

"So what did Ammu find out?"

Cornered, Mrs. Rao came up with a new lie. She had not wanted to say it while Ammu was on the phone.

"Darling, what do you want to know? You really surprise me, dear. Don't you have anything better to do at the university? Ammu was just talking to me about Dipu's appointment with the French Department at the university, and I was simply expressing surprise that she knew about it, that's all. Please go tell Satish that I do NOT want that dog playing football in my house."

As soon as Brinda left, she quickly called her daughter-in-law on her cell phone.

"Sorry, I had to go myself and stop that dog from making so much noise. He nearly tripped me this morning."

"Santosh loves that dog."

"Ammu, who told you that I had a meeting with Panayappan? I hadn't mentioned it to anyone. None of the children knew."

"Why did you see him?"

"But who told you?" said Radhika, feeling angry. "It's too much. I must know Ammu, it's a serious thing. I think I'm going crazy. Unless I talked at night in my sleep and someone entered my room at that moment, that's impossible. How did you find out?"

"I don't know who mentioned it me. Let me see if I can remember. You had just left, and Satish said . . . "

"Satish!" exclaimed Mrs. Rao as if it were a magic word.

"He told me that you didn't want him to get you a rickshaw, and I asked him what for, and he said to go to Malar Hospital. And that it concerned someone in the house who was sick."

"Oh!"

Undoubtedly, he had his finger in every pie, and it didn't entirely displease her. It was her fault after all. She had whetted his customary curiosity and Ammu had called just then. Confronted with the burning memory of her encounter with Panayappan, she decided to put a new lie to the test. She didn't even have a choice in any case. There was no question, she could not afford to reveal the real motive for her visit. They would never pardon her.

"Yes, I consulted him. I don't feel very well these days. Nothing major, but you know, one can never be too careful. Just a small lump, but he was very reassuring. It's nothing."

Ammu was speechless.

"A small lump! You are sure?"

"Yes. Nothing to worry about. He said it very categorically."

There was a long silence.

"But . . . Satish told me something different," Ammu blurted out finally.

"Satish, Satish, Satish, it's unbelievable how in this house people listen to Satish more than any other person. It's as if he were a deity, or a family guru," she attacked. "I don't care what he may have told you, my dear Ammu, it is what I tell you that counts," Mrs. Rao persevered.

"Hm mm."

"Anyway, don't mention the lump to anyone, because it's not there."

"Satish told me he thought that your visit had something to do with Dipu."

Mrs. Rao was flabbergasted. She was absolutely sure that she had not dropped the slightest hint, even in her dreams, that her visit had something to do with her son. She feigned disdain.

"You should not have such detailed conversations with him, I'm really shocked, Ammu, it encourages him. He is already so spoilt, and I can hardly get him to do anything. He spends half the day making three miserable chapatis, and the other half watching that silly dog that he has brought home to play football. On top of that he has the impudence to talk to you about Dipu! Why is he meddling?"

"Ah!"

"What? Just because I refused to talk to him about my health problems, he went ahead and invented something else. Really, I have other people that I prefer to confide in, rather than that servant! He pretends that he is not interested in anything, and he finds out everything that goes on. It's . . . it's really becoming . . . "

Despite the tug of war with Ammu notwithstanding, Mrs. Rao was not displeased. Never before had she lied with such conviction, with that much credibility in her voice and words. Her story was good.

"You're sure there isn't any tumor? He really made sure of it?"

"Completely. Yes!" Mrs. Rao assured her with bitterness, remembering how Panayappan had refused to be bothered by her son's case.

Ammu noticed it: something was fishy. She could not put her finger on it on the spot but her mother-in-law was hiding something. There was no doubt. She had a tumor in her breast that she had tried keeping from Satish. And now she was hiding it from her. Feeling stricken, Ammu asked her mother-in-law if she wanted anything.

"Yes," chirped Radhika. She was in her highest spirits.

"What is it that you need? Just tell me."

"Don't listen that dunce Satish anymore. Don't forget how foolish he can be. You forgot what he did to the cat?"

"That's beside the point!"

"You asked me if I wanted something, and I'm giving you my answer," intoned Mrs. Rao cleverly, in a small voice.

"I promise!" Ammu replied regretfully, mortified at what she had learnt.

8

A New Haircut

"Mummy has breast cancer!"

A meeting of the Security Council had been convened at the Suneet's behest. As the eldest son of Rao family, his voice was clear and firm. Brinda buried her face in her hands. Abhi breathed in deeply (as he had been taught by his master). Dipu let out a cry.

"How do you know? She hasn't said anything to me."

"As if you should automatically be the first to be informed of everything! She hasn't said anything to me either," Brinda snapped.

"Neither to me," added Abhi.

"Nor to me," chimed in Dipu.

"Shut up!"

"What did I do?" he protested with a red face.

"You . . . Nothing," Brinda controlled herself.

"How do *you* know?" demanded Abhi.

They had gathered outside, on the verandah. It was ten o'clock, and it was becoming hot already.

"Ammu. She told Ammu."

A very long silence ensued. Everyone evaluated the news his or her own way. Dipu was the most devastated. Nobody asked why the *bahu* had been taken into confidence, and who had authorized her to spread the news. Their heads were reeling. The words *breast cancer* continued to wreak havoc on their psyche.

They felt like hostages.

"Refreshments!" announced Satish, as he popped through the door.

There was an electronic beep. Brinda rushed inside and flung herself on her seat in front of the computer. Vanessa had come online.

"OMG, Vanessa!"

"What's happening?"

"Oh My God," she typed out all the letters this time.

Outside, Pradeep was sobbing. Abhi put his arm around his shoulders. Suneet started to speak.

"She doesn't know that we know. So don't breathe even a word. Basically she only conveyed it indirectly to Ammu. Let's just keep it a secret for now."

Politics was already gaining an upper hand.

"It's going to be very hard to pretend," remarked Abhi as Satish came closer with his snacks. Thanks, leave the tray here, Satish."

"But why, why did she get it just like that, all of a sudden, just when I arrived?"

"We don't know, maybe she's had the tumor for a long time, but never said anything to anyone."

"Mummy's not strong enough to keep quiet about it," whined Dipu, as if he were talking about his double. More tears sprang from his eyes.

"That's arguable. She can be strong when needed. Remember when Dad . . . how dignified she was at that time."

Lalli came up to Suneet and rubbed against his legs. The atmosphere became less tense. "Who wants to play football with Kuchu?" asked Abhi, changing the subject. "Look at him, look how he's waiting to play football."

"This is really no time for jokes, Abhi," exclaimed Brinda crossly as she joined them again. Oh Lord, what a catastrophe!

Anyway, there is no ball to play with anymore. Satish confiscated it, right Satish?"

He almost jumped to attention.

"Yes, Memsaab wanted me to. I keep it in my room. He only gets it once a week, according to our agreement. He had it the day before yesterday, so he cannot get it today."

Kuchu could have diverted their minds, but as Bira had remarked, this wasn't the moment.

"Who is the doctor she is seeing?" asked Abhi.

"Panayappan."

"The nutcase who treated Papa?"

"He did whatever he could, Dipu. He can't be blamed." Suneet continued to play his role as the eldest sibling.

"Well, now we'll just have to see. We will observe carefully. That's what Ammu says, and I think she is right. There are all kinds or tumors. Some are benign; they are not all fatal, so first of all, let's not panic."

The word itself was enough to trigger the emotion in the others.

"Mummy is ill, she has fallen sick," moaned Pradeep in a doleful voice. "I feel like dying."

"Stop it! Please stop him!" snapped Brinda. "We'll get her treated, don't turn it into a tragedy before we know for sure."

The IT professional didn't look very convinced. He had not even touched the refreshments that Satish had brought.

"If something happens to her, I'll kill myself," he announced to the group.

"Children don't die before their parents! Will you calm down and be serious for a few minutes?"

"Don't let such thoughts enter your head," continued Abhi as he gave his brother a compassion-filled smile.

"Mummy is sick," repeated Dipu, sniffing.

Nobody dared to contradict him anymore.

"Let's stay united and let's be strong. Let's love her even more. All will be well. We will have to cry for her one day," said Abhi the rishi consolingly, "but the day hasn't come yet. There is no need to live in anticipation."

"Well said! Dipu is jumping ahead, and it's not right," Bira reminded them as she hurriedly got up in response to another alert sounded by her computer.

"Yes, Vanessa?"

"rrxebngfgjigtiutoioiyiouyiouyiouyiouyioyioyoyiouyiouyiuoyiouyoiyoing."

"OMG! It's hardly any better here. Dipu is acting like he doesn't want to live anymore. It's too much."

"OMG," continued Vanessa for whom the three letters were a rather practical tool for expressing sympathy (she was preoccupied with her own problems and not concentrating so much on her friend's).

"What exactly do we know?"

Abhi was beginning to see that the meeting wasn't going anywhere. He felt annoyed by Satish's attitude. The servant had heard the bulk of their conversation by loitering around the table, but had not said a single word, nor displayed the slightest emotion. Abhi felt hurt on behalf of the family. Radha trusted so much in him, and this is how he was reacting to the news: he was carrying out his duties as if it was no big deal. He was going about doing things with his customary contemptuous expression. Worse, he was showing detachment where he ought to have shown compassion and sensitivity. He had never performed his duties as noisily. Well, he was nothing more than a servant after all, in spite of the many years he had spent with them. *He doesn't like us, while we love him and want to keep him!* Abhi pondered a bit more. It would take more than a cancer to shake him, which was a good thing. He at least knew how to remain calm. Whether one liked it or not, sooner or later, he would become indispensable. He already was.

"And you too, Satish, by the way. Don't you breathe a word, you heard what we said. We are all counting on you. You are her loyal servant. You don't know anything, okay?"

"That won't be difficult."

Accustomed to the strange and enigmatic answers of the servant, Suneet and Abhi didn't react.

"Naturally it won't be difficult for you because you are not one of her children like us," insinuated Dipu, outraged at the remark.

"That's not what I meant," Satish defended himself.

"Very well. I'd like to know what exactly we know."

"You mean about her cancer?"

"Yes."

"I'm very disappointed with Satish," Abhi declared once Satish was out of range. "You saw how indifferent he seemed? Unbelievable!"

"I never liked him," Dipu commented.

"Oh you, you don't even know him. I don't know how you can say such a thing. You don't even live with us," attacked Brinda, breaking the truce.

"Thanks, I know."

"Satish is part of the family," she reminded her brother in order to provoke him, without really believing in the words she was saying.

It was the right thing to do, repeating the official theory dear to Mrs. Rao's heart, especially since she was not present.

Just then, as if the theory needed further validation, Mrs. Rao appeared in person. She crossed the garden towards them, clad in a pale pink sari that had flowers and stars printed on the top part. She was escorted by Tommy. They were followed by Satish, with Kuchu in tow who was barking furiously. He had been deprived of his ball and was on a leash.

"She's had a haircut!" exclaimed Brinda.

"What rubbish!"

"No. Just look."

Mrs. Rao collapsed on a chair, beaming, next to Pradeep.

"Satish, start serving," she ordered. "What has she prepared this morning?" she enquired. She had not had the time to talk to their cook before her departure.

"Chana masala."

"Okay. Start serving. I'm terribly hungry. My bad haircut has given me quite an appetite."

"It's not all that bad," said Brinda cheeringly, though she thought just the opposite. "In six days it will look wonderful."

"Oh, really?" Well, in seven days I'll be going back to the place where I usually get my hair cut, to my old hairdresser. I don't know why I listened to Satish! You all have such a serious look on your faces."

"Yes. You are right," Brinda blurted out.

Abhi and Suneet stared at her. All the resolutions were already going up in smoke.

"How did he put it the other day, this Philippe?" Mrs. Rao tried to recall. "Ah yes, in his country they say that people are making a 'funeral face.' Well children, that's how you look today; you are making that kind of face."

"No!" exclaimed Dipu.

"That's not how they say it? I may have gotten the expression wrong. Did I make a mistake?"

"You didn't make any mistake," Dipu assured her in a choking voice.

Mrs. Rao found the atmosphere around the table very strange. She opened her purse and rummaged for her mirror.

"Well, I'm not going to meddle in your affairs, you must have all fought, just look at Brinda's face. All I do is leave for a couple of hours," she continued as she inspected her haircut, "and you start fighting like cats and dogs! What will it be like when I'm gone?"

The hearts of all the children, with the exception of Suneet, resounded in unison: "Oh!"

"Don't say that," said Dipu. "Don't say such things!"

"It's inauspicious," added Brinda. "Don't say such stuff."

Mrs. Rao appeared mystified and fidgeted with her hair.

"Aren't you exaggerating a little? What is it? I find Philippe's expression, this funeral business, interesting. Oh well. I don't want to get involved in your silly matters. By the way, Philippe isn't here today?"

"Um... er . . . "

"They are not married," Brinda chuckled.

Mrs. Rao attributed the maliciousness to their hostile relations. "Not that I'm missing him, mind you. And this *chana masala*, when will he bring it?"

The question that was burning on everyone's lips was finally articulated.

"How are you feeling, Mummy?" asked Brinda, in her sweetest voice.

"Exhausted! Absolutely wiped out! Can you imagine, the municipal authorities have had the funny idea of giving a two thousand rupee award to anyone who catches and brings them a stray cow, and it's creating more traffic jams than ever before. There is chaos everywhere. I got caught in the middle of a convoy while I was out. The rickshaw couldn't do anything. People have it in their heads to round up all these cows, and we just have to be patient about it. Well, let's eat. Thank you, Satish."

Radhika helped herself and passed the dish to Pradeep, who wasn't hungry.

"Why did you get your hair cut?" he asked, on the verge of tears.

"Ask Satish!" she replied pointing towards him. "He had one of his brilliant ideas, as usual. He recommended this new beauty salon that has just opened. The name should have been a warning to me, I should have been more cautious: *Honest Hairdressers*."

"Of course," confirmed Brinda. "Why would you even go there? *Honest Hairdressers*? I would have run away as fast as I could."

Her mouth full, Mrs. Rao just listened meekly.

"That's true, but then I'm not my daughter, that's the problem. I thought that Satish had found something decent, he does sometimes come up with good discoveries sometimes."

No one said a word. Satish did have good qualities, but "coming up with good discoveries" wasn't exactly one of them.

"Memsaab, it's a very good haircut," he suddenly lit up.

"Ah yes? Thank you very much, Satish."

Abhi fumed in silence. Not only did their servant have a cold heart but he lied to their faces with impudence in order to make himself look good. And poor Mummy, she couldn't even notice it.

"No," she said after he had left. "I didn't want to say anything in front of the poor fellow. He would've felt bad, poor fellow, but this haircut is atrocious, isn't it?" Anyone hearing her grumble about her new hairdo would have thought she was the maharani of Jaipur complaining about the traffic problems besetting her capital city for the last three decades, with its streets packed with as many cows as cars. "Hah, Satish can keep his hairdresser to himself. *Honest Hairdressers!* With a name like that you can be sure it's going to be a disaster, don't you think?"

"You said that already. Don't let it upset you."

"Yes, Mummy, don't let it affect you. You know we love you the way you are, and it makes no difference to us the way they messed up your hair," said Abhi on behalf of everybody as he put his arm around his mother's shoulder.

Mrs. Rao's astonishment knew no bounds.

"Well, it looks like I need to go there more often. It has obviously made all of you a little more considerate towards me."

"Lucidity is a form of suffering." The words of René Char[3] arrived in the dining area of an unpretentious little restaurant near Egmore station at about the same time as the huge crêpe that the waiter placed in front of Philippe along with the traditional steel tumbler filled with water. Philippe hesitated, then drank it all up in one gulp. After all, he was an Indian. Not quite. Almost. In any case, when it came to drinking water like that, he definitely was! René Char's idea seemed to him as nourishing as the *dosa* stuffed with vegetables that was in front of him. He attacked it with a fork. That did not do it justice. Since when did one eat a *dosa* with a fork? He got up, made his way to where they told him the tap was, and meticulously washed his hands.Back at the table he began eating his *dosa* with gusto, using his right hand. Stuffing his mouth with the chillies and spices, he pulled out his inner calculator in order to compute his happiness. Not only was he madly in love with this country, this city, Pradeep, his family, Mrs. Rao's rigidity, Indian culture, the bewildering chaos that prevailed with nascent modernity on one side and powerful traditions on the other, but he was also thinking about René Char! And if this wasn't bliss then what was? Inventing it, going somewhere to find it would be an exercise in futility! The juxtaposition of elements as diverse as a giant crêpe, thiiiiiiiiiin as a gauze and wrapped around vegetables, which easily crumbled into tiny bits on his plate) and the superior thoughts of a genius liberated from the limits of boundaries. Wasn't this what real plenitude was, the successful transcendence of appearances minus the burden of indigestible

---

[3] A 20th century French poet who described lucidity as "la blessure la plus rapprochée du soleil," the wound closest to the sun.

pain? "I'm inventing a happiness that I don't have," he told himself bitterly, as he returned to the sink to wash his hands.

The tiny internet café that he entered was empty. He quickly checked his messages. There was a lot of junk mail, and only four or five real emails. One of them, from an unknown member of a mailing list that he subscribed to, intrigued him: "I live in Noida. Anybody in the area who will be my Krishna? I am waiting." The person who had sent it had signed his name as Charan Patni and had also added the postscript "Foreigners are welcome."

"What is this? What are you reading?"

Philippe turned around. Pradeep put his arms around Philippe's neck.

"How did you know that I was here?"

"You weren't in the restaurant. I knew I would fine you in the nearest internet café, so I looked for it! I know them all around here."

They both laughed. Philippe paid twenty rupees to a man whose pale yellow dhoti, tied tightly around the waist, made his stomach appear even fatter.

"You're corresponding with a Krishna devotee?"

"No."

"Watch out, foreign sahib! You have no right to tell lies!"

"Hare Krishna, *mon amour*."

"Hare Krishna, my love. I believe in nakedness, the baring of the soul to the body, and of the body to the soul," Dipu suddenly revealed, inspired by the evocation of Krishna.

"Strange. What does one have to be to think like that? Indian and gay at the same time, perhaps."

"You better believe it."

They came out of the shop..

"You saw how he looked at us?"

Pradeep shrugged.

"I don't care, even a bit. I don't give a damn. That's why I want to live in France. Even my mother doesn't look at us like that; it is she who matters."

"That's because she doesn't know."

"She doesn't want to know. Being poor or being gay, it boils down to the same thing here: you are suspect."

Philippe stopped dead in his tracks.

"It's the same everywhere. Don't think it's like that only over here. There, one hides it. One hides everything. Look at my family; they are such experts at pretending. That's how they give themselves importance. It's important to give oneself importance, how else to live? You think they have tolerance? It's only because it's fashionable."

"Not in my opinion. You just need an excuse to live here, that's all," diagnosed Dipu coldly. "As for me, I want to live over there."

"Naturally," commented the sahib, observing the belly of a cow walking nonchalantly in the middle of the road, oblivious of the cowboys that the city had unleashed in her pursuit. "She must have swallowed all the plastic bags lying around, just look, Dipu."

"They die from the hundreds and hundreds of plastic bags that they swallow over the course of months and years."

It was sad, but there was nothing they could do to help the cows except salute their courage and give credit to the administration for trying to remove them from inside the cities, for trying to displace them, protect them. If they ate so much plastic, it was better if they got sent away from a place where there was so much plastic lying around everywhere. Philippe couldn't help but identify with the cow occupying a good part of the left lane of the road in front of him. He was also going to be "displaced" soon, or half-killed, in other words. Deprived from the sovereign freedom of being a prisoner of his land of birth. This was the definition of a displaced person. He imagined being in India for real, for good. Without the problem of having to renew a three or six month visa. No more hassles, no more waiting at the consulate. It was really funny, all those people crawling up to the window almost like beggars, pleading for a piece of paper, a permit, no, a symbol, a symbol of the force of a truth loftier than the peaks of administrative ineptness. He also imagined, in front of him, a competent official who did not need to be bribed, who would solve his problem once and for all. *We deliberated on your case, we have decreed, it's as if we were giving you an award, are you ready to receive it?* That was the crux of the problem. Accepting to receive what one had a right to. They would give him the psychological equivalent of a diplomatic passport, the freedom from depending on a drowsy official whose job consisted of "stamping" the whole day (and being yelled at, the poor fellow, whenever problems arose, which was inevitable). None of that! He was free to come and go, like in the good old days when all this did not exist. He was at home everywhere, Bombay, Madras, Paris, it was essentially the same city, just with a different name, with different people and cows with whom one might not exchange a look, and despite the relative resemblance they made you leave once your time was up. They give you six months. It's a long time, one feels, and then it's over. Who asked for such a definite period of time? These visas were a joke. *We'll give you anything but that.* Traveling had no use, it did nothing for you, yet it did everything, it made everything possible.

In this manner, he imagined himself in India for good, for real. Not like a flaky tourist acting like a divine *sadhu* pursuing spiritual bliss, doing the Goa, Pushkar or Kerala circuits - a role which alas he loved playing - the heavy fake pearl necklaces that reached down to the navel included. All that had just nothing to do with the real Indian life, which existed - just like French or English real life exists - without the temples, but which all the same fills your head to the point of making it feel that it's going to burst.

"Sometimes," said Dipu suddenly (he was not thinking of his mother), "I wonder what you are trying to say."

"My pain at being displaced without having asked to be displaced, just like this cow in the near future, but for her it's probably not a big deal."

"You, displaced? Who is displacing you? What are you talking about?"

"Nothing! I'm just talking on behalf of all those famished people who left their country one day without understanding - nobody explained anything to them - they just wandered about pretending they did while another country foolishly tried to console them, with academic degrees, successes, failures (to make them believe that success was important), and all of that meant nothing, it was worth nothing other than what it represented. That's all. It was all just a pretense, nations playing their colonial games. I'm talking about mine, basically."[4]

"Come on, let's go to a temple, it is there for you," assured Pradeep, holding his friend's hand as they do in India, without the gesture signifying physical intimacy. "It's there just for you."

Sometimes he never understood a word of the rambling monologues that Philippe launched into. He ascribed these moments of incomprehension to gaps in his own knowledge of French. It wasn't anything esoteric, at any rate. They simply had different ways of thinking.

Seeing another cow walking languorously on the road, the sahib suddenly asked himself another absurd question as he often did: what was it that made the English, the French and the Indians different from each another, just like their cows? Were

---

[4] Reference to France's relationship with the Pied-noirs.

the differences real? Space, nationality, beliefs . . . none of those seemed important. Didn't one live with all this baggage simply because of convenience? Philippe was reminded of the words of a Taoist master: *If we really look at our existence, we will find only a thin layer of varnish over an immense ocean of insignificance.*

They entered the temple and took their shoes off. Philippe watched Dipu disappear into a haze of incense smoke as he sat down to wait in the shade of the temple courtyard. He watched Dipu appear and disappear again, inside. He vaguely remembered a forgotten poem. *Wearing crowns of thyme and marjoram the joyful elves roam in the fields* ··· [5] He had spun around with so much grace in the narrow passage inside the temple. Observing him, Philippe remembered that he had also been suspecting for the last few days - although he did not have any proof - that Dipu was angling for a job with his father, which would explain his almost obsessive wish to "return" (he had even dared to say that he was missing France - what a nightmare - like a true son of the Republic!). This was diametrically opposite to the plans that Philippe was nurturing to live in India. Among all the reasons for wanting to return to France that Pradeep had brought up, there was at least one good one: the legitimacy of their union. There they were a couple; here they were nothing! Radha sometimes went to the extent of pretending that she understood but then would revert to denial by taking recourse to humor. Even Satish had better self-control. She might hatch a plot against him; she was quite capable, thought Philippe.

As for Dipu, he was missing the Deputy-Mayor, his future "father-in-law," the European legislator whose political work was incidentally helping consolidate the usage of this new terminology. The elderly politician had a special fondness for the programmer from Madras. Despite his age, the crafty

---

[5] From a poem by José María de Heredia.

Delcourt Senior was slated to win in the upcoming elections. His influence had not diminished; it was just that his children took no advantage of it. In this old country, as Mrs. Rao would have described it (without being able to put her finger on it on a map), where nepotism and its derived privileges were like sacred cows and constituted an *exception culturelle*, and where the caste system of the *Ancien Régime* was chugging along just fine, Olivier Delcourt had often succeeded in placing his protégés. It was proof of his social and networking skills. Finding a good job for a young and brilliant Indian would have been one of those challenges that the elderly Delcourt would have gladly met head on if he had had Philippe's approval. Philippe had however seemed keen on delaying the operation for the time being. Rumors circulating in diplomatic circles said that if the *Yes* vote passed the following May, the Deputy-Mayor would be likely to assume new functions within the Council. It wouldn't be just France but the whole of Europe where he would then be able to exercise his influence. He had a clean record, he hadn't had a part in the fake job scandal; he was not a *persona non grata* in Bruxelles. Obviously, all the European requirements, all the new puritanical ethics that the French would be forced to adhere to would complicate things somewhat, but Delcourt, the astute politician and first rate manipulator that he was, knew the ropes. The one to catch him with his hands inside the cookie jar had yet to be born. His opponents had tried all sorts of tricks. One of them who had briefly had the chance to serve as home minister between two elections had even had his phone tapped in order to pick something up that might incriminate his victim. In vain.

Because of all these reasons, and a few more - like Philippe's indecision about whether he wanted to live in France with Dipu, their stay in Chennai was beginning to feel like a fake holiday. India was a challenge that he wanted to take on. There was something so impossible about two men living together in India, be they devotees of Krishna or not (unless one were willing to face the harsh difficulties of such a life, or unless one chose to live in Bombay - outside of India), that he felt more and more attracted by the idea, the desire, unless what it really signified was a quest for *an elsewhere*. Was it? If yes, wasn't this reason after all the most precious of them all?

9

Letter from a French Father

She was sick. There was no way he could leave. Not right away, at least. He had been hoping to spend the New Year holidays in France, in Suresnes, with the father-in-law, the snow . . . Impossible, she would need him.

That bungling idiot Satish! With his retarded smile and his negligent habits he was quite capable of poisoning her. Bira? Oh Bira, she could not be relied on either, what with her attitude and her way of programming their mother's cancer into her daily schedule as it were some kind of an extra burden that kept her from spending time with her computer. And Abhi? In his typical nonchalant style, he would only pray to Shiva twice as much, which, unless a miracle were to happen, would neither cure their mother in three days nor help take care of her needs.

Fortunately, I'm there. The faithful son! Destiny had brought him back to her at the opportune moment.

Philippe couldn't conceal his joy when Dipu informed him two days later, in a very solemn tone, that he had changed his mind. They were staying on in Chennai.

"That is great, Dipu, that is great!" Philippe exploded in joy.

He was applying a white powder on his forehead, tracing lines, three parallel lines with his fingers as advised by Abhi.

"Great?"

"Yes, I'm . . . I'm . . . I'm simply thrilled; nothing could be better news, if you know what I mean. I was secretly hoping, secretly of course, that you would agree, but I didn't dare think that you would, and now you here you are, thinking just like me! We can now live here! You'll see, everything will be fine! First of all, I really like your family," he gushed. "I think I like your folks more than my own who are really very narrow minded. You will say that your mother is narrow minded too, but that's just not true, and moreover, she is starting to appreciate me more and more. Dipu, you've made me the happiest man on Earth, and you'll see . . . "

"Have you had your say?" his Krishna cut him off impatiently.

"I am overjoyed. You will be able to reestablish ties with the French Department at the University and tell them that you have changed your mind, they will hire you for the next semester, and maybe . . . "

"Are you finished?"

"You better not count on me working here. I think it's going to be very difficult for me to get a job here but I'm going to email my father and ask him to send me money and . . . "

Pradeep couldn't get a word in. He got up from his big armchair, determined to put an end to the feverish outpourings of the Frenchman, to his Indian delirium. Walking up to the window that overlooked a courtyard, he managed to clarify that he hadn't changed his mind over the basics. He still had the intention of "returning" as soon as possible, but his mother, as he had just learned, had developed cancer.

"What?"

"She hasn't spoken to me directly about it. She told my sister-in-law..."

"Ammu?"

Dipu nodded.

"Wow! Just like that?"

"Yeah. I come back from France after seven years, and this is what I learn. Fortunately, I am here now, near her."

"Of course," insisted the Frenchman, greedily anticipating the long months, perhaps years, that awaited him in India.

Radhika's illness. Ideal pretext! What could be better? Everything served a purpose in this base world.

"I need to talk to you."

Philippe turned around, surprised.

Mrs. Rao's supposed illness was continuing to have an effect, on Pradeep especially. A hallucinatory drug, it was making him swing between numbness and optimism. The previous night, he had dreamt of the ocean. A gigantic wave rushing in. He kept his balance on the surfboard, mastered the wave. A sudden tumble and then he was sinking, losing consciousness. Revival on a deserted beach. He had been washed ashore miraculously. He had woken up with a start. Nightmares were a horrifying habit that his system seemed to be acquiring.

"I hope you aren't blaming yourself!"

Guilt . . . A subtle traveler. It began with your own self as its starting point. It left you, invaded others, and came back to you. It roamed the whole earth on its wings. Philippe sensed it circling over Dipu's head. Like a fallen angel, masked, disfigured, manipulative, but resplendent all the same, an old actress making a comeback, bewildered, pretty. The model couple that Dipu and his mom were suddenly led him to imagine a Hollywood-like scene: Mrs. Rao in the place of Gloria Swanson in *Sunset Boulevard*, with a huge red dot in the middle of her forehead, coming down the majestic staircase of her residence.

"Blaming myself?" he asked, feeling disconcerted.

"That's not it? No guilt, I hope."

Dipu came and sat close to him. Yes, he was feeling guilty, but the guilt didn't date back to yesterday, or to the time of the announcement. That was not the issue. He wasn't guilty of anything. It is the nature of paradox to rear its ugly head in

119

extreme situations, when one is under threat, when logic packs up and leaves, knowing it has lost.

"Let me tell you something straight off. You are in no way responsible for your mother's illness," Philippe declared, in an almost menacing tone.

"And what if I had listened to you and told her about us? What would have happened? I prefer not to even think about it; it makes me feel really sick in the stomach!It's a good thing I realized in time what she needed to be told: nothing."

"Nonsense! You wouldn't have been responsible for anything. And you would have spoken the TRUTH."

He figured that during his three or four visits to Adyar, he had dropped enough hints. The dear obnoxious Mrs. Rao surely had a fairly good idea of what had been cooking with her little boy lost in France (and now in Chennai under her eyes, barely twelve minutes by rickshaw). Dipu brushed him off.

"I disagree. You are completely wrong. You are seeing things from the point of view of your panic mentality. It's not like that here."

"I know."

"You are seeing things like a European. Our being recognized isn't my goal. I don't have a western point of view. You really think she understood your talk about *pacs*? Not at all! Your explanations are too subtle for her. She actually thinks you're a clown."

"You're letting your mustache grow back?"

"Do you realize where you are?"

"Tell it to her plainly once and for all," he insisted, irritated.

Pradeep's face crinkled up with stress like water on the surface of a river when it is touched by wind and a ray of sunlight. His expression revealed the panic Philippe's horrifying words had triggered in him.

"Never! You're full of violence." he defended himself.

"And because you are not, life is passing you by."

Dipu had never heard anything more terrible in his life. He fought back the tears welling up in his eyes. He wasn't however going to relent or show any weakness.

"She'll be very hurt," he said in a very matter of fact way.

"Ah, so now we are going to spare her feelings?"

"You think she won't be hurt?"

"Are you trying to plead her case?"

Pradeep did not get sidetracked: "What does she see? I live abroad, she doesn't know what I do, who I mix with and I am not married . . . "

"But I'm marrying you!" exclaimed Philippe, laughing. "It can't get any simpler in Europe. Especially for us. My father is ready to rouse the journalists in Suresnes, your picture will be in the papers . . . "

"Your dad is insane," he reminded him. The idea of a civil union was not very pleasing to Dipu, especially if it meant there were going to be photographs in circulation. With her internet skills Brinda would surely find them, and Mummy would feel shocked and dishonored. "He's thinking of his career."

"Not really. At his age, it's more about getting attention and taking advantage of another opportunity to triumph over his adversaries. He does like you a lot, you know."

Dipu blinked. He also liked his father-in-law. What a great personality he had! Somewhere between that of the Duke of Edinburgh and Philippe de Villiers, a synthesis, with three hours worth of make-up . . .

"So he doesn't need it in order to advance his career?"

"How did your father die?" asked Philippe brutally.

Pradeep remembered, just as he was interrupted, that he had been meaning to talk to Philippe about something.

"I want to talk to you about Satish. You know, I've been wondering a lot about him ever since I've come back here. I don't trust him. Mummy has complete faith in him; it's illogical.

121

He doesn't seem very reliable. Brinda is hardly any better. They are always in raptures when that idiot is around, and . . . "

"So what's the problem?"

"The problem? He's not the kind of person she needs to be with now. She is sick, she needs someone else. I don't dare bring up the question with her. I'm wondering if you could be very discreet and knock some sense into her. I get the impression that in that house Satish has become a VIP. He acts with impunity. He provides the worst possible service and they all look up to him as if here were a god."

Philippe thought for a minute before coming up with a solution: "I like him, he's quite funny, your Satish. Don't count on me to say anything negative about him."

"That's not what I asked you to do."

"Looks like you are afraid of him, because you aren't able to manipulate him. If I were you, I would turn him into ally."

"Never!" exclaimed Dipu, as if he had been told to make a pact with his worst enemy.

"Suit yourself."

Two days later, wearing an impeccable cream-colored dhoti, a visibly agitated Dipu presented himself at Philippe's.

"These auto *wallahs* are terrible," he said complaining about the rickshaw drivers. They are getting worse each day. He wanted sixty rupees! It's not even two kilometers . . . "

"You make them bring down their rates. That's how I've been spending my time."

"I got so annoyed that I refused to bargain. Do you know what I told him?"

"That he was asking for too much?"

Dipu paused briefly.

"The opposite! I told him: Sorry, I cannot get inside for less than one hundred. I will have to refuse. His jaw dropped."

Philippe made a whistling sound. He wasn't in a hurry to

give him the news that he had.

"She's bringing us some tea."

"Thanks."

"I got an email from Papa."

"He's sending you money?"

"It's not that."

"Then what?"

Philippe handed him a crumpled piece of paper that looked like it had been read over a dozen times or else tucked away deep in the folds of a dhoti.

"Read it to me! We'll have to show it to your mother. I had vaguely talked to him about our wedding plans, and he sends me this. It's the speech that he prepared for the Assembly. Take a look and tell me if it's well written or not."

"Show me," said Dipu flatly.

While Leela was setting the tea in front of them, they joked about sending the text of the speech to Delhi, to Sonia Gandhi's office.

"*I address you, my dear colleagues, as we enact legislation to protect the rights of individuals of the same sex who want to marry. They are amongst the people who are very close to us. For the first time in our country's history, we are extending what we know to be the happiness of family life to our neighbors, to our colleagues in our workplaces and factories, to our friends, to members of our family. We are in the process of creating a more just society, a society that chooses to no longer humiliate its members.*

Like the Spaniards yesterday, we, the French, are today attempting to respond to the aspirations of those among us who, for the longest time, have been humiliated, their rights denied, their dignity trampled, their identity negated. I ask you why? Today, the simple fact that we are here questioning this injustice obliges us to find new answers, answers that remind us that the road to freedom also passes through the books of law. Today, our society, following the dictates of an inner impulse that, though difficult, is unstoppable, is choosing to guarantee these fellow citizens the respect they deserve, choosing to recognize their rights, to affirm their identities, and to restore its basic character to freedom. Freedom which, since the dawn of civilization, has always had to struggle to stay alive, has always had to struggle against the crushing force of tradition.

Dear colleagues, it is true that we are dealing with a minority, so why change the law, you could ask. Because that's exactly what it's about! A minority! The victory of a minority is always the victory of all. The triumph is ours, including those who are fighting against this bill. They will realize it later, history shall prove it. It is liberty that triumphs, and certainly not one group of people against another. Their victory makes us all, even those that are combating the new law, citizens of distinction, responsible and vigilant, civilized in a true sense. Our society, as I believe and say to you, will only emerge greater. Tell me, what damage are we causing to the institution of marriage, to the concept of marriage, by legally allowing two people of the same sex to marry? None! It is strange that the question generates so much spite, mockery, arrogance, and especially condescension, the worst of crimes, as if our laws were made so perfect that they could never be changed. Of which law of the strongest are we talking? We cause no harm to the institution of marriage by allowing such unions. On the contrary, we would finally be giving to each the opportunity to organize life as they choose, with the rights and privileges that come with marriage. In this present hour which is calling upon us to decide, the idea of family must be reexamined. How could the new law be prejudicial to the institution of marriage if, on the contrary, it is only strengthening it?

I am fully aware that in our country some people are in strong disagreement with us, with this change. Are our legal family codes unchangeable? Some would have us believe that. They are wrong. Our concern is simple: spare our fellow citizens unnecessary suffering. I have always believed that a society that takes care of its minorities, that works to eliminate needless suffering, is a society on the path of progress. Such a society doesn't crush its members and is not afraid to proclaim its first and foremost value: freedom . . ."

"He's repeating himself," declared Dipu, as he put down the printout for a moment.

"It's meant to be a persuasive speech," defended Philippe.

"Hmm."

"This law makes it possible for our country to reaffirm its commitment to freedom, to tolerance, in a profound way. Some will say it does so in a provocative way, but it is freedom that is provocative, not us. Women's rights, divorce, these were the issues of yesterday. Today, we cannot even imagine it, but till very recently in our history women did not have the same rights as men. Could we have let such a situation continue? Should lawmakers not one day have allowed those who want it the equal right to be separated from the person they are bound to by law? Today, we have the extraordinary opportunity to create a new freedom that will be available to those who need it. They have fought to receive this right. I am here in their name. They dictate my words. There has been a maturation process, all this hasn't happened without effort or sacrifice. They fully deserve what I hope they will indeed receive from the representatives of the nation.

Today, I would like to convince you, dear colleagues, that with this law our society will become more mature, more open. It will create new bridges, more tolerance; we will be ensuring greater justice by refusing to accept the suffering and humiliation of a category of our fellow citizens. There is suffering about which we can do nothing, suffering that we alas cannot eliminate. This suffering, on the other hand, predicated on exclusion, rejection, and hatred, is possible for us to end. It is in our power to do so. We must all be equal in front of the law: marriage is the concern of all those who decide to contract an alliance.

I salute all those who, sacrificing their lives and undergoing countless sufferings, mental and physical, occasioned by their sexual orientation, and facing family ostracism in recent times, have today made this change possible thanks to your vote for the welfare of all. We are not the first but I'm sure we will not be the last. Other countries, the whole world, will one day follow our example, guided by two irresistible forces: freedom and equality."

Dipu finished reading the speech and silently folded the paper. Philippe noticed that he looked pale.

"Dipu, translate it into English and show it to your mother, okay?"

"Very funny!"

"Then I'll show it to her myself."

He was joking again. Dipu shrugged.

"What did you think of the speech? Well written, isn't it?"

"What a fool your dad is!" he fumed. "It's heavy, dull. It needs to be rewritten. I'm not judging the content, I quite agree, in fact. But coming from him, it's a little surprising."

"You bet!" exclaimed Philippe who still hadn't gotten over his father's great artistry, his new style of transforming himself into a paragon of virtue and tolerance.

"I thought he was completely preoccupied with the referendum."

"It will be a *Yes*, he's sure about it. He wants to be ready to tackle marriage right away after that, before anybody else gets the idea."

"I see," said Dipu, feeling more and more doubtful.

The special morals rampant in politics were not a new thing. It was like the real estate business. You had to be the quickest. Market realities had their dictates. Dipu felt a strange elation, as if he had found a secret planet inside an impenetrable solar system.

Redundancies aside, the speech thrilled him. As much as he felt restrained by the social and family ties that he was a prisoner to, the excitement that he felt on reading the letter was beyond the ordinary. In Paris, encouraged by the high society living that he was accustomed to, he would have celebrated. In Chennai, he was incapable of celebrating. The content of the father-in-law's speech, even before being a bomb in the eyes of the average Indian was as grotesque an idea as all the cows disappearing from the streets of Delhi or Jaipur in less than twenty-four hours.

"Should we mail it to Sonia? Those two are colleagues after all."

"Very funny! Stop it! I don't want a conspiracy hanging over my head."

"A conspiracy hanging over your head? Anon?

Dipu gave him a furious look. "Don't call me that, it's silly, ridiculous, like your idea to send this speech to Sonia. I don't want you to call me by that name anymore." And to soften the effect of his anger he added, "honey."

"K," responded Philippe, leaving out the O out of sheer laziness.

"So is that all?" continued Dipu, sipping his cold tea.

"Do you want to read the letter my father sent along with this? It's worth reading."

He dug into the folds of his dhoti and produced a new piece of paper, better preserved than the previous one. Dipu glanced at the letterhead and began to read:

"*Well son, what do you say? What do you make of it? I snitched a few ideas from Zapatero, but not too many. They would not have worked for us. I don't think Bush or Blair will be taking borrowing any of my ideas. By the way, will you be kind enough to time the speech for me, you do it so well, or ask Pradeep to do it, I know he enjoys such things . . .*"

"What makes him think that I enjoy such things?"

"It doesn't matter. Keep reading. You don't have to do it. I don't plan to either. He's just being pompous."

"He is excited about it," Dipu corrected him.

"I'm taking this opportunity to thank you for your silence! Bravo! How long have you been gone? I don't exactly remember, early November, that's right, or maybe October, and not even three lines, don't tell me that they don't have the Internet in Madras. I met Jean-Bernard yesterday and he did not enquire about you. It shocked me at that moment and then I realized that all four of you have reached such a degree of indifference that I think that it's finally a good thing, all this indifference. There is something positive about it, you all have stopped pretending. I hope that you are not taking it too badly and that you will allow me my comments. This is what I feel. Nadette thinks the same, besides. To think that you did not even go and see your brother when you and Pradeep were in Florida! By the way, Beatrice is expecting, we just found out. Allow me another little remark (you don't really have a choice): I don't understand why you didn't go to meet Christopher. If you are still upset with him, what can I say further? It's because you don't put yourself in his shoes. If you put yourself in his place you would no longer be resentful towards him; all recriminations and reproaches would vanish, this is the old sage speaking."

"He is right!" commented Dipu.

"Of course!"

"It gives an old father, they say, great pleasure in being the mediator between his offspring (even though that is not a father's primary role, I agree). In keeping with that, I am giving you news that you can get from your sister, Carole. Surprisingly, she asked about you, but it was because she heard about a train accident in north India, and her knowledge of geography being what it is, she got worried about you. I reminded her that as shown in any atlas, there is always a north and a south, and that Madras was located far south. As for the new name, I should get used to saying Chennai like you, but what can you expect, I'm too old now for that. I have

noticed that you are acquiring good, almost political habits. All the rampant colonialism here, and these laws that they are pushing to recognize its positive role, are very unfortunate. The oppressed peoples will surely appreciate arrogance. Carole will be in Martinique for Christmas, and I hope the territory becomes autonomous or independent soon, the word metropolis is terrible. Hush! This is just between you and me. I recently had a discussion with the President of the island's Regional Council and he has convinced me. You see, Philippe, what is anomalous is that we are getting ready to legalize gay marriage but we are not concerned about extricating our country from colonialism. If I were a logical person, I would first begin by fighting for the people who are still under the paternalistic dependency of the State, and only then would I think about individuals. The problem is that I'm not very good with logic, and your "feelings" for Dipu have caused me to change my priorities. Contrary to what you think, Nadine supports me on this.

How were your meetings with Dipu's family? He seems so attached to them. Our family needs to take a leaf out of their book. I remember how he talks about them, quite unlike us all, that's for sure. At any rate, you should take a close look. How is the mother? I mean Dipu made her out to be quite old-fashioned, I don't like the expression a bit, but I can't think of another. On a different note, the Yes campaign has taken off well, and the site is receiving a record number of hits, going by that one can assume that there will not be any problem. It looks like the campaign is going to be pretty boring, but we are used to that. Another thing, I heard that they are trying to remove all the cows in Delhi, and I think I'm being very selfish and irresponsible but I hope they won't do such a thing. I remember when I was walking in Old Delhi once, can you picture this, I found myself completely blocked, as if I were a vehicle, even though I was on foot. I couldn't move an inch. I was stuck between three cows, a three-wheeler and a fellow struggling with his cycle-rickshaw, and it was all happening in that typical calm Indian way. It was unforgettable . . .

One last thing. Don't think I'm trying to fan the flames but your sister-in-law Noémie came up with a real funny one the other day at the dinner table. She said that the gays were aping straight people by wanting to marry. I retorted that in the thirties women who wanted to obtain voting rights were also aping men. It was funny, all that talk about copying. She remained quiet after that.

With all my love,

Papa.

PS – I have accepted an invitation from that asshole of a TV host, I never remember his name, ah, Georges-Denis Garaut, in fact I think his first name is Georges only and he added the second one because it looks very CHIC. Don't tell me that you are also going around with a name like that. His parents gave him the names separately, without the hyphen. These TV people will go to any length so that people talk about them. A little bit like me . . . "

Philippe took the letter back. "It tickles me, the way he ends the letter: He sets me up against that bitch and then he flaunts all his love."

"He loves you dearly," lectured Dipu, making use of his ponderous common sense which always smacked of a lack of imagination when it came to expressing general principles about family.

"I would like to know more about how great his love for me is. He has capabilities that I'm ignorant of, given the history between him and me. It is ambiguous, to say the very least."

Dipu remained silent.

"Doesn't my father's speech make you think about what you could say to your mother?"

"On the contrary, no!" he replied in a provocative tone.

"Use it, since it is there! It's a unique opportunity. There aren't many people in India who have that kind of luck."

"What luck? How modest of you! That your father is a

politician? It's more of bad luck than anything else."

"Oh, you really think so?"

Dipu stood up, walked to the window, came back and sat down, this time on the floor, against Philippe's legs.

"I have been away from my country for almost seven years. I used to cry almost each time I used to talk to my mother, and you want me to announce it in her face that I am gay? And that too, and this is beside the point, when I have just found out that she has cancer!"

Philippe Delcourt caressed his hair. The Honorable Senator-Mayor's grand speech had not yielded the result he had expected.

He could not win against Dipu, he knew that.

"Such psychodrama!" he sighed.

10

Waiting for *Laddus*

Mrs. Rao found it impossible to put the newspaper down. She clutched it close to her as if the act of holding it tightly would lessen the effect that the news had produced on her. Suneet had thrust it under her nose. Even Satish wouldn't have done such a thing. No, he would have been incapable of it!

"No! Let me read it again. I still don't understand. It must be someone else. There is no chance of that, you think?"

"None whatsoever!"

She heard, in the next room, the opening notes not of an opera but of a session of Windows 98. She found this "music" irritating. It meant that her daughter had returned home and had turned the computer on without bothering to come and say hello first.

"Howdy?" chirped Brinda, poking her head into the room since she had nothing better to do while she waited for the computer to get fully booted.

"Tell Microsoft to get rid of that music, I'm ready to sign a petition. How can they subject people to such a horrible sound? But that's not the problem today, darling."

To entice Brinda, she flourished the newspaper in front of her, like one tempts a dog with a biscuit, and burst into tears.

"You're reading the newspaper?" asked Brinda, incredulously. "That is something new! Are they talking about Kuchu's performance in football?"

That morning Brinda had woken up with a fever. What a horrible night! Would he win? She felt optimistic. He was the best. Well, in her dreams at least. She had seen him win. He was crushing his opponents. Even Satish hadn't been able to stay still. He had paced up and down with Lalli in his arms. Hmm. Leave that kitten alone, will you. Don't touch her at all. Not being able to contain herself, she had left the house. Satish was also concerned and was wondering if . . . The anxiety, the suspense, the incredible injustice in case of a defeat, it was all too much. There was nothing that could be done, except wait, wait for the hours to pass while the clock ticked. The moment of truth would arrive. The moment when HE would be declared the winner of the ultimate television contest title: Indian Idol! The two words were enough to stir the depths of one's heart. Indian Idol. It was with a big sob that Brinda learnt late that night that HE had indeed won. She recalled the overwhelming, mind-blowing words of humility HE had spoken during the past few days in front of the cameras: "I'm sure I will be the number one. I'll make it to the top," the prodigy had declared. Satish too had wiped a tear, in her dream . . .

Mrs. Rao buried the newspaper in her bosom once again.

"Go back to your computer. Stay in your room. At least you, my darling, are not doing anything bad with it."

"Neither is he," pointed out Suneet.

"Who are you talking about?"

"I would definitely like to believe that is the case," said Mrs. Rao, giving her son a hopeful look. "It's very serious, dear."

Brinda, taken aback, hesitated whether to enter the room and waste precious moments or retreat to her den to download music from Kazaa as she had planned.

"Your brother is in prison," bawled Radhika all of a sudden.

"Nonsense!" Suneet contradicted her. "Not at all! He is totally free."

"FREE?" exclaimed Brinda, entering the room. "What are you talking about? Wait, just give me a minute. I need to pee, can't wait anymore. By the way, where is Satish?"

"I sent him to Pondy Bazaar to buy curtains. We'll see what he brings back. I sent him before I found out . . . "

"Found out what?"

Mrs. Rao seemed to think that leaving some suspense in the air would help Brinda digest the shocking news more easily.

"Go to the bathroom. Hurry up." she ordered her daughter.

They remained silent. Radhika stricken, had the newspaper pressed against her heart, and Suneet, vulnerable, repeated a mantra without moving his lips.

"I'm back," announced Brinda.

"She is back," echoed Mrs. Rao, turning towards her son.

"Can I see it or is it some kind of top defense secret?"

"Ah," sighed Mrs. Rao. "If only it were."

"Sit down."

"You bet I'll sit down," she retorted rebelliously. "I have other things to do. Keep your secret to yourselves. I have a million important things to take care of."

She marched off back to her room taking care not to close the door behind her. This way, she would be able to rush back if she overheard anything interesting.

Mrs. Rao was not entirely dissatisfied with herself. She had not revealed anything to her daughter since she was still speculating over the actual implications of the story. It all seemed so complicated. Three short sentences, nothing more, evoking so much. At the same time news item also seemed so remote, so insignificant, as if it were just story that had nothing to do with her at all. That was why she never read the newspaper, unlike her late husband and her children. All these events, these stories, these anecdotes, pouring in from all directions. Soon they would be coming from Mars too. But what about her problems, where did one have to go to read about them? It was quite enough that she watched TV once a day, when they presented the news. For entertainment's sake; it was interesting to see how the presenters spoke, what they wore...

Three lines, completely meaningless! She read them once more, aloud, as if to uncover their real import. "*A young . . .* "

Satish, all breathless, suddenly appeared in the doorway. Tommy welcomed his arrival by leaping all over him.

"What have you brought?"

"I'm not happy with what I found, Memsaab."

"Show me. Why? The place where I sent you has wonderful stuff. You did not go to some other place, did you?"

He unwrapped the package that he had brought.

"No."

"Let's see. Oh Satish!"

"Memsaab likes?"

"It's lovely! Beautiful! Let me see. You brought the right thing. It will go nicely with the tablecloth . . . how strange . . . it looks . . . looks like it's torn. Oh no! How could they sell you a curtain like this? It is torn. Impossible! I know that store. Everybody in Chennai goes there. I'm going to call them right away. The scoundrels! They saw you and they took advantage of you. They gave you their torn curtains."

Satish fidgeted a little.

"It's not because of them."

"Then because of whom? You buy a magnificent piece of fabric, you bring it to me, and it's all torn. I don't see any other explanation."

"No..."

Mrs. Rao shrugged impatiently, picked up the telephone and started flipping the pages of her telephone directory.

"It's because of Kuchu," he announced, looking crushed.

"Kuchu? What are you blabbering?"

"I entered the garden, I had forgotten to tie him on his leash, he jumped on me and I lost my balance. I dropped the bag and when it fell to the ground it opened, and one corner of the cloth was sticking out, and Kuchu jumped on it and tore it."

"Oh no!"

Overwhelmed by all the emotion she had been experiencing since morning, Radhika, her newspaper still buried in her chest, began to cry in front of the impassible Satish.

"That's it! The dog is real troublemaker. He will not get the ball anymore. That's it!"

It was hardly a consolation! She studied the canine's fang marks on her beautiful fabric.

"Listen carefully, Satish. You will go back to the store immediately with this and explain to them what happened. Buy more of the same material, the same length."

"Not possible, Memsaab."

"You are really testing my patience! Isn't it, Suneet?"

Her eldest son nodded in agreement. "Go back and bring the same material like you've been told," he repeated.

Satish hung his head without replying.

"Do something, Suneet. You see what I go through from morning to evening with him. It's like this everyday," she exaggerated. "You tell something simple and he says it's not possible, *not possible Memsaab*," she imitated. "He drives me crazy."

"Do what you've been told, Satish!" exclaimed Suneet with annoyance. "Why did you let the dog ruin the fabric? Now do what you've been told."

Satish looked up. A faint smile appeared on his lips which quickly disappeared thanks to the gravity of what he still had to confess.

"I will not go back there."

"You see, Suneet, you see!"

"I can't go back. They threw me out. They went too far. They really treated me very badly."

"Badly?"

"They threw you out? That can't be true, Satish."

"They told me there was no need for me to come back. They said they didn't need customers like me."

"Oh!"

"They made such a big fuss just because I haggled to save every rupee. But they had to give up. I managed to make them part with it finally."

"I don't see anything wrong with bargaining for something," Mrs. Rao reasoned. "We all do it. Who doesn't haggle?"

"They did not like my style."

"Go back and just explain everything."

"It's not possible, Memsaab. Not after what I said to them." Satish was an expert in the art of suspense.

"What did you say?" Radhika demanded, expecting that Satish was overreacting.

"I told the salesman that he was a big fat good for nothing and that he could go to hell and . . . "

Mrs. Rao and her son gave each other horrified looks.

"Okay, fine. Leave the cloth here. Let's just forget about it, I'll take care of it myself. I'll go there when I get a chance. It will be all right, they know me. You go and make sure things are okay in the kitchen."

"Yes, Memsaab."

It was the last straw. Mrs. Rao at last let go of the newspaper and tossed it onto the side table next to her. Without waiting for an invitation, Satish picked up the paper and calmly read the three lines that had been underlined in red.

"Our Pradeep?"

"Go, get lost. You meddle in everything! And we are seeing

the result."

The phone bell rang. Suneet picked up the receiver.

"No, he's not here at the moment . . . I'll ask him to call you back. Thank you."

"Who was it?"

"It was from the Police Commissioner's office. I know his son quite well. We were in school together."

"In that case you better cultivate friendship with him. We might need him. What did he want?"

"He wanted to talk to Dipu."

"To Dipu?" repeated Radhika.

She picked up the paper once more and read out loud:

"*A young Indian, Pradeep Rao, a long time resident of France, accused by the United States of hacking into military websites was taken into custody for questioning by the Chennai police and subsequently released after being cleared of all suspicion.*"

Brinda charged into the room.

"Did I hear it correctly?"

"*A young Indian, Pradeep Rao . . .* " recommenced Mrs. Rao, ready to pursue another reading for everyone's benefit.

"No need to drill it into us. Can I have the paper?"

Radhika regretfully handed her the newspaper.

"Listen, don't they say that one should not believe everything they write in the papers?"

"Yes, that's true."

She didn't insist further.

"We can be proud of him," quipped Brinda, trying to lighten the atmosphere.

"Be quiet!"

"Not everyone would be able to do what Pradeep has done."

"Be quiet!"

"Awesome! He's great, my brother. Hacking into military sites, wow! I can't wait for him to come and tell us about it," she said as she prepared to leave.

"Tie your shoelace," admonished her mother for lack of a better argument.

Feeling stricken, she called out for Satish.

"I will not be having lunch. I've decided to fast. Just bring me two *chapatis*."

"With?"

"Plain."

Suneet had to leave for work. He got up and promised to come back soon.

"What I don't understand," enquired Radhika, "is how they managed to find him at Philippe's, and not here, when they took him in for questioning."

Suneet had no explanation. How had the city police found out where he was going to be?

"They got to him through France. We will find out more very soon."

"Ah, that's why he didn't sleep here that night. I was so worried, I hardly slept," she said untruthfully.

She accompanied her son as he walked out, returning to the living room hurriedly when she heard the phone ring.

"Hello," she greeted the caller in an anguished voice. "Yes, who is this? Who is calling?"

"It's Ammu."

"Ah."

"How are you feeling?" her *bahu* asked her in a tense voice.

"You're all getting on my nerves. I'm fine. I'm not sick or anything."

"Why did you cut your hair?"

"I felt like it. That's all. We should be talking about Pradeep instead. And stop worrying about my health, it will end up bringing me some problem."

"We're not worrying," Ammu replied in a hurt voice.

139

She recited, rather incoherently, the three lines that she almost knew by heart now, to Ammu. Ammu couldn't understand anything, so Mrs. Rao picked up the newspaper again. Her daughter-in-law was very shocked, and speechless.

"Who would have ever imagined!"

"Me," Mrs. Rao felt obliged to reply. "I knew something was up, but nothing like this, of course. I didn't even know he was doing so much computer-work. Can you imagine, what did they call it? Hacking into military websites . . . ."

"It's unheard of."

"I tell you I don't believe a word of it," she continued, contradicting what she had said not even a minute ago. "Pradeep is incapable of such behavior. His sister is rejoicing, but I don't see there is anything to celebrate."

"There is a contradiction in these lines," Ammu said after a few seconds of silence. "On the one hand they say that he is being accused by the United States, and on the other they say that the Chennai Police has cleared him of suspicion. The report is too brief, I don't feel entirely reassured. It looks like the newspaper people didn't have enough information so they just published a vague story without verifying the facts."

Despite the three hours that had elapsed, Mrs. Rao's thoughts had not made it that far.

"I think they have done their job correctly."

"Just read the last part again, after *subsequently released*."

"*After being cleared of all suspicion* . . . Ammu? Ammu, are you there?"

There was no response from the other side.

"Ammu!"

"I'm trying to figure it out."

Fearing what her *bahu* was going to say, Mrs. Rao expressed her impatience by coughing noisily.

"It's surprising that they absolved him so quickly for such a huge crime."

She surely was a talented *bahu* when it came to saying things that one didn't want to hear.

"It's possible, my dear Ammu, quite possible. As far as I'm concerned, I'm happy. I must let you go, Satish is bringing my dinner. Well, actually I'm fasting."

"You eat when you are on a fast?"

"Only two chapatis with some tea so that I don't get a headache."

It didn't take long for Ammu's suggestion to make its way into Radhika's empty stomach. Why only three lines in a newspaper that had so many pages, so many illegible articles? To whom were they trying to prove that her son did not deserve a more detailed treatment? Three lines!

Since she was holding a newspaper in her hands for the first time in such a long time - the last time was when Sushil had died - she decided to browse through it, like a catalogue. A nice pastime for someone on a fast. Four columns on the top half of the page were devoted to an article on the French President who, she learnt, was named Monsieur Chirac. Funny, our cousin in Rajkot, his name is Chirag. I must tell Dipu about the coincidence. Interesting name! She had never heard it before, well maybe on TV, when the Iraq war had started, but she wasn't certain. Neither did she know the name of the Prime Minister of Sri Lanka. Great Britain and Pakistan, yes. It wasn't reasonable to expect one to recite all the names by heart. Especially an old country like France!

The French Chirag had been given so many columns. She found it very unfair. Dipu lived in France just as much and also in Chennai, and he had only three lines, vague to boot. She didn't really feel like diving into the article. She adjusted her cushions and opted for a quick skim. It had something to do with people's right to display religious symbols which was being challenged. The Islamic scarf was part of it. So were the traditional colorful Sikh turbans. And some of the huge crosses and the Jewish kippah caps too. They had not been banned on the street, just in the schools, all for the sake of a principle that she had never even imagined existed: *laïcité,* French secularism. The newspaper was struggling to explain it. A matter of social cohesion. The conclusion of the article was that the new law was out of touch with the times.

"I will not go and live in France," she announced to her idle servant who was hovering around, trying to find a way to engage a conversation with Memsaab. "You don't have anything to do?"

"The newspaper is very interesting?" he said, cleverly changing the topic.

"I will not go to live in France. Can you imagine, it's very difficult to practice a religion there if it is not theirs," she explained to him.

"Can I read?"

"There is no need for us to go and live there, isn't it Satish?"

"Except to go and visit Dipu."

"What are you saying? Our Dipu will stay here!"

"And Philippe Sahib?"

Mrs. Rao was so stunned by Satish's words that she almost broke her newly repaired titanium glasses once again.

"What are you saying, Satish? My son and the French sahib are two different people. My son has a life here that is waiting for him, a good marriage, a nice job, and the sahib has his own life to lead. Like Brinda said very correctly the other day, they are not married. So kindly don't mix things up. If the sahib wants to live in India, nobody will stop him, and he can wear a huge cross, as big as he wants. What do you think of the three lines in the paper?"

With every passing month his opinions were becoming as important, if not more, as those of Ammu.

"They will not succeed in extraditing him," pronounced Satish.

"What! You believe all this is true, this silly story that they have printed? His extradition? Rubbish! You're talking rubbish!"

She looked at Satish as if he held the key to the meaning of the most important words of the day. As she put her glasses it occurred to her that Pradeep would perhaps no longer be able to go back to France because of the legal complications that the narrow minded authorities there had created, such as the banning of turbans and the risk of extradition. That's what he meant, that not-so-foolish Satish! Three revolting lines, and each person was interpreting them so differently in his or her own way. She came to the conclusion that she needed to start looking around as soon as possible for a nice young girl for him to marry. He wouldn't be going back to his Chirac any time soon.

Luckily, Suneet was friends with the Chennai police commissioner's son. Things would definitely get resolved.

"Satish, I cannot find my sleeping pills. Where are they?" she asked, anticipating an evening that promised to send her hiding to her bed with a headache like a bad speech by W. Bush.

"Sleeping pills? Haven't seen them, Memsaab. Everything will turn out okay, Memsaab. Pradeep *bhaiya* is not in danger."

"I have never thought that he was in danger," she answered haughtily. "You know, sometimes I think he would be better off in prison than spending so much time in the company of this Philippe."

Satish did not agree.

"The best thing would be if they both went to prison together. It would be less difficult for Dipu."

She finally found her sedatives under a pile of underwear.

"You are really sick, that's not what I meant, my poor Satish! Both of them in prison! Who is going to believe me? My poor

Satish. My poor Satish," she repeated, surprised at the comforting feeeling that these three words gave her. My poor Satish, my poor Satish . . . "

Five times, it was enough. He tiptoed out of Mrs. Rao's bedroom with dignity.

"Poor Satish," she continued all by herself. "Poor Satish, this time I will put them in the top drawer of the nightstand, and if I need them . . . Poor Satish. Fortunately, he has us. What would he do if he were all alone, being without a family as he is? He too would be better off in prison. Come to think of it, it's amazing how many people would be better off in prison, instead of being left by themselves. My poor mother, when she spent her last days in that old age home, she was in prison. It was a prison, which is just as well. Not that I didn't want her here with us, it was she who didn't want to be here. Well, both she and us. My poor mother!

After her mother, it was the turn of her children. Poor Brinda – there was a hint of anger in her voice. Poor Abhi – incomprehension. Poor Suneet – a hint of respect due to her acknowledgement of his responsibilities as head of his family. Poor Ammu – invisible and crazy! A true daughter in law! And poor Dipu – abandoned, in France, reduced to a state of having an old sahib without a mustache for a friend.

After her children it was the turn of her neighbors. Poor Mrs. Menon – must be so handicapped by her foolishness! And her Gopal, poor chap, she still hadn't been able to find him a girl. And the poor cobbler on the street corner – he is *really* poor, he never has anything to do, God knows where he sleeps!

After her neighbors, it was the turn of her compatriots. All the poor people who had to deal with the floods, all those who lost their measly little huts which they would really miss because nobody would try to relocate them, all the poor people who drowned in Bombay, their bodies floating in the water...

144

After that, it was the turn of the leaders of the country. Poor Prime Minister, poor Sonia, and poor Rajiv!

After them, it was the leaders of other countries, the few that she knew. Poor Chirag, who did not like the scarves of the Muslims and the turbans of the Sikhs. Not to mention the poor Bush who couldn't put together three intelligent sentences.

She suddenly understood: it was the fast that was attacking her, making her delirious, suffocating her. That was where it was coming from, her litany on behalf of the poor! She got out of her bed and sent Satish to the market to buy a box of *besan laddus,* those tasty sweets made of sugar and chick pea flour that she could count on to produce all kinds of miracles, including stopping her from seeing the world from the limiting perspective of poverty.

"Bring me one full box. Twenty *laddus* at least! They stay fresh. Dipu also loves them. Make sure they're very fresh."

"Yes, Memsaab."

Freed from her visions of poor people, Mrs. Rao regained her confidence and returned to the living room staggering with hunger. She couldn't wait for him to return with the sweets. Nothing else could guarantee that she would be safe from more invasive attacks of poverty on her brain, her poor brain . . . . No! She had to act. She went out into her garden to admire her trees. The poverty quickly disappeared.

The sun was going down. A few rickshaws were passing outside, on Greenways Road. Out of a thousand sounds all around she could very well distinguish the almost toy like sound made by the rickshaws on the road. She heard one stop near their gate, *phut phut phut,* as always. The driver turned off the engine, perhaps expecting a member of the Rao family to appear. Brinda was a huge consumer of rickshaws. Abhi, a little less. The place was peaceful, perfect for a little snooze. Sometimes Radhika, or Satish - a little more brutally - would end up having to rouse a dozing driver. Mrs. Rao appreciated the fact that the area around her house was a preferred destination for rickshaw drivers who wanted quick naps. It bestowed a certain calm and pleasantness on this tiny section of Greenways which were not to be found further ahead where there were always too many crowded buses going towards the bridge on the Adyar River.

She closed her eyes and breathed deeply. She felt peace dawning on her as the driver outside was probably converting his little vehicle into temporary sleeping quarters. Even the craving for sweets went away. She was finally feeling more comfortable in her fast. The most difficult moments were over. Her state of mind was changing little by little, as if under the influence of alcohol. Mrs. Rao, the mother of four children, was dozing off just like the driver of the rickshaw outside. She glimpsed, on the other side of the garden, a scantily clad young woman who was leaning on a cane, a mirage, a young girl, turning in the blink of an eye into an adolescent (funny how she resembled Brinda, though she appeared less sophisticated, like an obsolete version of the Windows operating system), metamorphosing into a young woman advancing towards her who had married Sushil against her family's wishes and had paid a heavy price for this act of defiance: severance of family ties which had lasted for many years. And finally, this shadow of a mother, a terrible mother with an impeccable hairdo. Her whole life in a couple of winks. Her eyes were closed, and perhaps because they were closed, her children approached her. Suneet, or maybe it was Abhi who took her hand and murmured something that she had to strain to hear. You know, we have decided, we want to give you back some of your former freedom, take it back, we have lots of it, we all are undergoing change, yes, yes, even Brinda, and look, look, Pradeep doesn't even live with us anymore, we are growing up, so you also grow up. Leave me alone, I don't want to talk about it! I don't want to talk about freedom. That is not a family's purpose. I refuse, I do not want your present, I cannot accept it, my children. It's over, I don't have the strength to accept your freedom. You are asking me to turn back and become who I was twenty years ago, Radhika at twenty . . . She does not exist anymore, I don't even recognize her face. Photographs tell so many lies. Why are you offering me all this freedom? To finish me off, right? I don't want it. Isn't one, on the contrary, supposed to gather all that has been good in one's life as a parent, never look back, and remain a mother till one's last breath? That is my plan, it's as good as any other. I will not change it.

She sensed some agitation around her. Did they *really* want a change? Did they want her to disappear gradually, a little each day, a mother who has been shown the door, who dissolves like a lump of sugar in a cold liquid. She shivered in her sleep. I am not human, I just exist. Life, society have created this strange entity that is me, who goes about from one room in the house to another, from one end of the garden to the other, dressed in one of the numerous saris that I buy in Pondy Bazar or somewhere else. It depends. Pondy Bazar isn't the only place, right Satish? It is difficult to turn over a new leaf finally, my children. It is difficult to say farewell to oneself.

My whole system, and not only mine, is conditioned by my children. How can it be any other way? I have noticed, you see, Sushil, my life is more complicated, more agitated, when Pradeep is near me. On the one hand I miss him the way a mother duck misses her duckling, when he is in Europe, so far away. I have no way of controlling him except by asking him on the phone what he is doing, who he is meeting, and he answers what he wants. On the other hand, I'm more peaceful once I put the phone down. He liberates me. And when he cries, he liberates me even more.

His absence, she mused, was not an issue. Her other children led ordinary lives that she could apprehend because of their proximity. Even Abhi, despite his mysterious loftiness, did not cause such disquiet. He went to the temple everyday, meditated with his bizarre friends under the guidance of this self-proclaimed guru whose holiness was inscribed in his title, at least in his title. What was his name again? His Holiness Sri Sri Ravi Ranganath. She appreciated Abhi's good nature. Ever since he had joined this organization where he practiced his kriya yoga, he had become more direct, more open, less rigid, even if he had become just as evasive. It would seem that all the exercises that he practiced, locked up in his room (Brinda, Satish and Mrs. Rao herself were forbidden to cross the threshold), had changed his approach to the world. She would have to ask him to show her the breathing exercises one of these days, they might help her not devour so many *laddus*. The problem with Abhi, she admitted, her eyes still closed, was that he was becoming more and more reasonable, to the point of being insufferable at times. It was almost obscene. She ought not to think like that, she was his mother, but then it wasn't even clear if she had the right to say anything or not. Another concern, he didn't seem keen on getting married. So that's not a concern, well, all right. So what was it then? What was the use of knowing how to breathe so well if he did not use it to take advantage of it in order to get married? I'm narrow-minded? It suits you to think that way. I have experience. Yes, but Abhi at least, you understand, he doesn't live in Paris, he lives in Chennai, and he doesn't have in his circle of friends an unsavory character like Philippe whom he drags around. He kept up with his childhood friends - he was in touch with even those that he had in Bombay; his humbleness was always genuine.

Her introspection came to an end when she heard the gate creaking. She had many shortcomings but this was something new. She had never before indulged in introspection consciously.

148

As the sun set, for the first time in her life she regretted that she had never done it. Introspection, everyone practiced it, even fools. They did it their own way, in secret, in silence, without even realizing it at times, in shame while donning a mask. One hid oneself in one's car, or in a bus or a bed, one did not aver it. It caused one waste to time; sometimes it bestowed extra time. Introspection, it was a little like lightening in the sky on a stormy night. One became aware of things that usually remained hidden, in a dazzling way, and surely the brutality of the unexpected thoughts was proof enough of their truth. Right? Maybe not! Who knew?

Satish's arrival was preceded by that of the rocket named Kuchu. He charged right into Mrs. Rao who let out a scream. Even stray dogs were accustomed to shoving her!

She opened the box, inspected the sweets and closed the lid.

"I'm not hungry," she told him. "I'll continue my fast till the children return."

11

The Hacker

"Here's a bottle of Glenmorangie," said Philippe a little shyly, without actually stretching his arm and offering it to her. Mrs. Rao looked at him with panic, as if she was sure he was trying to poison her. "It's the finest kind, and it's a real stroke of luck that I found it here, near . . . "

"Indeed, a real stroke of luck," repeated Mrs. Rao. "I have fasted the whole morning and I'm definitely not drinking any whisky, even your Glen-whatever-it's-called."

"Not even a drop?"

Radhika sized him up from behind her glasses. She couldn't help finding him likeable. That was the worst part - whenever he was around she never felt bored; he made her laugh. Although she had done her best, the first few minutes, to show him his place - she had been colder than the Queen of England in the aftermath of the passing away of the much missed Princess Diana - he sure knew how to lighten her up. She made an effort to remember the three lines but she couldn't. Not when they were talking about scotch! The newspaper had disappeared from the living room. Brinda had probably taken it with her. "On top of it all, he's an alcoholic," she concluded. "He encourages my son to commit crimes on the Internet, and he makes him drink." A painful headache put an end to her ruminations.

"Well Pradeep, what is all this? Do you mind telling us what is going on?"

Bira suddenly came out of her room and seeing her brother ran up to him. "Congratulations, Dipu. Brilliant! You are a genius. Those assholes should not have gone and made such a mess out of Iraq."

"Brinda!"

"Yeah. Well, it makes me very upset, what they did in Iraq. Don't try to argue with me on that."

"That's not why I did it," said Dipu, feeling uncomfortable. "When I began, I didn't know that they would go into . . . And even . . . "

"That's what you say!"

"He's telling the truth," insisted Philippe, defending Dipu.

"It doesn't really matter if he is."

"Are we going to be discussing politics?" asked Mrs. Rao in alarm suddenly remembering that a box of saffron and cardamom-scented *laddus*, sweet and moist, was waiting in the kitchen.

For her, politics, in a discussion, represented a danger mark similar to the ones used to measure water levels during monsoon floods.

"No, it was just a causal remark."

"No politics in our family, Mr. Philippe," she said, addressing Philippe in a rather solemn tone. "We never talk politics, isn't that true, children?"

"That is true," acknowledged Brinda. "Except when we do."

Philippe appeared embarrassed.

"It's different back home; it's Papa's profession . . . "

"Yes, of course," remembered Mrs. Rao. "It's different. You probably discuss politics like other families discuss sports, right?"

"Quite right," he agreed, closing the subject.

Radhika suddenly spoke up with animation. "I know your French president," she exclaimed triumphantly, to everybody's great surprise.

Philippe gave a start.

"You know him?"

"Chirag. His name is Chirag."

Dipu burst out laughing. "Oh yes! You certainly know him! It's Chirac, with a C. C as in clown."

"By the way honey, you remember our cousin in Rajkot? I was thinking about them the whole day today. We have completely broken off ties with that branch of our family, it's so sad. Chirag must be married by now; I'm sure he has really beautiful kids."

Dipu looked up to the sky and rolled his eyes. Back to Mummy's biggest obsession.

"If they had arrested me in September," he announced, "they could have given me up to seventy years in prison."

She looked at him with incomprehension. They were talking about Rajkot and Chirag's marriage and he was talking to them about prison!

"Seventy years? That's a lot, no? Did you really do what they are accusing you of, then? It was not a joke?"

Brinda was indignant.

"Of course it's not a joke!" she exclaimed. In less than three hours she had deeply involved herself in the incident, alerting her friends on the Internet, the most loyal ones, that is. Having very little information, she had embellished the story and had painted her brother as a hero, a victim of imperialism, saved at the last minute by the BJP, the party in power.

"Here, see what they are saying in *Hindustan*..."

Who would get to read it first? Weakened by hunger, Radhika was a few seconds late. She let her arm drop heavily. Suneet stretched out his hand, but Brinda was like lightening. She grabbed the newspaper so fast from Pradeep's hand that the page got torn.

"Shucks! It's all right, the lines devoted to you are still there."

She distanced herself from the others by another meter.

"*Pradeep Rao, the young Indian accused by the United States of hacking into its defense systems, underwent detailed questioning in Chennai, according to various ministry sources in Delhi. It seems that Rao traveled to the United States last autumn, with his papers in order. He was not stopped at the time of arrival or departure at the airport in Tampa. The FBI has refused to comment on the allegation that his information was not communicated in time to the authorities. Till very recently, the Unites States had been hoping to secure the extradition of this brilliant IT genius.*"

"No way!" exclaimed Brinda, leaning against the door. "Pradeep! You are a genius."

"Show it to me," ordered Suneet, with irritation.

She resisted his attempt to take the newspaper from her.

"Wait. There are three more lines. It's very short but it's incredible," she promised.

"Let me see it," said Mrs. Rao without much hope.

Brinda resumed reading: "*The events are believed to have taken place three years ago. Rao is accused of illegally penetrating and damaging fifty-three computers belonging to the US Army...*"

"Fifty-three!" marveled Brinda.

"Fifty-three what?"

"*...and NASA between 2001 and 2002. The damages caused and the subsequent repairs are estimated to have cost one million dollars.*"

She withdrew to her room - the newspaper page serving as her armor - after announcing that she was going to repair it with scotch tape.

"Satish!" cried out Mrs. Rao. "Bring us some snacks. I think I'm going to end my fast. I'm feeling weak."

Suddenly, in the midst of this family where he was neither accepted nor rejected, where he was at best considered a natural calamity, inevitable like an ineluctable karma, Philippe began wondering what he was doing in that living room. He came from an incomprehensible broken family, and now he was surrounded by one for whom the word God held true meaning. He looked at the handsome Pradeep - it was not enough to reassure him. Why had he come to India? Was it not the question to ask, even though he did not know if there was an answer? Sure, the importance of traveling cannot be overestimated. Philippe had perhaps come to India for one thing: to understand what family was all about. How was it different from what he was used to? He could observe the difference everywhere, even on the street, as if he was discovering new monuments. He was not disappointed to say the least. All the "monuments", whether they were Mrs Rao or the Taj Mahal, symbolized something which he had slowly seen disappear in France, just the way dams give way when powerful hurricanes pass. The family that he had come from had exploded, and the search for unity, whether real or false, was still ongoing inside, in the jungle of his contradictory feelings.

To dissipate his malaise vis-à-vis the Rao tribe, he poured himself some whiskey, sitting in his corner at the table, after all his companions had one by one declined his offer. Surprised, and as if pleased by his presence, Mrs. Rao smiled at him.

"How come Chennai Police ended up locating you in order to get hold of Pradeep, and you, dear, why didn't you tell me about this before?"

The second question obviously seemed more important than the first. Philippe began drinking his whisky; methodically he explained what he knew: he had received, three days ago, an alarmist phone call from his father. It had all started in Paris with the RG, the French intelligence service. They had received a complete file on Dipu sent by the FBI. The case had been solved early November, as they were leaving for Chennai. They had quickly found a lead to Olivier Delcourt by cross-checking things against the information that had been furnished by Pradeep's former landlady. Officials closest to the Minister of the Interior had been quickly alerted. What were they to do? How were they to deal with the press? The position of the Senator rendered the investigation problematic. It was not in itself a very unusual event, a new kind of offense. There was nothing insurmountable about it. Their American colleagues, operating out of their quarters close to the Embassy, seemed determined. Keeping the French press away at that stage of the investigations posed no difficulty. The connections between Rao and Delcourt's son were almost unknown, and the position of the senator in favor of an overhaul of the family code had been widely disseminated in the media early that summer. In was inconceivable to booby-trap the political debate to satisfy the needs of an American investigation. Interests much bigger than the fate of an individual were at stake. The Referendum being just around the corner, the astonishment of French services, despite their excellent relations with their American counterparts, was proportionate to their lack of resources to hush up the affair. It risked spinning out of political control. They tried to detect, in vain, what the contents of the file signified in terms of the future relations between the two countries. The accusations leveled by the Pentagon were beyond negotiation. The hacking had been executed in France, the nationality of the culprit was less important than the place and the logistical support that he had surely enjoyed. Before launching its own investigation, the FBI, in the person of Patrick French, one of the officers in charge of European affairs, demanded a meticulous preliminary investigation into Rao's identity, the reasons for his presence in France, his connections. Confronted with the unexpected political complexity of the affair which had to be underplayed in order to be kept secret for a longer time, the Interior Ministry, in accord with the surprised Senator, decided to temporarily wash its hands of the file under the pretext that Rao was on a trip to India. They could not have hoped for a more convenient solution to the problem. Now they only needed to transmit to Delhi, through the usual channels, the minor documents, some not even translated into English, leaving out most of what had come from the FBI.

With his customary curiosity, a silent aspect of his role as a domestic servant in the Rao household, Satish was not the one to miss all the fresh details being given by Delcourt Sahib. Opportunely planting himself by the living room entrance, under the pretext that the hour to clean the aquarium had arrived, he devoured the information while forgetting to feed the fish. He almost caused a spill by swirling the water in every direction, which made Memsaab feel slightly angry.

Focused and anxious, Mrs. Rao gobbled up two *laddus* as she listened to Philippe recount, sentence by sentence, what he understood of the story that had been told to him first by Dipu and then by his father. Dipu had denied that he had misbehaved, as if that was the main reproach, he had never imagined that they would be able to trace it to him. He had perhaps been a little unaware, okay, it had happened so many years ago, why would he have talked about it? Philippe insisted. Why the silence? Why would he have talked, and of what? He had even forgotten the details of the events, which went back, as regards the active phase of the hacking (and not espionage, it was important to make a distinction!), several years. He repeated it at least four times. How could he have remembered, since he had not had any intention to cause harm?

Mrs. Rao of course did not retain much of what Philippe had said. His discourse had been so rambling and confused. She turned to her son:

"So, all this is true?" she concluded severely. That was the only thing that mattered, the details, the blah blah, all that was

like journalism – without any value. "Well, so we can say that...
we can say that..."

"Just say it," whispered Abhi.

"I have always thought that these computers really do our
lives no good."

"How did you come to this conclusion?"

"He hacked into the computers, didn't he?" asserted Radhika
feeling sure of herself for once. "Isn't that what he did?"

"It was just to keep myself occupied," Pradeep finally
acknowledged as he helped himself to some whisky. "I was
twenty, or something like that..."

"Older. You were older!" exclaimed Mrs. Rao whose obsession
with dates was especially evident when they concerned her
children.

"Okay, a little older. I got lucky, I wasn't sleeping much at
night-time, I was getting bored in Paris, far from my people, far
from you..."

"Oh!" cried out Radhika, moved to tears. It was too much,
unhoped for. The cry from Dipu's heart had come at most
appropriate time. The party had been spoiled by an explosion
that had not claimed any victims. Not up till then.

"I was spending sleepless nights in front of my computer."

"Sleepless nights?" repeated Mrs. Rao, stupefied.

"Why didn't you come back right away? You should have
come home immediately," she added as if it were an operation
that took only a few seconds, "instead of fiddling about inside
those military sites. Why were you so interested in the army?
That too the American army!" she burst out as if she knew how
to distinguish between the armies of the world.

"What did you discover?" added Suneet whose burning
curiosity was growing by the minute.

Dipu promised them that he would tell them everything a
little later, he was very tired, the interrogation had exhausted

157

him, he did not remember very clearly what he had read on the sites of NASA and the army during those long insomnia filled nights. A lot of things, some that were really very boring, some which he had not been able to understand, and lastly, some which had surely appeared interesting at the time but now escaped him

"This whole affair, you understand, I... I was not actually trying to break in, I was just playing around. When I realized I was inside NASA's network, I was unable to stop myself. I had even forgotten about it. Until... Even Philippe, I never told him about it."

"What do you mean even Philippe?" pointed out Mrs. Rao immediately. "I don't understand why you are saying this. Even Philippe!"

The sahib poured himself some more whisky. This brutal two word accolade -*even Philippe* - might prove to be useful. *You still don't understand, Mrs. Rao? Why don't you just put two and two together and find out what it really means? It has deep psychological significance. Cool, isn't it? Words almost say what they want to say, they do as they please. They just need an excuse to reveal what is in the heart.* A disguised coming out. Dipu immediately back-pedaled.

"I live in Paris. If I had to talk to someone about it, with whom would I have talked, other than Philippe? Don't you think it's obvious?" he added.

His damage control effort was successful.

"You are just like me," acknowledged Radhika susceptible to his reasoning, even if it meant throwing common sense out of the window, she knew it secretly, like everybody else, they could remain in denial if they wanted to, their perverse good feelings could also go out of the window. "I, for example, when I'm faced with a big problem, what do I do? I call Ammu."

"Exactly!" concluded Dipu. He had succeeded in bringing

the ship safely back to the port.

What is my life, Philippe lamented to himself contemplating his glass of whisky at same moment. Anguish had begun to gnaw at him. What is my life? They tell me that I travel, I fly, to escape into the future, but it's not true. I don't have any other choice. Wandering fulfils my real needs.

... What can I do? Over there, in France, I am not recognized anymore. Son, brother, uncle, an unidentified cousin, a UFO. Meaningless titles.

Here, I have another family. They see me as a stranger. She is right. A UFO.

Titles can always change. One family that I don't recognize, another that sees me as a stranger. Whatever the titles, one ends up being the same. Nothing catastrophic here, since one is ready to give me what the other is refusing.

"Ah! Here's the newspaper at last! We can read it now!" exclaimed Radhika who had never before spent this much time reading the news. "It's my turn, isn't it? Brinda, please give it to me."

She passed it on to her mother via Satish who did not dare to keep it even for a few seconds.

In September, just before leaving for Florida, they had together attended the birthday celebrations of Lord Ganesha in Paris at the city's only Hindu temple in "Little India."

Little India comprised only three or four streets, not more. The shops along the sidewalks had gradually been bought over by members of the Tamil community who had opened their businesses there - travel agencies, restaurants with names like "Gandhi" and "Pondicherry," silk boutiques and grocery stores. Specialties both from the south and the north, mangoes, spices, incense, sandalwood soaps, ayurvedic toothpastes, rosewater, coconut oil, Dabur shampoos, sacred chants of Shiva, CDs of

Ravi Shankar stocked on the shelves reminded the people of the neighborhood of their nostalgia for India.

Little India, also known as *Rue du faubourg St. Denis*, situated near the *Gare du Nord* train station was closed to traffic that Sunday, the 5th of September, at nine o'clock in morning. When Dipu and Philippe arrived, the storefronts had already been decked with garlands. The festival was starting. Offerings of bananas, areca nuts, betel leaves, incense, camphor, and a variety of powders had been arranged on the table stands. A mixed crowd of Indians and Europeans, which kept getting bigger, awaited the arrival of the floats. Sunbeams kept piercing through the dark clouds. Small mountains of coconuts had been erected along the sidewalks. Philippe wanted to know why. Near the floats, men were taking the coconuts and breaking them forcefully by hitting them on the ground. The asphalt of Paris was strewn with brown shells and white pieces of shrapnel. It was part of Sri Lankan ritual that with each coconut broken, a little bit of the ego, at the collective level, got destroyed - it was to remind each participant in the Ganesh festival to open the heart, to abandon selfishness. The sound effect was deafening. One awaited the elephant god while eating *samosas* and *laddus* and offering others meals and glasses of milk flavored with rose syrup. Everybody was there; the entire Hindu community of Paris seemed to have congregated in Little India that day. Everybody seemed headed in the direction of La Chapelle and the temple. Philippe was mesmerized.

"Is it going to be like this when we are in Madras, your hometown?"

"No," said Dipu. "Not really. There's no comparison. Well, perhaps just a little."

And now he understood. He wasn't comparing anymore. There was nothing in common between the few streets granted by the Parisian authorities and the real sentiment of India that one could share with entire families in the few places of pilgrimage that he had already visited. He had just spent two days in Kanyakumari, at the southern tip of the continent, alone. Dipu had declined the invitation. In the morning, before dawn, he had descended to the beach, preceded by pilgrims waiting to worship the sun. The hawkers were also there, ready for business. He avoided them. They were selling tea and coffee for two rupees. He moved away and climbed up the rocks at the end of the beach. Members of a family had taken their place on a rocky promontory. He suddenly lost his balance and one of the sons rushed forward to help him. Dawn was breaking. One could now discern the small islet where the memorial consecrated to Vivekananda stood. A woman wearing a green sari was stood on a rock, praying, her palms joined together. As the light became brighter, she sat down, her body seemingly amorphous, and her hands still joined in prayer. He photographed her from the behind, forgetting to ask her for permission. He had never in his life seen such a vision. It was not just the beauty of the sun rising in the horizon that they had come to celebrate, it was for something more than a spectacle. For these pilgrims, it was an act of communion, with earth, the sky, all that which escapes while being so close. What could one do, except say nothing, and just watch. Just be.

It pierced Philippe's heart like so many things that pierce one's heart in India, one doesn't know why, and it's painful sometimes. He knew that when he returned to Paris, he would hardly be able to believe it, he would need the photo, and then he would want to scream, cry, destroy it, beg for mercy each time he would see this slight woman with her hands folded. During the two days that he was in Kanyakumari, he did not come across any Western tourists. He was alone in the midst of the Indian pilgrims. He stayed at the Vivekananda ashram. It was a very ordinary residence, almost like a military barracks, yet it was perfect. Neutral. Without any seduction to sell. The desire to stay and then to run away overcame one very quickly. There was something oppressive about their simplicity, their fraternity. Was he seeing it through his Western eyes? He felt less and less sure. What kind of a Westerner was he? Sometimes one is no longer anything, one is no longer from a certain country, one is no longer from anywhere, one sees a scene for a few seconds and one knows, one feels a belonging beyond the conditioning of one's birth. One is so much more than a national of any country.

In the ashram, there was a museum devoted to Swami Vivekananda. He offered two rupees to a very dignified looking old man seated behind a big desk. To his surprise, the officer did not take the money, and looking at Philippe straight in the eye asked him, with a smile, "Why have you come to India?"

He had the presentiment that the magic he had felt on the rocks was about to reappear in a different form. The face of the old Indian appeared to radiate a halo. So this is Kanyakumari, thought Philippe barely able to contain his emotions. Instead of accepting your money they first ask you a question like in a fairy tale. Why are you here? What are you seeking? Can we help you? Can you help *us*? Where are you going? What do you think of your life? Are you satisfied with it? Where will you go after seeing this exhibition? Will it change anything? It's not certain, is it?

Philippe gave a reply. "I have come because I was curious." The elderly man gave him a big smile as he directed him to the rooms where the displays were. He did not accept the rupees.

In Paris, there had been a slight shortage of space for honoring the son of Shiva and Parvati. Of course, there were some streets: Perdonnet, Marx Dormoy, Ordener, Labat, Marcadet. All these streets at the service of the elephant god for almost five hours—that wasn't bad for a city that had not been designed for such noisy processions. The roads had been washed with rosewater sprinkled with saffron before the arrival of the floats, which were being pulled by barefoot devotees. The scent of camphor permeated the streets, and the storefronts were decorated with colorful balloons. The procession was led by flute playing musicians. Young Indian girls carried earthen pots containing camphor on their heads. The two chariots were finally brought inside the courtyard of the tiny temple situated on *Rue Philippe de Girard*. The deities were dressed in flowers and green clothes before being taken inside in palanquins. "I'm thinking of my parents," Dipu had said, becoming emotional. "I'm finally going to see my mother again at last. The holy scriptures teach that one must worship one's mother, father and guru first and only then God, afterwards. In that order. You cannot worship God first. One's parents and teacher come first. God does not want your worship if you are not capable of honoring your parents."

Philippe bit his lip to hold back his tears and did not say anything. He continued looking at the motley and colorful crowds and at the gods who were being prepared for the ceremonies. All this augured well for his upcoming trip to India. Wasn't Ganesh the one who removed obstacles and guided one on the correct path (to the extent that one knows what the correct path is)?

When he returned to Chennai two days later from Kanyakumari his decision was made.

"You are right," he told Dipu. "You were right all along. Let's not say anything to your mother, or to anyone."

"You changed your mind? Serious? Is this one of your jokes?"

"No, look at this."

He took out his digital camera from its case and scrolled through all the photos in the viewfinder till he found the one he was looking for. Dipu was introduced to the woman in the green sari lost in her contemplation of the horizon.

"Look at what?" he asked in surprise. "You spoke to her, and she convinced you? You're trying to be funny?"

Philippe remained quiet and took his hand.

"I don't want to cause them botheration, you have been right all along. Nothing is the same here. And that's what I am liking. I'm not doing anything the same. My eyes are not seeing the same things, my ears are hearing other sounds, I'm laughing like I don't laugh anywhere else . . . "

Dipu made a funny face.

"What, Anon, what?"

"I checked the emails; there was one from your father. And the morning you left for Kanyakumari, I received a summons."

"A summons for what?"

Philippe was dumbfounded. Dipu told him about the hacking over the course of months, the obscure details of his Parisian past.

"A real catastrophe for my father!" exclaimed Philippe. "Did you do it on purpose?"

There was nothing unpleasant about the idea. The senator being in hot water because of him was not entirely a displeasing thought. Since the previous night, which he had spent on the train to Chennai, he had changed his mind about getting married in France. "No question about it!" he decided shivering in the dark as he lay on his sleeper. If he was going to have a union with Dipu, it would have to be nowhere else but in India, in a temple devoted to Krishna, in collusion with a helpful priest. He was not keen at all on the fuss that a western marriage would involve, such as blessings by the green pro-environment deputies - no kidding! -and now also by his own father, or his secretary. He did not want any of that comedy, and too bad for his wonderful speeches. What he wanted was Krishna, nothing less. Krishna. Hare Krishna. If I get married, it will be with him and together we will work for Krishna's devotees. Hinduism was far from being hostile towards gays. And even the sluggish Mrs. Rao had an ambiguous attitude, to say the least. And didn't Vatsyayana's Kama Sutra make allusions to all the forms of love? And wasn't the adorable Kartikeya, Ganesh's brother, Shiva's other son, who sat on a peacock, venerated by some as the god of masculinity, as the celibate god? Could one imagine the Mahatma Amma in her lagoon refusing to hug them? An idea suddenly materialized in his mind, maybe they could make a trip to go see Amritanandamayi, in Kollam in Kerala, and ask her discreetly, this livewire of an Amma, to unite them? She was known to organize marriage ceremonies for the needy, for couples who did not have the resources to arrange decent weddings for themselves. It was more exciting to imagine oneself being blessed by Amritanandamayi than by Noël Mamère[6]. He began to dream, on the overnight train that was trundling towards Chennai, that Amma would apply sandalwood paste and saffron powder on their foreheads.

From this seductive perspective, the whole new American twist had not come at an entirely bad time.

He hurriedly left the apartment in Alwarpet and logged on to the internet in a café down the street. He read the email that his father had sent. The mayor's office in Suresnes as well as the Senate were safe from scandal, they had no reason to panic, except if the Interior Minister[7] tried one of his dirty tricks, which at this stage of the investigation seemed improbable. Nobody wished for Delcourt to reverse the situation to his advantage

---

[6] Former journalist and Green deputy who gained notoriety by going against French law and officiating at a same sex marriage in a village of which he was the mayor. The union was repealed by a judge.

[7] An indirect reference to Nicolas Sarkozy who was the Interior Minister in 2003-07 under De Villepin's government, before running for president.

and win new points in the battles that would take place after the Referendum.His no barred support for a YES, while so many of the other cowards were preparing themselves for the opportunism of a NO, was also something that was discouraging the government from rummaging in the garbage can of an issue as absurd as the hacking of an American military site.

The sarcastic tone of his father displeased him. It was nothing new. He pretended to fear nothing. But it was not difficult to imagine what he really thought and what he must have told his other children, especially his favorite *bahu*, that pesky Noémie.He would use it to wax ironic about his choice of friends. All of a sudden it seemed that Pradeep was no longer in his good graces as much, in spite of the prospect of a really chic marriage which would floor more than a few among the small Parisian élite close to power who happened to be more homophobic than met the eye, and who especially, especially, were always ready to follow a fashion without the least amount of reflection unlike what, despite everything, the Spanish democrats had done.

12

Over Lunch

"It's all his fault!" snapped Mrs. Rao, losing her patience. Brinda was caressing Lalli. The cat had survived the ride in the machine without showing even a sign of a scratch. The veterinarian, without masking his skepticism, had contented himself by merely administering a little ointment.

"How can you even make such an unfair accusation, Mummy? He didn't even know him, his Philippe, when the whole thing happened, when he – he's so brilliant – hacked . . . "

"There is no need to say *his* Philippe, dear! He did not know him at that time and that's precisely what I mean," she continued her tirade. "That's precisely what I mean."

"Okay, if you say so."

"I mean . . . If only he had found Philippe instead of meddling around with computers he would not have visited those sites, and he would not have dragged our name into the mud."

"So, whose fault is it? I don't get it!"

Her hair still not fully done, Mrs. Rao flared up.

"It's their fault of course. Your attitude is really aggravating! If only Dipu hadn't spent his sleepless nights in front of the computer . . . "

"He would have spent them with Philippe then, is that it? Really, you surprise me more and more each time. Is that what you are suggesting? It's not funny, Mummy. Sometimes your logic seems very . . . "

"I NEVER said that . . . "

"You . . . "

"Never never never. I never said that. I said, if Philippe had been the good son that he is not . . . "

"Whose son? Yours?"

"Let me finish, Bira, otherwise I will have to call your brothers. If he had met him a little sooner, we wouldn't have had to go through all this, that's all! After all - and you have a right to think as you wish - a sahib with such regal bearing whose father is a minister would not have let him break into military sites. This is unheard of. The more I think about it, the more I feel I'm going insane."

"As if you aren't already! Don't worry, Mummy. You are not going insane."

"I'm calling your brothers."

"I think the Chennai police were not given all the information," she continued, tackling the heart of the matter. "The French authorities must have withheld the key elements so that things don't become worse for him. They'll wait for the affair to die down."

Mrs. Rao looked at her daughter with disbelief. When had she become a detective? She would certainly be successful working for the police, she told herself, instead of wasting time on her useless studies at the end of which she would not even be able to find a job. She would just end up with a bunch of degrees, jobless, like many others among the youth of the country.

"Yes, Miss Sherlock Holmes! I don't understand a thing. Even Satish understands whatever is going on better. And you, you say things that are complicated beyond belief! Can you go and find me the newspaper, dear? I wonder what we will get to read this morning."

Since the past one week, each day had been bringing new

light to the whole business. Mrs. Rao's daily schedule had turned completely topsy-turvy. Instead of spending two hours on the phone, she was spending four. This morning, for example, she hadn't even been able to finish getting ready. She returned to her bedroom and began her prayers. Late! Finally, as a religious symbol attracting divine force and spiritual illumination (something which she had never ever before been in such dire need of, or perhaps just as a make-up accessory), she smeared some sandalwood on her forehead and applied a pinch of red *kumkum* powder between her eyebrows on the third eye chakra, like she did every morning.

She heard the telephone bell phone ring and in her rush to get to the phone she almost overturned the *kumkum* container. She hurried to the living room where she collided into the poor Satish who had been left to his own devices near the aquarium.

"How are you feeling?" Ammu dared to ask.

Allusions to her presumed cancer had long been discontinued. That was already old history. The cancer had been superseded by Dipu's interrogation. She considered herself to be the chief victim of the internet scandal in which her son was embroiled.

"Exhausted!" she exclaimed, grateful that the word existed. "I wake up in the morning feeling exhausted. I think it would be much less taxing if someone beat up."

"I believe you. You should ask Satish to give you a thrashing."

Ammu's response made Mrs. Rao laugh.

"How do you feel about all these unfortunate things happening to us, dear Ammu? We have been dishonored all the way up to France, isn't it? I still don't know where France is exactly, but the dishonor will never fade away," she sniffled.

"You're exaggerating, as always."

Her eyes on the goldfish, Radhika made a peeved face. It wasn't a complete pout, just a sulky expression. Didn't she have the right to exaggerate? Her son faced the risk of spending sixty-odd years in prison! Besides, her exaggeration was not something new to them.

"If you categorize catastrophes according to a grading scale, you know the way they do it with hurricanes," went on Mrs. Rao (she had picked up a lot of new concepts by reading the paper) "- category1, category 5, and all that, I wonder Ammu, what category would we be in? Category 3, but we could easily go up to 4 or even 5."

"Don't worry, the embankment won't break."

There was no guarantee when it came to fortifications. Storms, when they raged, had the power to wreak havoc. They discussed the event of the day: in a dilapidated building that housed the intelligence wing of the Chennai police in Numgambakkam, Pradeep Rao, the Indian hacker who had operated under the alias of Panagalpondy was undergoing a fresh round of questioning. Since Philippe's apartment was relatively closer to Sterling Road, he had taken his mother's permission to spend the night there. Not only had Radhika not objected to the idea, she had encouraged him to go wherever he pleased. "You definitely don't need my permission as long as we are in the glare of this vindictive investigation." The guardian of morality had decided to give her son a break.

"I can decompress better over there, you see."

"*Achha*, okay."

"I fine-tune my answers with him . . . "

"*Achha beta*."

"It helps me prepare better. Over here, it's not the same, the atmosphere of the days when I did all that is missing."

"*Achha*, my dear. *Achha*."

She felt there was nothing in the world that she would have refused him. It would be *achha* all the way till the crises was resolved. Family solidarity! Domestic employees included! They would support him till the very end! There was nothing more beautiful. Wasn't family spirit the next best thing that had been invented after God?

Invited by Mrs. Rao, Philippe decided to walk to Adyar without realizing that it would turn into an expedition. The more he stopped to ask for directions, the more he got lost. He devised a new technique. Instead of following the directions given by the first person, he asked several people. The result left him flabbergasted. They made him turn left, turn right, go forward, go backwards, without any remorse. All directions were possible. And whenever he asked out of ignorance, "Is it still far?" he was told: "Two minutes!"It was always "two minutes." Covering such long distances on foot didn't seem to be a habit with the locals. Two minutes? It didn't make much sense.

As he walked the streets of Chennai - it was the sixteenth of December, exactly ten days before the catastrophe – he thought of the people that he had left behind in Paris: his brothers, his sister, the wives of his brothers, Carol's partner, his nephews, his niece . . . He stopped there and refused to include the rest of the family in his stroll, the cousins, second cousins, uncles, aunts. He needed help, how far would he have to go, was he supposed to turn left or right? Adyar? All right, make a left! Thank you! "I should have used a map," he realized, "although, map or no map, it would have been the same thing."

Family? He had a family, heavens! The mantra came back, a milder version. And suddenly, whoosh, darkness. The candle was extinguished.After a laborious passage through lit space, the stalactites of wax, fragile and brittle, the magma of lava were the only remnants of brightness. In an instant the candle of confidence was snuffed off. Right in the middle of Madras. Instead of smiles, it left behind ugly wrinkles, instead of serenity it left behind creased lines, instead of illuminating the face, it left behind a mask which wasn't even carnivalesque. The smiles

171

and the happy sounds were transformed into muted and painful indifference, ethically unassailable but inhuman. Decades worth of ties of fraternity arbitrarily rejected, forgotten and ultimately betrayed. The flame of confidence had no choice but to die out.

What really exasperated the sahib and plunged him into this abyss of perplexity was the mass of convictions and beliefs acquired generation after generation by the people in his family (and one could imagine that the phenomenon affected millions others as well). They clung to it, from father to son or daughter, like lifebuoys that are supposed to save you, but drown you slowly instead, in an ocean of inanity. Belief in truth was gone from their hearts; denial of real feelings offered them practical advantages. Their obsession with what was OFFICIAL, with "what will people say," was what the Delcourts were driven by. Modernity - if one believes that it saves one from drowning - had not yet reached the shores of the Delcourt family. Philippe, still lost on his way to Adyar, reminded himself that modernity was, at times, so hard to figure out. He suddenly had a shock when he thought he saw his favorite *bhabi*, Noémi, in the guise of a tourist, a "westerner" as he called them, whom he passed. *Oh my God, what is she doing here?* He recovered quickly and brought his hand to his heart. Calm down, calm down, it's not her. The real one must be fitting a dental prosthesis or ordering her assistant to prepare a filling at this moment. And suddenly anger welled up inside him. She had plotted against him to get her apartment back. Directly or indirectly. The whole life of that bitch, he recalled without the least compassion, revolved around one single thing: making money. She even used her free time to regain strength so that she could get back to making more money, and then some more!She would do this relentlessly, until she was six feet under, or at least until she made it to a four star retirement home, heck, make that five star. It would be managed like the showroom of a prestigious car dealer with its floor managers and mechanics, car repaired, hearing-aid cleaned, a decent end assured in exchange for a few thousand euros. The senior recycling plant, a way of abandonment characteristic of the so called rich societies, creating new jobs in full swing...

He once again crossed the fake Noémie as he had to turn around and proceed in the opposite direction. She needed go away, she needed to scram, she was in the wrong country! His temper continued to rise, becoming more intense. Ever since he had arrived in India, this was the first time that he was experiencing the opposite of what he had experienced in Kanyakumari for two whole days. Why did he have to make eye contact on top of all this? In his excessive zeal, he began thinking LIKE HER. Like Noémie! To think like someone else, could there be a worse nightmare? He was sure she thought him crazy. There was no evidence, he nevertheless was certain. Not crazy in a clinical sense. Crazy in a way that some of the mediocre psychiatrists understand the term to be. He thought that SHE viewed him that way because it simplified everything for her and sheltered her from a more complex reality. For example, the previous ninth of April must have been for her another opportunity to gnash her teeth and mutter under her breath that he was crazy. Why? On a spontaneous impulse of affection he had sent her a little birthday card, with carefully chosen words, a vast palette of colors, empty, stripped of all ambiguous connotations. It was an effort wasted. He imagined her great surprise and her attribution of his gesture to his "madness." Only a nut like him could have sent her a card given the nature of their relations. She had responded with silence which had made him feel utterly humiliated. She hadn't even taken the trouble to thank him.

Hrrumph! That quite justified his resentment. His sullenness. Wasted energy. The mind doesn't have ecological awareness.

Demoralize him, that's what Noémie and her ilk wanted to do. Make him stumble, trip over. Nothing new and nothing too serious! Murderesses always ended up being arrested. War, screams, bitterness... wasn't it better to just find refuge in silence, to grab it and stop the infernal machine from creating new fears, new monsters, surreptitious, on the lookout for new ammunition, and to work for peace even if it meant impoverishing oneself? To not let the wheel of karma turn indefinitely. Wasn't that the best path to follow?

"Philippe has arrived?" she enquired after a moment's silence.

"He had said nine thirty, I'm a little worried, Ammu, my dear."

"Worried?" she asked feeling bewildered.

Since when had the Sahib been enjoying the privilege of being able to make his mother-in-law feel worried?

"Yes!"

"Worried . . . ?"

"I know what you're going to say. I often know what people will tell me, it's interesting, when it involves my children. We . . . we have a certain responsibility towards this Sahib, I think. Basically, aren't we, in one sense, his family... while he is in India? Don't you think so?"

"Hmm..."

"Yes my dear Ammu, yes! I feel a little bit like . . . how should I say this... a little bit like his mother."

"Hmm..."

"All the more so, when you think of it, because this investigation which has poisoned our lives has ruined his vacation. He was supposed to go to . . . I'm not sure where in Tamil Nadu, and he had to change his plans. I must tell you, Ammu dear, I do feel responsible for the fellow. And Dipu still has to keep going for all their questioning. I'm so fed up! I can't imagine

174

what else they wish to find out. He has already told them everything. I'm waiting for Brinda. I sent her to get today's *Indian Express*. All he did was entertain himself with computers; it's not a crime!"

"For them, it certainly is!"

There was silence which was quickly pierced by a cry that came straight from Radhika's heart. "I'm dying to have some *palak paneer*! Satiiiiiiiish," she yelled. "I should let you go now, Ammu dear."

The desire for *palak paneer* had to be quickly fulfilled.

"Satiiiiiiiish . . . "

"Memsaab called?"

"Change the menu. It's not too late! Tell the cook to make some *paneer* with spinach."

"And the Sahib?"

"What about him? Yes, for him also. Hurry up!"

She let out an exclamation. They had printed Pradeep's picture next to the article in the newspaper. At least half the people in Adyar who read *Indian Express* would know what was going on. She rapidly skimmed through the article. She felt more surprised at the fact that Philippe was late than at the sick manner in which the journalist had taken delight in exposing the facts.

"Accused of illegally hacking into American defense sites, Pradeep Rao was once again questioned by investigators in Chennai . . . India has categorically rejected demands for his extradition. The brilliant programmer lives in Paris, where apart from carrying out his exploits, he is also pursuing his studies in language. The French Government has expressed surprise. A very brief communiqué issued by the French Home Ministry has emphasized that Rao has not been brought under investigation. Rao is not denying the allegations which, although serious, have led investigators to believe that Rao's motives were innocent. The hacker had acknowledged that he was "having

175

fun" by breaking into military sites which has infuriated the FBI authorities whom we were able to join by phone. Rao denies that he had acted out of criminal intent."

"Absolutely ridiculous!" she fumed. "Criminal intent!"

"The incident involves, to recall the facts, at least forty-two computers belonging to the American Army, twelve to the US Navy, five to NASA, two to the Department of Defense, and one to the Air Force. If extradited to the United States, Rao could face as much as seventy years in prison. When questioned about the consequences of the intrusion into the US defense system, a spokesperson confirmed that Rao's actions might have caused six hundred machines in Washington to go offline for three hours in October 2002 . . . "

"Three hours! All this fuss over only three hours! What is three hours?" exclaimed Mrs. Rao who was accustomed to wasting thousands over insignificant things.

"I better not say anything otherwise I may explode," warned Brinda. "They are raising such a hue and cry over three hours, it's a real shame, Mummy."

"Calm down, honey. Philippe will be here soon."

"So?"

"It's just that you are so upset, it bothers me, dear."

In a certain sense, the crisis had afforded Brinda a taste of political mobilization for the first time in her life. She left the house to go to her class and encountered the Frenchman in the garden. Professors, students, and everybody else in Chennai whom she knew had already been informed. Mrs. Rao put away the paper without finishing the article.

"Namaste! I'm sorry Mrs. Rao, I got lost on my way here."

"Namaste Philippe," she responded joyfully. She felt upbeat that it was only three hours.

Soon they were very seated at the table. *Palak paneer, samosas, masala dosa* were all on the menu.

"I'm going to tell you a story," she told him as she motioned

176

him to help himself. "Very few people in this city know it and you will not find it in any newspaper. It was all so long ago. I'm very happy with my children despite the absence, alas, of my late husband. We are finally happy, except for this whole thing about Dipu."

"Of course!" he responded feeling somewhat anxious.

What was she cooking now?

"I don't think Pradeep has ever told you the story that I'm going to tell you. You could consider it a family secret though I don't know if it can really be called that because it's not a dishonest secret. Family secr . . . Satish, what are you doing here, listening to us? You've already heard this story before."

"Yes, Memsaab," he admitted, without budging an inch.

"Then don't keep standing behind my chair. Go watch the TV or attend to the dog. Not Tommy. He will stay here. That other creature in the garden!

"Should I give him the ball?"

Mrs. Rao had not foreseen this delicate situation.

"Give it to him and then take it back," she advised breaking from all logic. "So that he understands it's exceptional."

Satish saw an advantage in playing dumb. "I should take it back without giving it to him?"

Flabbergasted, she pushed back the *palak paneer* on her plate.

"No, of course not! You let him play for ten minutes and then you take it back from him. It's amazing how he never understands anything!" she exclaimed, turning to Philippe. "So I was telling you . . . "

"You were telling me a story."

"I think it'll surprise you, Philippe. Even here, it's extremely rare. I think, moreover, that most of our neighbors will prefer not to know that it ever happened but I don't regret anything, because I did it for the sake of love."

Satish made his exit and Philippe seemed embarrassed at

where the conversation with Dipu's mother seemed to be headed. She was still a stranger to him and this sudden revelation of secrets seemed abnormal, as shocking as a river changing its course. Unless it signified a new passport, a permanent authorization. A foreigner being given a glimpse of naturalization. Or the right to vote in local elections.

"I am listening."

His solemn tone must have pleased her.

"I didn't marry my husband right away, I first married his brother!"

Whom had she married? He opened his eyes wide. His brother? He felt his heart beat faster. Wasn't she too entitled to her share of unsuspected secrets in life? Why not? His own father had been with a good number of women. A dozen at least. And three among them - Bernadette, Domitille and Laetitia - had given him progeny.

"Satish, don't forget. Don't leave the ball with him. Santosh will be arriving soon, I don't want him being knocked down."

"Santosh loves to see him dribble the ball."

"When I met my husband, we were both eighteen. It was love at first sight. But we had to wait, wait till we turned twenty-one, of course. Unfortunately, my family was not in favor of the match. We were not of the same caste. So I decided to elope. I was nineteen, and had the legal right to marry."

"Why did you marry your er . . . husband's brother?"

"Because we had to wait till he turned twenty-one. A boy cannot get married before the age of twenty-one in this country. So I asked Ramesh, who was older than my Sushil, if he would, and he accepted. He contractually agreed to divorce me two years later. I was thus able to live with my in-laws as Ramesh's younger brother's future wife. Everything is different now, right? Such a thing would not happen these days, I think. Do you understand?" she enquired laughingly.

"You lived for two years in the same house with Ramesh and Sushil?"

"I had my own room," Radhika specified. "I waited until I could marry Sushil soon after his birthday. Suneet was born a year later."

Dipu had not said anything. He had not mentioned all his hacking adventures either. Philippe wondered about the reason for his silence. No, they were just trivial details, legal minutiae. Why would he have talked about it? The same went for the computers. He had not known about the consequences.

It was the official version.

"Do you still see your brother-in-law?"

"He died, four years after our marriage. In an aeroplane accident. He was on his way to Dubai where he had found work as an engineer. He was twenty-three years old."

She too then, in her own way, had fought the law, fought her parents. Radhika Rao! She had fought two battles. One against society, and the other against her parents!

"It feels as if it's not a real story," he commented. "I know that it's true because you said so, but it seems as though it could not have happened to you."

"Have I become that old?" she laughed.

"It's not that, I didn't mean that, of course not."

"I understand, Philippe, I understand."

"It's so surprising."

"Isn't it? You will, I hope, continue to appreciate our family. In spite of its . . . Ultimately, each family creates its rules, its laws. There is a government, and I am the Prime Minister. Satish! Satish! Can he hear me with that dog making so much noise? Satiiiiiish!"

"Do you want me to go and call him?"

"Satiiiiiish! I wanted him to let the cook know that I'm not happy. The *palak paneer* wasn't very good. She must have left by now. Well, it's not important."

The time to demonstrate allegiance was ripe.

"I liked it. It was very nice," said Philippe with tactful politeness.

Would she share a family secret with him at each private meal? It would be highly surprising if she only had one secret. Secrets had a tendency to multiply, plurality suited them better. He had an intuitive feeling that she had other secrets as well.

"Do you know the great M.S. Subbulakshmi?"

"No."

"You have to listen to her! I'm sure Abhi will be delighted. She just passed away, on the eleventh of December. She was born in Madurai; she sang at our wedding. And we will never forget that, I never will. What an extraordinary woman! I can listen to her for hours. She did not accept money and asked my father-in-law to send a check for the renovation of the temples in Rameshwaram. It was she who paid the musicians; she didn't accept a payment from us."

The memory seemed to sadden her. She brought two fingers to her lips, gave a nostalgic smile, leaned her head to the right and got lost in her memories.

She began to sing. *Radhe Govinda Gopi Gopala*. A bhajan, she explained, a devotional melody that Mahatma Gandhi liked. Then she fell silent again.

"Which is the one word that you prefer the most in your beautiful language?" she asked him suddenly. She loved such quizzes and felt the need to lighten the atmosphere. "Don't they say that French is the language of love? Tell me, is it true?"

Philippe had difficulty answering her. He took a few moments as he reflected on the first question while she proceeded to clear the table. One word? He tried to think hard, but nothing came to him. Blank. Just then it occurred to him - the word *love*. But surely, that was not what she wanted to hear. He suddenly thought of another word which he found irresistible because it was so grotesque.

"*Oeuf à la coque.*"

"Goodness gracious," she chortled, when he explained that it meant soft-boiled egg. "That sounds so funny!"

"It's my favorite word."

She seemed enchanted. He bet his life that the "egg story" would soon be doing the rounds of the Rao family. He was happy to make her laugh. Things were getting better day by day. The more she laughed the better disposed she would be towards him. Life could be so simple sometimes. The investigation had also proved to be such a wonderful ally. Not only was that androgynous Dipu of his stuck on Indian soil for now but he was also in an emotionally difficult situation, everybody's eyes were on him, which gave Philippe new reasons for hope. He could see it in Mrs. Rao's eyes. She had never been as amiable with him as she was that day. She was treating him... like... a son-in-law, what other word could be used? He still sensed some reticence, but it seemed almost perfunctory. Of course, they would not broach any topic that might offend. Didn't the resolutions made in the train to Kanyakumari still vibrate up and down his spine when he meditated after his morning cup of tea? Initial prejudices had disappeared from the horizon, just like the rain-filled clouds. The situation no longer called for inopportune and foolish confessions, neither was marriage under the auspices of Krishna a priority anymore.

"Can I ask you a question?"

When a question begins with such a preamble, shouldn't one fear nothing? And allow preconceived ideas to break down? Memsaab's mood was mellow, although with her it was wise thing, verifying what meaning she gave to words. They had entered a pacification phase with consequences unknown. Were they genuinely opening up to each another? Was she now going

181

to end her game - one step forward, two backwards? Was the ancient monument that she was trying to renovate itself? Not three brisk strokes with the paintbrush, but excavations, painstaking archeology. To uncover the essence of the real Radhika, the Radhika that she had been when she was twenty years old. He looked at her as attentively as he could. After the errors of the first few weeks in India, he could not claim to make sense of everything anymore, and especially not when it came to her.

He hadn't forgotten his first meeting with her. He had brilliantly succeeded in alienating her by telling her stories that she had pretended were amusing. He was not going to tread in that direction again. There had been a change. Perhaps, she had now started believing that an alliance with the Delcourt family would be beneficial, like a transit by Jupiter or like a herbal infusion. The blessings would shine on all, even on Brinda who might enter into matrimony with some cousin that they might find suitable for her in an old French province. As long as the stars were favorable! Why couldn't a French branch be developed? And on Abhi too. Abhi who was still single! He was very capable of turning into a *sanyasi* thanks to his guru who didn't even allow him time to wear his shoes. She had nothing against him seeking God, but at twenty-nine he was too young. Not without getting married in any case, if possible.

The more he studied her face - which was less impassive than usual - the more he wondered whether such an alliance between their two families was what she wished for the most, deep inside. Money, trips, new horizons, tons of consideration, everything would be there. If only Philippe had been a woman! Life never gave you a fair deal. If only! He could see her game perfectly. *It's not going to work this time, Radha. Sorry! If you are not capable of accepting that which is real for what it is, why did you dare marry your husband's brother? You knew then how to give it a chance.*

"Please, go ahead."

"You don't think, I hope, that Dipu had malicious intentions when he hacked into those military sites?"

"I don't believe it for a second."

The visit ended shortly thereafter. She had become cold and distant during the last five minutes as if to erase the other impressions that she might have given him. She'll never give up, he thought with a heavy heart as he walked across the garden, Kuchu leaping all around him. Mrs. Rao's question occupied his mind as he made his way back, this time on a rickshaw. *Ram Ram. A detour via Marina beach, please.* The sun was setting and hundreds of families were out together on the beach. It was a sublime picture. He descended from the vehicle and walked towards the sea.

A few smiles exchanged and he returned to the little yellow rickshaw that was waiting to take him to Alwarpet. *That's all, I just wanted to stop here.* Dipu, a crook? All depended on what one meant by the term. The most dangerous crooks were not those who committed these kinds of crimes, neither the counterfeiters. On his moral scale, crooks were elsewhere: among the hypocrites, the liars, the false friends, the selfish humans, the phonies. Still, did Dipu have criminal intent when he had attacked those American sites? How had he been able to keep such a big secret? Philippe remembered how one day he had asked him why he spent so many hours on the computer and Dipu had mumbled something vague. He had hesitated, he could have taken the opportunity and told him everything, but no, he had been evasive, as usual. Secretive.

The following night, he had a dream. He was meeting a North Indian on the Internet. He saw the face move slowly; the image generated by the webcam was blurred. A few hundred hours of connection later, and after many days of passionate conversations, Suman suddenly asked him for money. Officially, it was to come and see him in France. The dream accelerated. Philippe, confused and disoriented, turned red, shivered. His back, head, and legs hurt. He refused the demand. *No, Internet is Internet, and real life is real life, they cannot be mixed. Buy your ticket and I will reimburse you once you are here, when I see you in person. I will not send you any money. There are too many scams. You say that you love me, that you want to marry me. Come here first and we will see if we are compatible.*

The telephone rang in the middle of the night. It was his father. Patrick French, the FBI agent in charge of European affairs, had expressed his desire to meet him. Philippe murmured thanks and put the receiver back.

13

Quality Time with Mummy

Before leaving the house in order to join his brothers, the enlightened Abhi had a talk with his mother. She was waiting for Satish to serve breakfast. His *rangoli* still unfinished, the servant had no intention of hurrying up. Radhika had been feeling bored. There wasn't even a newspaper handy that she could read. She ambushed the first person who materialized. The person was trying to creep out of the house . . . on tiptoes. So now they were trying to elude her! That was the price one paid for being someone from whom nothing escaped.

"Where are you off to?" she harpooned him. "Can we talk for a few minutes?"

"I'm in a rush."

"Me too."

"You don't look like you are. What is it?"

Radhika made a grumpy face. Fine! They could all get lost and leave her alone with that moron, Satish. They never allowed her to talk about the problems that gave her sleepless nights.

"Nothing!" she said, avenging herself. "Go."

"I'm listening. I do have two minutes."

She got up, looked at her reflection in the mirror and sat down again. She patted her hair that had been gathered into a bun. Thanks to her insomnia, she had a look that was less severe, but more beaten.

"Two minutes. That's what I get, two minutes? I feel like

one those beggars on the footpath behind Malar hospital, people give them two rupees; I'm getting two minutes."

"You don't plan on acting like this everyday, I hope? Don't compare yourself to them, Mummy. It's not proper."

"Not proper?" she mumbled, quite agreeing with her son. "Listen to what I'm saying, my dear . . . "

He began to fear the worst.

"You are twenty-nine years old. That's right, twenty-nine! Soon you'll be thirty, and . . . "

"Oh, great!"

"Sit down, will you? Do you want Satish to bring you some coffee?"

"I have to leave in two minutes."

"I know, you've already told me. Don't worry. You can leave in two minutes. Satish, quickly, bring some coffee."

Abhi flopped into an armchair.

"It's not urgent, of course, but . . . all the same, Abhi, all the same. When you are past thirty, it won't be the same. Doesn't it scare you?"

"What are you talking about?" he asked.

He had understood.

"Aren't you concerned?"

"I . . . "

"Yes, of course you are. I should tell you it's urgent. I'd rather be honest with you. Poor Mrs. Menon, our neighbor. Look what is happening with her son, Gopal. Is that what you want? I want you to realize it yourself. I will handle everything," she continued, switching into a more pragmatic mode. "I will find you a girl who . . . "

"Our two minutes are over."

"You want to wait until you aren't the right age, is that so? And I'm not in a position to help you? You'll come asking me for help, and . . . Oh, you are all so difficult, even Bira. She is

186

impossible. She has become so rude and unpleas . . . "

"You are the one who is being difficult."

It was a weak counterattack. Out of the four it was Abhi who was the least expert.

Skilled at manipulating (her manipulations were directed at her children for their own good), Radhika rebelled. "Me? Difficult? That's a good one! I am not being difficult; I'm trying to help each and every one of you. Before it's too late."

"You *are* difficult," he insisted obstinately.

She decided to give up for the time being, deciding to move her pawns more effectively later.

"I am a difficult person, okay, but why? I'll tell you why. Because I love you," she lashed out without guilt. "Because I love my country and believe in its values of tolerance and compassion, and in marriage. Yes my dear, it's my fault that I'm like that and want you to get married. Difficult! Ask Ammu if I am difficult," she suggested, furious.

Her good relations with her daughter-in-law - unexpected as they were thanks mostly to the *bahu's* patience - were to her proof beyond doubt that *she* was NOT difficult!

"Let's not involve Ammu in this."

"And Dipu? You don't think I'm fed up with that sahib who has no business coming to our house. I tolerate him because . . . "

Abhi didn't let her finish. He got up and left. She had exceeded the daily limit that was allowed.

Poor Mummy, abandoned by all. She clung to anything. It was as unbearable as the sight of those kids in Adyar who asked for alms near the bridge instead of going to school.He passed them everyday wondering what he could do for them. Nothing. The same scene repeated itself everyday. A bitter truth about the India that they lived in.

Did they have to let her manipulate them under the pretext

that she had already decided how events should unfold in their lives? Perhaps, yes. Tears welled up in his eyes. He was twenty-nine, and would soon be thirty. The harassment would increase in strength for a few more years, and then like a weakening cyclone, after thirty-five, it would blow over; that would be the end of the loving hostilities. Peace by default! Age would take its toll, perhaps. Or she would no longer be in this world, who knew? Out of a sense of contradiction, he might then be able to take THE decision because family and social pressures would have collapsed, whoosh, just like a house of cards. Abhi was a saint and a rebel; he was both, he carried both the impulses. He was the two extremes together. He had on occasion talked about this with his guru. The answers given by Sri Sri had not enlightened him. He would continue living life, like Suneet, Dipu, Bira. To each his (or her) own. Sadly, their paths no longer intersected. Childhood was over. What remained was rebelliousness and wisdom.

He quickly recovered his centeredness. When one lives in an environment where poverty breathes at every street corner such that it becomes an extension of ones own self, one ceases to succumb to despondency because it risks dragging you to a zone where even the poorest among the poor do not enter. It gives rise to strange feelings that mutate into a backache. Anger of the vertebrae against suffering. Dashed hopes hammered into the flesh by the bumper blows dealt by life. In conjunction with his backaches, his cranium reflected more and more light each passing month, preventing his hair from recovering any lost territory.

Dipu's recent escapades didn't help either. *She's focusing on me because she cannot handle you right now, Mr. Smarty Programmer. She is working on Abhi till she can take aim at you again.* She is out of control, our Mummy. And you, you don't cease to amaze us, Dipu. You are so alike. Panagalpondy, you infiltrated the

188

site of an army, that too not just any army, and you picked a nickname to do it, it brings fame to our city.

Panagal was the name of a rather gloomy park in Chennai. It often remained closed and was the starting point of the famous Pondy Bazaar cloth market with its neverending haggling. It was a mecca of open air commerce that stretched over almost three kilometers. Teeming with people, its streets of the bazaar were also used by a few Ambassador cars, rickshaws, carts, scooters, and stray cows indifferent to the tumult.

It would have been a different story if he had managed to learn one or two things about NASA or discover the secret plans of the biggest army in the world. Not even that! Not that it would have changed anything. Preoccupied with the investigation that he was undergoing, Pradeep had an intimidating influence on his two brothers. They were rallied around him in solidarity, happy to miss out on the scoops that they could have enjoyed in the evenings had they been more interested.

"You definitely went the whole hog. Our family is in the public glare," Suneet had pointed out. "It's very disturbing. Our family can't be in peace anymore. I'm not accusing you, Dipu, but people are pointing at us. We will never be an anonymous family again."

His brother's moralistic tone had surprised him. How was he responsible? His only fault was that he had felt bored in Paris. He hadn't made any other mistake. Unless Suneet was using it as a pretext to fault him for returning to Chennai along with Philippe. Such underhand methods were not entirely impossible. He was using the hacking incident to judge him. A new chapter in the manipulation initiated by his mother. His brother was participating in the *air du temps* of December 2004. A *procès d'intention,* a trial on the basis of probable cause. On the basis of unsubstantiated allegations. It was one of those trials where the accused was not even informed. Everything happened behind one's back.

"Please don't accuse me, Suneet. I didn't commit any offense against you," he had defended himself. "Everything will turn out fine, you'll see."

"Yes, probably. After your trial. How are we going to keep our heads high?"

Dipu hadn't been sure if he was being castigated for something else, a more intimate matter: his love life. He had felt ready to advance all the ideas that his spiritual perceptions at times spawned within him, whenever his feelings for Philippe blocked his Indian identity. He had felt ready to inform Suneet that he was convinced of one thing: *God didn't love him any less. And that He didn't give a f***; for Him it was all the same. Doing what the majority decided in the name of all was not spirituality; it was the real offense!*

"I don't think there will be a trial. The situation is very complex. None of the three countries will be able to find an easy way out. And Suneet, there's no point telling Mummy, but I have connections."

"You must put your life in order," Suneet had admonished, changing his tune, just as Dipu had expected.

He had put up with it in silence. It was a conspiracy, using a public affair as an excuse to target him on a different level.

He had felt tempted to defend himself through religion, by reminding him that he also did his *sadhana*, like him. That he was a devotee of Krishna, like him. That God loved them both just as much.

"What bothers me is that you have been lying," Suneet had continued.

"To whom?"

"To all of us. To me."

Dipu had realized that his brother was setting a trap. He was trying to make him talk in order to manipulate him better later on. He had found it very hard, terribly hard to resist. Suneet was the eldest. He had felt an overpowering urge to discuss God with him, but it was impossible. His brother was inventing a god who was none other than him and who spoke through his mouth. Manipulation yet again, a mistaken belief in powers that one didn't have! In verity, Suneet was combating the truth about his younger brother more than his alleged lies.

"I don't think I understand what you mean," Dipu had replied, trembling inwardly. "You are mistaken."

Looking at him, Suneet had realized his brother would not divulge anything. He was striking at water with his sword. It had relaxed both of them. In the final analysis, lies suited them all. Even the judicial authorities. Believing that ONE truth existed was what made it really dishonest. That was the real fraud.

The specter of dangerous revelations had vanished. Dipu wasn't ready, Suneet no more than him. Using religion was essentially a tricky enterprise. Even the most experienced gurus didn't risk it often. Evoking the body as this or that, evoking successive incarnations, the soul incarnating as female and getting accustomed to a role, all these secondary truths of spirituality, they had no significance. One couldn't stop oneself from being what one was. This was the first and only obligation. As for the rest, it was nobody's business. Evoking god for a yes or a no according to one's own convenience was a pathetic reflex.

Suneet had smiled, reverting to his previous state which was what Dipu had wished for.

"Don't worry *bhaiya*," Dipu had cleverly smoothed his brothers ruffled feathers with just a pinch of guilt. He had been able to resist his older brother's inquisitorial attack which was what really mattered. The worst was over.

Horrified at what he had been on the verge of disclosing, he had broken into a cold sweat. It could have led to justify himself in the worst possible manner, reminding his brother that he, like him, was a Hindu, that his intimate life was not prejudicial to his faith which remained untouched. Society lacked tolerance, what could he possibly do about it? *And Mummy, and Bira, what can I do to make them all more tolerant? It's not my job to play that role.* What a miserable gift it was, tolerance. One did not end up in prison, that was all. It was nevertheless a social prison, the "closet" as they said in France. And what would really have been corny is if he had told Suneet, "God made us, both you and me, so why all these hang ups? We will both go back to Him."

At least, he had reasoned, he still piqued their interest. They were asking him questions; they were trying to have a dialog with him. He appreciated that. In France, he had met with indifference. The noose of indifference. They killed people slowly with it, little by little. A magnificent weapon, used for bringing people in line. The weak ones, always the weak ones, they took revenge with its help. They venerated its existence. They bombarded you, fired at you with the insidious machine gun of indifference, rat a tat tat. You didn't expect it, it did not cause pain, it was like an anesthetic, the foretaste of a slow death, not brutal, almost generous. The delights of the most refined vengeance, the most ridiculous as well, were to be found in the peaks of indifference, triumphant and sovereign, that he had experienced in Paris. Already, at his age, he had become familiar with it, what would it be like when he was fifty? What would it be transformed into? Indifference, he knew it well, he had tested its ravages over time. She was a bitch, more devious than alcohol. That is why he had decided to unite with Philippe, to thwart its attacks more effectively, to protect himself, like one protects oneself from ones best friends. The war of indifference sometimes opens with the weapons of friendship. It was better not to be its fool.

"Satish," came Mrs. Rao's mellow voice. "Come here, I want to tell you something."

She knew how to be sweet (and just how much) when she had to, whenever she needed him for his services beyond the call of duty (to the extent that he was capable), whenever she needed him as her witness, or whenever she wanted extract an audacious opinion which would torture her afterwards. Even with Ammu she never obtained such results. With Ammu, she had to wear kid gloves, modulate her voice, and accept that eighty percent of the things she said would be divulged. But nothing of the sort with the servant. He was only prone to making vague allusions which generally were so incomprehensible that they just reinforced his reputation as an idiot.

Until the Day Judgment arrived with regard to his presumed foolishness, he was indispensable to Radhika. Pouring ones heart out to him was like savoring a delectable cheese *naan*, one didn't feel like stopping.

If there was anyone who knew her better than her own children, anyone who didn't fall into any of her traps, it was Satish, of course. The fact that he never participated directly in any of the debates that agitated the family put him in a privileged position. It made him seem like some kind of a royal personage floating above all the confusion, an emblem of the Nation observing in silence without retaining anything. He himself would have been incapable of visualizing himself not huddling close to the door or in the kitchen in order to listen to the latest developments in the family. Radhika understood. If she objected to his staying planted in the living room it was only out of formality (it didn't look good!). Wasn't this better compared to knowing that he was hidden in the next room?

"Come here."

"What is it now?" enquired Satish, approaching.

For issues "beyond the call of duty" he had the right to be insolent without offending Memsaab.

"You'll never guess what I saw in my dream," she challenged.

Realizing that they were about to start a new guessing game, he placed his hands on the back of a chair, sighed and leaned forward. Mrs. Rao was pleased with his body language.

"You saw Dipu in prison?" he mumbled. It was the easiest answer.

She shrugged it off in silence. Wrong ! He obviously wasn't in form that morning.

"Brinda is going to marry a very rich and tall sahib who will come from America?"

The idea merited more attention.

"I don't have to dream of that, I'm sure it will happen. Hopefully it will not end in divorce. It's amazing, isn't it, how quickly people get divorced these days. Besides, our cultures are different."

"Not too different in the case of Brinda," Satish reminded her. "One would think she is American."

"You think so? Time will tell. But that's not what I saw in my dream."

"Ammu will give birth to twins?"

"That would be delightful, but it's not that either. What's the matter today? Normally, you guess right away."

"I guess Memsaab's dreams?" he asked in wonder. "I don't recollect. Not Memsaab's dreams. I normally guess Dipu's or Brinda's . . . "

Mrs. Rao was beginning to feel impatient. She had not even started opening her heart and here they were, wasting precious minutes.

"Abhi left the house and joined his guru's ashram? His future is staring us in the face." Satish observed.

"You go clean your face! Your nose looks so dirty."

"I give up," he avenged himself. "I cannot guess."

"Try!" she encouraged.

The servant shut his eyes tight in concentration and assumed a most inspired look. Mrs. Rao waited for the right answer.

"The late Sushil Sahib came to Memsaab. He told her that fortunately he was there to protect the children from Heaven, because Dipu would not go to prison for long and that in the end he would marry the . . . "

"You are so silly," she snapped. None of that is correct. What did you say? Marry whom? What are you raving about? I don't wish to dream of my poor Sushil at all, he is better off where he is. I can say this to you: I wouldn't want him to come back."

"Memsaab was unhappy with him?"

"I was happy," she replied with embarrassment. "Of course I was. But it's better for him where he is, and it's better for me where I am."

Satish removed his hands from the chair and got ready to leave. The clock was ticking and he still hadn't started his work.

"Well, I'll tell it to you later. It's got nothing to do with all that. It's . . . much more interesting. You'll be very surprised," she tempted him.

"Yes, Memsaab," he agreed as he headed for the door. "I have . . . I found this paper, this morning, by the gate. I think it fell out of the Sahib's pocket yesterday."

"And you tell me now?" she scolded him. "Show. Show it to me, you fool."

As always, Satish's eyes opened wide as if he was looking for the person she was speaking to. He always reacted this way whenever Mrs. Rao brutalized him. He handed her the sheet of paper holding it with both his hands like a public prosecutor trying to convince the jury with a decisive piece of evidence.

"It's in French, I can't make out head or tail of it. Stop

pushing it under my nose like that. What could it possibly mean? How mysterious, no?"

"It is an email," was Satish's diagnosis. "It tells the date when it was sent. The Sahib's father wrote him a letter."

"Oh, the Minister! Okay, but that changes everything. And you didn't even show it to me. Let's see, who could translate it for us? Any idea, Satish? Who speaks French around here?"

"Dipu?"

"Dipu, yes naturally. But . . . I . . . How to say this, I . . . would like to keep it confidential, I don't want him to know, understand?"

Satish folded the letter back.

"That is illegal," he announced, stepping a few feet away from Mrs. Rao. "Isn't it shameful to read someone else's letter behind their back?"

Mrs. Rao was taken aback. Such wanton display of morality all of a sudden, that too from a servant who hadn't thought twice about putting a kitten in the washing machine, did not sit too well. Of course it was shameful, but pointing it out was even more so.

"I would like to know what the father is writing to the son. Is there anything wrong in that? Why didn't you throw it away? You can throw it away. No need to talk about it any more. Go, throw it away. Don't keep standing there," she said with resignation, mortified, hoping that her order would not be carried out.

"I can throw it away?" asked Satish, playing dumb. He had no intention of throwing it away.

Radhika hesitated. Getting rid of it would be one way of to get rid of the two sahibs, the father and the son, of throwing them into the sea. That's what they deserved. At the same time, she considered the discovery an unexpected gift from heaven, and she stretched out her hand to reclaim it. To her great surprise, Satish looked away.

"Let me have it. I'll throw it away."

He put away the precious document safely in his pocket.

"No, Memsaab. Not good."

"You are annoying, and that's an understatement. Give it to me. Don't poke your nose in things that aren't your business. Give it here before I really get angry."

He pulled it out of his pocket.

"How about we burn it?" he offered an alternative.

"Go and bring the directory so that we can find a translator. I'm sure we can find someone in this city other than Dipu who knows French. Maybe I should send you to one of those hotels where all the tourists stay. You will be able to find someone who can solve our problem.

"We shouldn't be ashamed . . . ?" repeated the defeated Satish as he handed over the letter to Mrs. Rao.

"Of course not, not at all," she interrupted. "You're mistaken. What is there to be ashamed of? To have a son who is not even married, like this Sahib who has come from France? There is no reason. You are out of your mind, Satish. You don't know what ashamed means. It's just a useless letter that he dropped, probably because he wanted us to find it. Let's take a look and see if I can understand it. What does it say?"

She put on her glasses and read the first few words aloud.

"I don't have the faintest idea what the Minister is saying to his son," she announced, without sounding surprised. "There is no reason to be ashamed, Satish. Why should anybody be ashamed? I've never felt less ashamed in my whole life than right now, at this moment. You know, sometimes . . . one has to doing things that seem to others . . . not very legitimate. There are crimes that are much more serious! Are we committing a crime? If only the history of the world was filled with such crimes! Let me tell you a story. Think about that poor emperor who built the Taj Mahal. His sons threw him into prison before killing each other like dogs and burying him where he didn't want to be! That is a crime! They scandalously economized on the construction of an independent mausoleum. And you're making such a big fuss over a simple letter that my curiosity, which is legitimate after all, makes me want to read. You think that is a good reason to feel ashamed?" she concluded, satisfied with her defense.

Satish had one more weapon in his arsenal.

"And Ammu?" he threatened. "We tell her?"

Mrs. Rao quickly forgot the fate of the Mughal emperor and became pale thinking of her own as she was reminded of her daughter-in-law.

"It's you that I'm ashamed of!" she exploded. "Of course we don't! Let one thing be clear between us, Satish. There is no need to say anything to anybody, especially Ammu. Otherwise, otherwise . . . "

"Otherwise...? Yes, it is clear. I won't breathe a word," he promised.

"I'm really disappointed," she continued in order to subjugate him further. "Tomorrow, you will go to Egmore Station with the letter. That place is full of tourists. You can look for a French tourist who will translate it for you.

"Into which language?"

She hadn't thought about that. They would need someone who also knew English. It wasn't that simple.

"We will see."

"Shameful," he mumbled as he withdrew, this time for Brinda's ears. She had just returned home.

"What is shameful?"

She deposited her things and a newspaper on the table.

"Hello dear. Nothing. Satish, you know how he is. He gets upset for no reason. We are going to look for a new servant. I'm fed up. I threatened to fire him and this is how he backchats.

You will pay for this, you are a disgrace, Satish," she threatened, calling out after him.

Brinda, fascinated with what she had witnesses, spoke up in his defense. She suspected a complicated settling of scores which involved secrets that had been kept from her.

"You've become very chummy with him these days."

"I think you're right" her mother concurred. "I must tell you though, that because he pokes his nose into everything, sometimes his opinions are interesting."

"I can see that!" Brinda retorted, unconvinced.

Radhika shook her head. The day had started off badly. A mysterious letter and . . . and she hadn't shared her recent dream with anyone. Only Brinda remained. It was terrible how all those dreams went waste over the course of time like the billions of stars that died as soon as their light reached the Earth. How could they be saved from oblivion? She felt a great sense of loneliness fall upon her. Why didn't dreams have a . . . special legal status? Didn't they deserve to be protected like an endangered species; were they not individual treasures, as valuable as any other form of cultural wealth? Although she considered Bira to be the last candidate worthy of such confidences, she didn't have a choice, unless she waited another hour till she met her five year old grandson at the beach.

"Honey, I had a really strange dream. I think you'll enjoy hearing it. I found myself at a polling station in Bombay," she continued without waiting for a reply, "with our labrador, Tommy. And you'll never guess! I had managed to get him registered in the voters list, yes, our Tommy!" she exclaimed confusedly. "His name was in the register, Tommy Andrew Rao, professional footballer, born 19th July, 1977, which corresponds to his four years if you convert them into human years."

"Oh," muttered Bira, taken aback. "I hope you're feeling okay."

Mrs. Rao was keen to spit out the contents of her dream before they evaporated completely.

"I kept him very close to me; he was very good, like he is always, and the officer in charge smiled at me. He informed me that Tommy was an eligible voter and that everything was in order but that it was not compulsory for him to vote. They just needed Tommy to enter the polling booth but it was up to him if he wanted to cast his ballot or not."

"And he barked in which direction?"

"I woke up. No, that's not it! After leaving the polling station, I was accosted by a police officer, a *Kotwal* sahib, who tried to arrest us. He said that the authorities were going to order an investigation. As Tommy's owner, I had committed many crimes including registering Tommy illegally on an electoral list."

"Satish, I want tea!" yelled Brinda.

"I heard," grunted the servant. "You should not worry so much about Dipu, Memsaab."

"And an *aloo paratha*," added Radhika, who was feeling hungry.

"I don't know if I should tell you what I read in the news this morning after all this."

"Wait till I've eaten," Mrs. Rao negotiated. "I'm feeling weak."

They had to wait patiently for fifteen minutes before Satish brought an unleavened flatbread stuffed with potatoes that Mrs. Rao had ordered for breakfast.

"Tommy does not like football, I regret. It's the other one, Kuchu," Satish mentioned as he unfolded a tablecloth.

"It's not properly cooked," complained Mrs. Rao. "Why is her cooking always so bad the day I'm starving? When I'm not hungry, she makes good food, typical of her, no?"

"Typical!" repeated Brinda.

"It's unfortunate. I'm really hungry. That's what you managed to gather from my dream? What an idiot!" she said, lowering her voice. "I don't care which dog it is!"

Brinda pulled out a page from the newspaper and dove into a new article devoted to Dipu. Mrs. Rao had her mouth full when she asked to see it.

"It is now established that Pradeep Rao, acting under the alias of Panagalpondy (reminiscent of the park bearing the same name in Chennai and associated with the famous cloth market of Tamil Nadu's capital city), might have also scanned the networks that he penetrated in order to crack the access codes of the system administrators. His actions resulted in preventing the American Army from accessing, for several hours, its own websites. Rao has accepted the facts. "It was just for fun," is what he reportedly told investigators. "I threw them in the trash can. I didn't save them . . . "

"There, you see. It was just for fun!" repeated Radhika with satisfaction.

"Hm mm. Read the rest of it."

"The American authorities are crying foul even as the Indians are claiming that they have not been given any significant evidence of the damage that Rao has allegedly caused. They are refusing to charge him. The affair is embarrassing the French government as well which, it is believed, did not respond in a timely manner to the repeated requests made by the FBI. Paris is all the more reluctant to indict the whiz kid since relations between the two countries have deteriorated after the invasion of Iraq and Washington's retaliatory tactics against French nationals have irked the government. According to the Administration, Rao's actions were premeditated - something which Rao refutes - and represent de facto a threat to the security of the American public. According to sources, the United States however recognizes the fact that the Indian national acted alone and that they have no reason to believe that Rao has ever participated in any terrorist activity. Moreover, no sensitive or confidential information seems to have been accessed or tampered with . . . "

14

Bapu of French Politics

"Meditation is one of the greatest forms of art in life; it is perhaps the supreme art. It cannot be learnt from anyone. That is its beauty. There is no technique, and thus there is no authority. When you learn to know yourself, observe yourself, observe the way you walk, the way you eat, what you say, your gossiping, the hatred, the jealousy - being conscious of it all inside you, ceaselessly, is part of meditation."

Philippe closed Jiddu Krishnamurti's book. Reading inside a rickshaw that was zigzagging its way forward at full speed wasn't very practical. The vehicle would succeed in avoiding two out of three potholes, and then bang! You got hit in the nose. There was no escape. Dipu descended first, hopping out with a light step, the way any twenty-eight year old might. The sahib had more trouble, he hunched himself to let himself out of the funny little yellow box. They joined the rest of the Rao family on the beach. Almost everybody was there; the only person missing was Ammu.

As pointed out by Mrs. Rao, Ammu was always to be found missing. Mrs. Rao was draped in a pale yellow sari and did not hide her pleasure upon seeing Philippe again as she acknowledged him with a light nod. She noticed what he was wearing - a cream colored impeccably ironed dhoti. It was not tied sufficiently high up above his hips which caused the lower part of the garment to keep getting caught in his sandals.

"What does *baba* mean?" Philippe discreetly enquired once they had begun their stroll on the sands of Marina Beach.

"What did he say, what is he asking?" probed Mrs. Rao. Her ears were not as sharp as Satish's.

"He's wants to know what *baba* means!"

"Ah!"

"Grandfather," replied Dipu. "Why?"

"This morning, when I was walking on the street, a vendor called out to me like that: *Baba*! *Baba*!"

"No, of course not!" exclaimed Radhika, shocked. "You're not a *baba*."

"Not yet," mocked Bira.

Being called out to in that manner had shocked him. Maybe it was because he vaguely resembled a hippie? Was it possible? "It's quite possible," Dipu assured him. "Who knows!"

It reminded Philippe of the gesture Indians used to express assent. They shook their heads as if they were saying no although they were saying yes, and it was the same for its so-called opposite, the *no*. They avoided saying it. It was considered an unfavorable omen, not too auspicious.

"I am not a *baba*?"

"A *baba*?" Mrs. Rao reassured him, feeling a little embarrassed. "A *baba*? These merchants will invent just about anything in order to entice tourists. You are not . . . you are not all that old," she declared with regret.

The indirect reminder that he was an "old" sahib - not young enough to be the friend of a son that they wanted to marry off - began to affect her mood. Fortunately, the innocent Santosh ran up to his grandmother and tugged at her sari. He wanted her to take him to where the vendors were selling their wares.

Seven days before the tsunami would strike under a similar blue sky, sweeping away thousands of fishermen in the Bay of Bengal and along the coast of Kerala, Mrs Rao had succumbed to the pressures of her children and had agreed to an outing on the beach. They had all insisted, one by one. She would have preferred to watch *Desperate Housewives* in her living room but another kind of curiosity had gotten the better of her. It involved observing the sahib in the midst of all her children. The first-class voter that he was, Tommy had also been allowed to accompany them on the trip to the beach.

"Look, Daadi, looooook," screamed Santosh.

"Look at what, dear? I don't see anything."

She was very busy keeping an eye on the sahib and was not paying much attention to all the activity on the unusually lively beach. In her opinion, Dipu and Philippe had no business holding hands in front of her even if it was the normal thing in India for friends to hold hands. Not them!

It got worse when she saw Santosh latching on to the sahib's other hand. An inaudible cry of jealousy escaped her, and her heart started beating faster. That was the problem with kids. They loved too easily, as easily as they kicked a ball!

"Daadi, why don't you let Kuchu come and play with us?"

"Oh yes, dear. We will bring him with us the next time," she prevaricated. "Hold my hand, here, come, let's go and buy your favorite cake."

Santosh let go of the sahib's hand and took hold of his grandmother's instead. She gripped it tightly.

They queued up in front of a pyramid of brightly colored sponge cakes. Radhika found herself stuck behind a short bald man muttering to himself. "If the hundred fifty million Indians at that time had all pissed in a tank, it would have been enough to drown the handful of Britishers who were here and Her Majesty's entire government as well," he muttered.

Brinda began to giggle. She scurried towards the water, her body bent over in laughter. Mrs. Rao beckoned to Suneet with a movement of her head which implied that she considered herself to be in danger. She immediately abandoned her place in the line.

"What an uncouth fellow," she murmured under her breath. "Come Santosh, don't stand near him."

"I want to, Daadi," he insisted.

If Brinda was laughing, why couldn't he?

"Come over here." She pulled him close to her.

"He's not wrong," commented Abhi. "In the period that followed 1910, the nationalists allowed . . . "

"Come and see which cake you want, my angel," interrupted Mrs. Rao, unhappy at how their excursion was turning out. "This one or that one? That one, right?" she asked, already regretting the fact that she had missed her TV show.

Santosh hesitated. He chose the first one and then asked for a different one before changing his mind again. They finally sat down on the sand next to Brinda.

Philippe had not heard the historic words uttered by the short man but he was feeling angry with Mrs. Rao. She had dared to detach the child's hand from him right when he was holding Pradeep's hand on the other side. Mrs. Rao was getting on his nerves. She was just like his French stepmother, without the western bourgeois quirks. And *baba*, which meant grandfather, simply took the cake. He, a grandfather? He had not even finished growing up! India certainly did not fail to spring surprises on you. According to the region, *baba* could mean father (phew!) and even spiritual father, guru (gosh!). He decided to go on the offensive - how did they put it? - give her a real cold shoulder. It would be the *hors d'oeuvre*, a prelude to the hostilities. It was winter after all, even in Chennai.

"You ought to help me get up," suggested Radhika, immobilized in the sand.

"How many did you have this time?"

"Daadi is a fatso," chanted Santosh. "Daadi is . . . "

Suneet caught hold of the kid. Kissing him on the forehead he put his hand on his mouth with a laugh.

"When I was a little girl, my grandmother used to tell me that her mother used to burn incense in front of Empress Victoria's portrait every evening, so I don't like to hear what I just heard, you see."

Santosh made a face after taking the first bite out of his cake. He got rid of it by burying it in the sand.

"In those days, many Indians licked the boots of the English, didn't they?" provoked the sahib. "The ones who became rich thanks to them."

Mrs. Rao stood up and gave the Frenchman a withering look.

"My great grandparents, Philippe, had a construction business during the British Raj, and they did very well for themselves. It was not the way you say," she declared solemnly with a hint of disdain in her voice. "Indian history is such, like that of your country perhaps," she added with irony "that we had a Muslim period, and a period of Sikh domination in the north, and many other things, and the British period was definitely not the worst, unlike what you might think. I know some young people today, in 2005 . . . "

"2004, may I remind you, we still have a few more days to go."

" . . . who would prefer to have been born before 1947. Whether one likes it or not! Obviously, it doesn't mean anything, except that we don't have to be ashamed of that particular period in our history."

Dipu squirmed in the sand.

"Interesting," continued Philippe, determined to settle scores with her even if it meant resorting to political debate. "So, basically you eulogize the foreigners who exploited and humiliated you for almost two centuries."

"The French played their part in all of it, here in the south," retorted Mrs. Rao. "But that is not what is relevant, Philippe."

"Doesn't it bother you, all those clubs reserved for Europeans, the compartments reserved for Anglo-Indians on trains, and . . . "

"Let's not talk about all this, please! English influence will not diminish so quickly, whether we change the names of our big cities or not. Indian pride doesn't depend on it."

It was Abhi's turn to squirm in discomfort.

"We have accomplished a lot since independence. It wouldn't have happened so quickly if that wasn't the case. We manufacture our own cars, trains, aircraft, er . . . our own nuclear bombs, we send satellites into space. And in the field of information technology that I'm very familiar with, we . . . "

"Okay," interjected Philippe Delcourt. "We know! We know about that. For the last five years at least your country has been experiencing an unprecedented economic boom. And at the same time, it is acceptable to you that tens of millions of your fellow countrymen live in the most abject poverty. Explain to me why it's like that, how can you accept it? I don't get it."

Mrs. Rao emitted a series of sighs which didn't augur well; they signaled that no pleasant response would be forthcoming from her.

"It's obvious you have never heard of demographics. Help me get up, Philippe," she commanded, stretching her hand towards him. "These discussions are making me tired. If I had known that we were going to discuss politics, I would have stayed back with Satish who, by the way, must have started getting worried. Which way do we go?"

"Ah good old Satish!" exclaimed Brinda who had been respectfully listening to the discussion of her elders. "Which way do you think we must go, Mummy?"

"We don't like these pointless conversations, right, my dear?" said Mrs. Rao as she slid her arm under her daughter's.

"YOU don't like them. I, on the contrary, love them. It's a refreshing change from all your fantasies about marriage for Abhi, and Dipu, and me . . . "

"For you?" asked Mrs. Rao in astonishment. "Have you ever heard me talk about it? Never!"

"I can see quite well that you are too occupied with the other two to pester me about it, but I'm ready to meet your challenges. You are just waiting for an opportunity to . . . "

"Bira! How can you say such a thing?" protested Mrs. Rao in a spectacular outburst of fake disbelief as if her pride had been wounded. "You are still so young. Plus all those years of further studies that you are planning . . . "

"Yes, thankfully I am still studying. Otherwise you would have already launched an offensive. You yourself got married at the ripe old age of twenty."

Radhika frowned and turned to look back at the four men who were following behind them.

"Times were different then. You people are all so strange and unreasonable these days. I wonder why Ammu didn't come with us. Santosh, hold my hand. Wasn't it yummy, the cake that Daadi bought for you?"

"No!"

Bira began to laugh.

"It's not your lucky day today."

"Hurry up, and find us a rickshaw, can you please? If I'm lucky I may be able to catch the end of the show. It would definitely be more interesting than the way Philippe insults our country. *Bharat Mata ki jai*, long live Mother India!"

"He didn't insult our country; he wants to live here and never go back to his own. Why would he insult?"

"He can say what he likes; I've noticed that he is only interested in Anglo-Indians like he said. He doesn't go anywhere else. He should first learn to tie his dhoti properly around his waist. Don't you feel shocked, Bira, don't turn around just now, don't look, see how your brother is holding the sahib's hand!"

"On the contrary!" she replied provocatively. "On the contrary! I would be quite shocked if he didn't hold his hand."

Mrs. Rao let go of Santosh's hand.

"Just leave me alone, you're terrible. What does he see in him, can anybody explain it to me? Greenways Road!" she ordered the driver.

She hauled herself into the vehicle with some effort. Bira climbed in next and sat beside her mother. Mrs. Rao bade her sons and Philippe goodbye with a wave.

"So?"

"I think my brother is very normal. Philippe is a source of security for him, which is something that he needs, especially in France. Affection, company, attention, love . . . "

The last word was too much, but Mrs. Rao didn't jump. They couldn't afford to jump anymore. Their means of transportation had no room for it.

"There you go again with your nonsense! Only some of those words are applicable, others are not! Impossible!"

"You have such unprogressive mentality."

"I don't think I'm mistaken when I say that it's not advisable, dear. I know about these things a lot better than you think, and in the case of your brother, believe me, it's not going to happen, unless he decides to break off relations with us, which is quite unlikely now that he risks losing his residency and even being convicted in France."

Brinda pursed her lips.

"Have a heart, Mummy! You are going to take advantage of what those idiots are doing to Dipu to force him to leave Philippe. That's so horrible!"

"I'm not going to force him. He can do what he wants. And he doesn't have to leave him, as you say, because as far as I can tell there is no particular reason why they spend so much time together. They are just friends. Moreover, Satish is of the same opinion as well," she pointed out as their vehicle made its way to Greenways.

"That's just ridiculous! I don't give a damn about what Satish says. To me, his opinions matter as much as Tommy's, do you realize? You are completely insane."

"You have developed a nice habit of telling me that I'm insane whenever I don't agree with you."

There were two men waiting at the gate.

"Namaste. Does Pradeep Rao live here? We would like to meet him."

"Who are you?" asked Mrs. Rao, taken aback.

"What's going on?" Brinda enquired as she paid off the driver. She had already noticed that the younger guy had a heavy-looking camera slung over his shoulder.

"I want to speak to him, you did not answer me on the phone . . . "

"We are not receiving," announced Mrs. Rao as if she had been in mourning. "Goodbye, we don't have time."

"B'bye," added Brinda shutting the gate.

Mrs. Rao pushed away the leaping Kuchu in an effort to keep her balance.

"Stop, you silly dog. There! What was I telling you? They are coming all the way here now. Where is Satish?"

Delcourt had spent the morning trying to get in touch with Philippe. With Christmas approaching, the senator had once again been rattled, almost as much as he had been five months earlier. Despite his age, nobody could have said that he had slowed down. Some of his colleagues, yes, but not he! A big supporter of the bicameral system, he did not subscribe to the idea that the Senate, in a democracy like France, was an anomaly.

He thought that, in a paradoxical way, it was in fact its guarantor. There was nothing archaic, he thought, if citizens piped down for a change and did not elect its members. *It is important that the mandate of Senators not be subject to the direct suffrage of idiotic voters* was attributed to him in a weekly that had published the line in its "Quotes" column - words that he denied having ever pronounced. Choosing to be provocative, since he didn't have anything more to lose (by his own admission), was a gambit that always paid off. His adversaries saw him as a pure cynic. Although it was only at the proposal stage, the legislation on gay marriage was not the only coup he had been planning.

In a realm where only petty mean-spirited statements or thunderous declarations made an impact, his methods had triumphed - at the very end of his innings.He had cynically hijacked the last Bastille Day celebrations to serve his political ends. The indignant septuagenarian had not hesitated to shock everybody by proclaiming his new-found hatred for patriotism. Interviewed at his own request on the twelfth of July, he had pointed out that along with North Korea, France was the only country that honored itself with a military parade on its national holiday. This was abhorrent, he vociferously said, completely outdated. Sheer demagoguery and propaganda! People were being subjected to the gigantic illusion of past colonial glory, he accused, in order to make them forget the unemployment affecting millions and the excessive conservatism of a society manipulated by unions. Pomp and spectacle did not amuse anybody any more! The refrains of past glory sounded more and more hollow each passing day;all those hijacked values were eloquent proof of their emptiness.

He added that such parades were tantamount to a collective operation of deception, or almost, a device at the service of the arms market, a free showcase, thanks to hideous brand of patriotism which was the laughing stock inside European foreign ministry circles. What words and deeds was the nation compensating for through such a puerile display that could only please a citizenry already benumbed by the incessant aggressive demagoguery of its politicians? The word spread quickly and the very next day a government spokesperson demanded a public apology on behalf of the insulted Nation. Delcourt repeated that the parade was nothing more than ostentation, an act of arrogance, a veritable insult to the countries that had been the victims of colonization. Many African countries wanted the day to be a day of apology instead of a painful spectacle of battletanks and Mirages and Rafales. The enthusiastic senator denied having crossed the limits - he had not taken up an extreme position at all! Avoiding television, he ranted on the radio that the July 14th parade was the apotheosis of the ideology of nationalistic extremism of the kind that prevailed in dictatorships. Wham! It had lasted long enough, he insisted. Behind the parade one could decipher fear and not pride, it smacked of a hunger to conquer, it was not an *entente* between peoples, it signified bitterness over the end of the colonial adventure, not apology; it was redolent of all those hidden fears that one experienced before embarking on a long journey. Nobody dared to ask him what those fears were. Globalization, perhaps?

Let us move on to other things, he had concluded. Let us turn the idea of Europe into an opportunity to stop the masquerade which no longer had meaning. The colonial past deserved something better than a parade. Competition with the United Kingdom and Germany was no longer relevant. Open your eyes, he had said. *What is a matter of great concern is that such an operation prevents people from stepping beyond their boundaries, their shitty hexagon.*[8] This last sentence was the last

---

[8] The French refer to their country as the Hexagon sometimes because of the shape of the country on the map.

straw. Several right wing deputies demanded that Delcourt be arrested for high treason. Pressured to issue a comment, the Defense Minister politely contented himself with passing the judgment that the senator's language was scandalous, a matter of grave concern. However, he added, one had to be open to debating ideas. Everyone had a right to express themselves. As a precaution, security around the senator was tightened. His assassination would have tarnished the image of the country overseas and had a negative impact in the next Referendum. The government chose to ignore the man, he was just a loner, abandoned even by his peers. Marching up and down Champs-Elysées, wasn't it the most beautiful fart that the Nation could emit, the passing of gas from one single collective anus? It was unimaginable doing away with it, the minister graciously declared with a cloying smile. We are going to fart till the end of time.

Worried all of a sudden that consequences for his career might end up more unfavorable than what his atypical trajectory already predisposed him to, Delcourt assumed a conciliatory posture, quoted Gandhi, and evoked his right to joke. He was awfully proud of his country, but the problem (problem indeed!) was that the notion of nation revolted him, each and every pore of his body was against it. It only gave rise to bloodshed and exclusion.He had started believing, only recently, in the pacifist principles as incarnated by Gandhi, the father of the Indian nation. *Bapu* also didn't have much faith in parades you know, or in tanks, canons, armored vehicles, airplanes, and all of that. Three days before he was assassinated, the Mahatma, a sage born into one of the oldest religions in the world had gone to meditate at the tomb of a Muslim who had converted tens of thousands of Hindus to Islam. The "fair thinking" man asked for forgiveness for the reprisals that had taken place in Calcutta and Delhi. On the eve of his death, his followers had sung, like they did every morning, his favorite hymn: "One who feels the pain of others is one who truly belongs to God." Delcourt made it known that he was sorry to announce loud and clear that he had never been a fan of the odious Marseillaise. It was not an anthem one could be proud of. What he stood against was the parade that symbolized a system based on lies and falsehood. The legalization of absolutism with the help of History. He was of the opinion that it was necessary to have a statesman like him to denounce the intoxication, all the "correct" messages that the nation was sending to itself, which only served to shroud its real greatness, which had nothing to do with weaponry.

The speech was a complete flop, and Delcourt, attacked by an extremist a few months later in a restaurant, turned his attention to the next battle: the Referendum. He had not anticipated that a certain Patrick French - a highly placed FBI official - would appear and strew thorns in his antipatriotic garden in the form of a politico-familial scandal.

It had been a rude shock for His Senatorial Highness.

It was twelve noon. He decided to write an email. With a little luck, his son would read it the same day.

"A funny incident happened, the other evening, at Lipp's. I was waiting for Bernadette who had gone down to the basement. A young looking fellow approached, he stared at me for a long time, and then all of a sudden gave me a hard punch that knocked me into a pillar. Before running away he shouted: This is what France says to you - or something like that! One of the waiters did try to catch him. I'll spare you the rest of the details. More than the actual pain it was the fear . . . When Bernadette came up, she began to laugh. In the car she told me that I resembled Captain Haddock.

Tell me Philippe, the gods are trying to have fun at our expense, wouldn't you think? Well, let's all stay calm. I keep telling myself to stay calm. Bernadette tries to cheer me up each time she sees me worried or depressed. This story about Dipu couldn't have come at a worse time. It's not officially out, and I'm banking on our democracy of hypocrites to hush it up, which, by the way, will be to my advantage for once. On the one hand they are trying to bring me down, on the other, the affair would hinder them; they have more than they can handle on their plate. For now, the Home Ministry is chumming up to the FBI in the joint bureau. The Americans have found a wonderful excuse to interfere indirectly in matters that don't concern them. There's nothing that they like better. One cannot understand foreign people, and much less influence them, if one does not meddle in their affairs . . . That's the reason why everyone here is hesitating so much. Nobody wants to get involved in this mess, but they are all dying to see my downfall. In my opinion, the government will not budge and will do the contrary as long as its credibility is not threatened. The French Secret Service is laughing up its sleeve and gaining mileage.

It's surprising, but I'm afraid that my inopportune declarations from last summer have roused the interest of the Americans - the allusions to Gandhi, his cry of revolt in favor of Islam. In these troubled times, the slightest tone of discordance causes concern. They did not miss even a fragment of the scandal stirred by my 12th of July statements. French did not hide his admiration. It would be quite unthinkable in their country . . . A denunciation of the American dream on the fourth of July by a senator? Their history is different. Why would it happen? It's too soon. I felt as if French was wondering about my real motivations. That someone who is almost a member of my family might be declared guilty of hacking comforts him. What interests him is not the hacking itself. As bizarre as it may sound, Philippe, I think he is convinced that I'm a spy. I don't know what sort of spy he imagines a politician like me to be, given my age! He is forgetting that for us, spying, as a part of a politician's career, is not a tradition. He is very direct, quite polite, and sharp. He seemed to think that I had used Dipu's services to get more information about their counter-terrorism plans. I looked him straight in the eye. What could my motives be? He smiled. What is grotesque from my perspective remains plausible from his. What he tried to *know is this: for whom? For which government, for which armed group?*

And all this because of a . . . moron, excuse my language, who got bored in Paris and didn't know what to do with his time. Mr. Pradeep Rao. This is what they are producing, these emergent countries who are churning out these little computer geniuses. Well, the question which still hangs in the air is this: did he act alone?French is convinced that the answer is no. I spoke to him about you two. The fact that you two are a gay couple did not help convince him, as if that too was a part of the machinations. So then I thought, listen to this Philippe, that a decent way for us to get this chapter closed would be if Dipu said that he was looking for proof of the existence of UFOs. Please think about it. It would be unassailable and it's such a widespread obsession among Earthlings. Less so among Indians thanks to their mythology which is already so rich than among Westerners, I agree, but Dipu could have been corrupted by some loonies like the Raelians who masterminded his searches. Basically, I think it would be a good idea if he threw the ball in the court of the Raelians; they will think twice before issuing a denial, given how hungry they always are for publicity. What do you think? All this is very serious, Philippe. We don't see any other solution here. It is ESSENTIAL to justify Dipu's break-in before it gets directed at me (probably after the Christmas holidays). If he pursues that angle and pretends to be a complete idiot - an inept dunce searching for aliens, the Americans will swallow it. They will probably even be flattered. And I will be able to get out of the jam with my honor intact.

Here is the plan I propose. I am sure that you will manage to convince Dipu. I will not hide it from you that in the present state of affairs I cannot imagine him refusing. Do whatever you have to, to convince him. Also remember that I will know how to express my gratitude when you both get married."

Philippe paused his reading. It was a threat. If Dipu refused, the senator sahib would cut off the supply lines. "The jerk," he exclaimed in a loud voice inside the internet café near Egmore station. "What a jerk!"

"*If you provide me any other good justification for the hacking of the military sites and those of NASA as well, I'll go with it. I'm game. With two members of my cabinet, we examined all the solutions. The only solution that we thought would work in the end was this one.*

I'm waiting for you to reply as quickly as you can. Today is 19th December. If you can send me a response in three days, it will be perfect. I suppose that the Indian investigation isn't over yet. Rest assured, both of you, there should be no indictment. Everything can be manipulated here. How is Dipu's family taking everything? It was amusing to read what you wrote about . . . let's call her your Indian mother-in-law. Not easy, tell me about it! A little touchy, it would seem. Is that good or bad? It's for you to decide. Both, undoubtedly. After the scandal in the summer, a journalist contacted me for a book of interviews on the theme (not very saleable, if you ask me) "only fools don't question tradition."Several publishers are being considered. One of the higher-ups belonging to the Movement for France said last weekend that my statements made him "feel like vomiting." You know what I said to myself? - You can go ahead and vomit. It will make you feel better afterwards. It reminded me of the extremist Hindu movement based in Bombay, I forget the name. Dipu will definitely know what it's called.

I have reread my letter, and realizing the importance of Dipu's approval I would like to make one thing clear: I am absolutely certain that for the sake of his own peace of mind Dipu better be prepared to tell this lie. If he refuses, I will not insist but in the event that he does, have him telephone me. Need I remind you, I did not choose to be put on the hot seat like this for such a pathetic reason. You have a responsibility towards me. As I mentioned earlier, it will make the bond between us even stronger. You still don't do a stable career. You know how to squander money but not earn it. I'm counting

on you. Do me a favor by not complicating things further.
   Your bapu father"

15

The Translator

"Hare Krishna, my love," he said, stretching himself leisurely.

"Hare Krishna, Dipu. Coffee will be ready soon."

Not sleeping was akin to undertaking a long journey: a means of fighting against one's identity, against all that is incomprehensible about oneself. Philippe had not slept a wink.

The senator's last email had been delivered so that the ultimate tax payment—one that is owed by the heart and compounded by miles of separation—could be extracted. One was never completely done paying these particular dues. Since the past eight days, the *bapu* of Suresnes had been trembling in his skin. He was nervous about his career ending in dishonor. Throwing in the towel with his head held high (lest it got buried in the tomb of ignominy, if he waited too long) was turning into a more complicated matter. Between three and seven o'clock in the morning, Philippe had wondered how the senator would save his skin with all the ferocious beasts prowling in the arena of public debate. Perhaps in his heart of hearts the Senator did not really care about scandals like everything else. But the human heart was unfathomable. And why did an old man have to be punished for the consequences of a crime that he had not committed? Philippe spent the night exercising his brain; it was the first time ever that he had felt compelled to worry about his father's fate. All because of Dipu!

He remembered the website that he had set up. The senator's

opponents, all the journalists, and even his friends would not fail to pounce upon him and link the hacking to the creation of the site in favor of a Yes in the upcoming Referendum. How else could he protect himself other than by making Dipu pass off as an idiot whose legal history he was unaware of (his legal future too, because the accused, in July, did not know, or claimed not to know, that he had committed a crime), and as a young degree-holding immigrant whom he had decided to give a chance? Fortunately, deception was the secret skeleton in the cupboard of politics. One couldn't live without it. It was a real drug! In certain cases, which at times were not the least bit important, it offered itself as a last bulwark against downfall. If the poor Filibert, almost twenty years ago, had publicly acknowledged that he had been informed of the operation that was carried out against the Greenpeace ship off the New Zealand coast, his brilliant career as a young forty year old would have quickly ended, which would have been a real pity for the Republic!

The logic of power would have called for his resignation. In between the Channel and the Rhine, there lay an unexplored deposit, pure gold, aggressively sought by the seekers of power, a bonanza that required little effort, the ultimate test of its strength. Filibert had emulated the example set by the Presidency and had resorted to lying with the vigor of a mountaineer determined to conquer Mt. Everest. There was no question of turning back. The faculty of lying, a tremendous natural resource, free and marvelous, was within everybody's reach - the cynics, those hungry for power, and the licensed manipulators. Children practiced prolifically, wasn't it proof enough that it was synonymous with life itself? Among adults, politicians cherished its innocent character. Lose his post over a sunken ship? Filibert had laughed. He would be remembered by posterity for other achievements, more perfect, before they opened the military archives to researchers in fifty or so years. No fears. A sunken ship? A photographer killed?Put his career at stake for a bungled espionage operation? What good was politics if it did not involve lies? The country's nuclear tests in the Pacific justified it.

"How's the tea? Need more milk?"

Dipu put his cup down.

"Perfect. I can't wait till I'm back in France, you know."

"Why is that?"

"I have my reasons."

"Could your mother be one of them?"

It took him a good five minutes before he finally admitted it. He had misgivings about her.

"What do you mean? What kind of misgivings?"

"Her apparent couldn't-care-less attitude notwithstanding, she is quite capable of creating trouble for me. It would be better if I just went away. In spite of my love for her. At the same time, she is unwell, even if she refuses to broach the subject."

"One does not automatically become hostage to someone if they are sick, that's just not true. And besides, that's not what she is doing."

"True."

"So why are you worried?"

Philippe went into the bathroom. *Bathroom* was an apt name for the place! The water flowed generously, like in a hammam. A translucent glass cabin would have assured anonymity and even lent a false sense of style. In Indian bathrooms one was not encumbered by glass cabins. Water did not flow in secret.

"You know, Dipu," he called out as he began to undress, "if I were a writer, and if I wanted to write about our story, I already know what I would never mention. But what's the use of telling it to you since I will never be writing the story."

"Say it all the same. What won't you mention?"

Philippe approached and stood a few feet away him. He was naked. Dipu noticed that he had gained weight. Not excessively. It wasn't evident when he lay in bed. With his dhoti, and depending on whether he was bare-chested or not, he resembled a cow. Which didn't really pose a problem. Indian cows were rather thin.

"Intimacy. I would hate to talk about it, like they all do. Sex laid out on paper. Of course, one has a right, that's not what I mean."

The extra kilos didn't matter to Dipu. How could esthetics come into play when this almost paunchy belly reassured him so much? It was important to know what one wanted. An abdomen that was flat like a slab of chocolate often came at a price - unfaithfulness and arrogance. He had experienced it before meeting Philippe. At the same time one could not always push away all the slabs of chocolate, their bitterness notwithstanding.

"What do you mean?"

"I don't know. I'm talking about style: *He was naked before him*, or *before her*, that kind of stuff. That's not what I would feel like talking about in our story."

"Nobody is forcing you to."

"Intimacy is not vulgar. On the contrary. But when you put it in words for others, it's likely to become so."

What he liked about him were his legs. Long, lean, muscular.

"If you recount it you are narrating something else . . . "

"What?"

He liked especially his eyes. The intensity of his gaze.

" . . . that you could just as well narrate differently. It becomes a big fraud. *And then he came . . .* "

"Huh!"

He also liked his arms. In fact, there was nothing about him that he disliked. The only thing was that one had to go beyond esthetics; one had to listen to one's real feelings, and forget about the fashion magazines with their attractive pictures that led to division and scams. Going beyond esthetics meant being willing to make the effort.

Dipu did not believe in the syndrome of the perfect body and the perfect spirit unified in the same person. Like politics, it was a lie, a practical invention, the dream of idiots, or of merchants who sold one with the promise that both would be part of the package. Sometimes, when they both did come in the same package, those in the business failed to recognize its worth, they continued their speculations—for the sake of more gain. The only esthetic necessary was self-awareness which the other detected instinctively. It did not depend on your features, the size of your waist, the color of your skin. Dipu was susceptible to what was perhaps a little foolishly called *style*. A bizarre appearance did bring one closer to the images in the magazines but it wasn't easy being at home there: the images of the idols, the actors re-enacting their own reality by falsifying it. Be that as it may, style was like perfume, it made space expand.

"Nothing. Let's not go into all that. It's basically a dark and stifling topic."

"Okay." said Dipu yawning.

An age difference of fifteen years! Did it matter? To his mother, yes. And to him? Gods did not have an age. There was no need to speculate about the future. How long would he be his Krishna? One could die at any age.

"One would have to talk about all the emissions."

"What emissions?" he asked distractedly.

"All the emissions. I'm just saying that in books and in movies they prefer sperm, they avoid the rest, except for Pasolini at times."

What was he raving about? He was probably pursuing an idea, just like he was pursuing his. Musings on form and age, the bitter question of age. Everyone saw their kingdom where they believed they saw it, heard and touched it. From the point of view of pure esthetics, Dipu reckoned that the sahib was carrying approximately three or four extra kilos.

"The director of *Théorème*?

"Yes."

Because of the age difference, Dipu sometimes felt like his pupil. It was as if he was supposed to "learn" from him, which was something wonderful and wearisome at the same time. But such knowledge did not interest him much. Happiness was much more important and it could not be postponed. Philippe's neither. His happiness was an irresistible force that even Radhika would not be able to obstruct. Realizing its might, she had readied the last weapons in her arsenal—emotional blackmail.

"They take sperm because it bolsters the ego, while other emissions are liable to debase it. With you, I want to neither boost my ego neither lower it. So if I were writing or talking to someone about you, I would not discuss sex. My lips would be sealed. Nothing about that stuff is interesting if it is separated from the rest."

"So then the rest of the stuff is not interesting as well, if it is separated from sex?" Dipu argued, just for the sake of logic.

"Not in my opinion. You can find passages on sex which are sometimes very long in books and films; it's almost never necessary, except for commercial reasons ostensibly. I must say that I find it a nuisance actually."

"I agree," said Dipu in order to close the subject.

He gulped down a big mouthful of coffee.

"So what would you talk about? They talk about sex because they have to talk about something, and then just like that, they draw you in . . . "

Taking advantage of the fact that he was on his feet, and naked, he interrupted him.

"I would talk about . . . about India, about your mother, your smile, about the old carcass that I am, about Bira, Satish . . . "

"Him again! What do you all see in him?" Dipu cut him off. "Why does everyone fuss so much over him? He's such an idiot."

"Because he's a fake idiot!" replied Philippe, laughing. "I would talk about the monsoon in Chennai in November, and also about your mother's secret idea that we should get married."

"You take pleasure in saying just anything, don't you? Wait, just a second. You saw the way she was looking at you when we were on the beach? She looked like she was ready to turn you over to the police."

"You can say that!"

"Because that's definitely not the impression she gave me."

Philippe let the water run, just enough so that it might flow on him without preventing him from hearing Dipu's voice.

"You see, same vantage point, two different perceptions . . . I'm sure she was just putting on a show like all manipulative mothers."

"You are exasperating. She will do everything in her power to get me married, of course, but to a girl! To a girl! Not to a guy, even if I tell her you are my krishna. Never! Where have you ever seen a mother in India who is ready to accept that her son wants to marry a . . . "

Philippe turned off the water and looked in Dipu's direction once again.

"But," he interrupted him, "this has nothing to do with the mothers of India. We are talking about her. I'm talking about Mrs. Radhika Rao. It's irrelevant to talk about India in general. She never says what she is thinking, so how do you know what she *really* wants? I personally think that she would like for me to become part of the family. And become her son-in-law. While she waits for Bira's husband."

"Hmm. You are reading too much into it."

Philippe poured some shampoo on his head.

"Do you know what you represent for me?"

"I need two seconds," answered Dipu, "let me think . . . Two seconds."

It was going to be a treasure hunt, a search for images and representations, each of them implying endless manipulations. Did human love always entail manipulations? One could hardly claim it. Not to such a large extent.

"I think I do have some idea. For you I am . . . I am an open window to India that allows you to breathe, and even when we are in France, you are still able to feel the air that comes from here."

The sahib closed the bathroom door and turned on the shower once again to let its glacial torrent wash away the tears streaming down his face. The words spoken by Dipu were the truest that he had heard in a long time; they rang so much truer than his father's, pronounced, as they were, by the infallible voice of love, the universal voice which connected with the divine.

After his shower, and before his *dhoti* ceremony—he could now tie his dhoti around his waist with a dexterity which was contested by only Mrs. Rao—Philippe joined Dipu in bed.

"You said a short while ago that you didn't trust your mother. Would you care to explain?"

"Do you know under what circumstances I came to Europe for the first time? I've never wanted to tell it to you but it's different now. You know her."

"What had happened?"

He rested his head on his chest.

"I'm going to be frank. I fled from her. I had a good reason for doing so."

"What was it?"

"She would have never stopped pressuring me to marry. But

now that since she doesn't have me under her thumb, it's more complicated. The first time, I escaped the marriage she had arranged by running away one month before the day of the wedding. The next few times, I was saved by astrology. Two girls got rejected because of serious planetary differences. I don't know the French word, but in our culture we say "manglik" and I think it's because of Mars being in the seventh house, or something like that, and luckily her plans haven't worked out after that. But this one time, everything was fine, she was born one day after me, under the best planetary configuration possible, so I myself accepted. And then, there was still a month to go, I looked at myself in the mirror and I said no. I would not make her happy and she would not make me happy either so I ran away, there's no other way I can describe it. I borrowed money, went to a travel agency, and purchased a ticket for an organized trip. We did a tour of Europe and Paris was part of the itinerary. That was my first visit."

"You said yes at first. Why?"

"You need to understand how things work here. It's our system, we are at its mercy, and one loves one's parents, and I think there is some good to it as well. There was something in it for me, I wanted it. Plus the astrologer had given the green signal . . . "

"And you went away anyway?"

"I said yes because I had been rejected by a friend from school with whom I had fallen in love, it lasted five days . . . "

"Oh."

"He announced to me that it was over after only five days. I no longer knew what was happening to me, we had spent four days together in Mahabalipuram, I had thought that it . . . he told me that it was over, that he only wanted me as a friend. Maybe he was also more or less under similar constraints to marry, I don't know."

"Maybe!"

"I became afraid of finding myself alone. I accepted my mother's offer . . . Except that the fear did not stop me from instinctively coming back to my senses in the nick of time. I found myself saying no, not possible."

Philippe looked down at him.

"I took off almost like a thief. Like a political refugee. A refugee of marriage, that's what I was. Humanitarian organizations would have their hands full if the concept of refugees was expanded to include all those who resist forced marriage. I came to live in France almost as an exile. To live the life that I could not have here. Even when I was in France she continued to show me girls each time I came back to spend a month at home. But as I told you, the planets did not match. That saved me."

"And with me, will the planets match?"

"I'm not concerned about that anymore. I don't know if our planets are in harmony, frankly I haven't even bothered to check. I don't know what Mummy's astrologer would say, though."

"We can make an appointment if you like."

"No. In any case, things have changed now, that was seven years ago. And this time, I can see that she has also changed. She has aged so much, poor Mummy."

The sahib gave a start. "Huh. Now you are exaggerating. She and I are almost the same age . . . "

"I mean to say that she has begun to understand that she's not going to have her way with me. Even with Abhi, she's not been successful. Speaking of Abhi, I don't understand it, I don't know why he's not interested in getting married."

In the rickshaw, Philippe pondered over his father's letter again. He wasn't sure if it was the best moment, but they had to act quickly, within three days, he had written! He fished it out from inside his dhoti, and unfolding it, said to Dipu:

"Take a look at this, especially the end. He's asking you for something. If you are not okay with it, telephone him. And if you want my opinion, I'll give it to you. Just ask."

He got down and went off to buy three train tickets to Kerala.

Mrs. Rao was having trouble locating her glasses. She was sure that she had put them on the little table in the entrance hall. Satish mumbled that he had not seen them.

"Well, since I don't have anything to read for now, there is enough time for you to find them for me," she tormented him. "Look for them. The house isn't that big."

"Not that big!" he grunted. "That's what you think. If I have to spend the whole day looking for them, I will not be able to get anything else done," he warned her, getting a whiff of the cushy day that lay ahead.

"You will find them quickly, I'm sure. Today, I'm only going to eat chapatis. I don't have an appetite," she murmured. "Ah look, Satish, somebody has left a newspaper here. What a pity."

Without enthusiasm, Satish offered to read it to her, but Memsaab declined and instead entrenched herself in her little prayer room on the ground floor. She looked at the beautiful image of Krishna in front of her, with his dark blue complexion that resembled the rain clouds, and whose enchanting smile did not fail to remind her of Dipu's sweet smile as a baby.

"Should I read it to you?" he insisted in a tiny voice.

"No! Find me my glasses."

Fortunately, she had Satish whom she could still dominate. Traditional hierarchy was disappearing - one of the perverse effects of globalization. And those American TV programs were also doing their bit in changing the equations. For now however, the vortex was sucking in just her children, not her servants.

"When is he coming, this translator of yours? You made it

clear that it was French?"

"What else would I say? Yes, French!" He replied indignantly. "He knows all the languages," stammered Satish, looking Memsaab straight in the eye, without reflecting any ambiguity. She had no idea how lucky she was! There was none other like him in the whole of Chennai. He would save the day.

"So we will finally find out," replied Mrs. Rao, all wound up. She couldn't wait to find out what this European father was saying to his son, and how close they were. She was prepared to write to him herself if the situation went out of hand. After all, she now had the Minister Sahib's email address.

A quarter of an hour later, when she had finished her prayers, the man arrived. He looked disheveled, as if he had just woken up, and was all smiles. Satish was in tow, radiating triumph. The enthusiastic dogs of the house that formed a noisy escort party brought up the rear.

He was served a cup of tea which he wanted. They sat him in the garden under a leafy canopy. The gardener was weeding the lawn. They also lit a few incense sticks. Finally they let him read the letter peacefully a number of times. Satish remained standing next to him. There was some nervousness as they waited for the first words of the famous Parisian senator to echo on the Rao family's property in Adyar.

Five minutes, six minutes, nothing happened. Radhika broke the silence.

"So?" she said, forcing a smile.

"It's coming," he assured her, without lifting his eyes.

"Some more tea?"

It was nearly impossible to tell with certainty if . . . No, he seemed so sure of himself, sure of his translation, he was taking all the time he needed. Maybe he was feeling embarrassed by the content? And what was that distinct whining sound emerging from his mouth? She turned her eyes towards the expressionless

Satish and being unable to talk to him openly in front of the stranger, gave him one of her frowns which signified "where on earth did you get hold of him of all people, you dunce!"

He responded to her with another frown which signified: "Just hold on. No need to get impatient and be critical so soon. We will find out whatever it is. And hear it too. He is preparing himself. One can't translate such an important letter without concentration. Have some respect! He knows his job." She resigned herself to waiting. Minutes passed. The man was still poring over the sheet. Out of politeness Radhika and Satish had ceased to look at him. There was no question of embarrassing him further.

"There are words which I can't figure out," he announced tugging at his mustache. "Is there any beer?" he enquired after producing another whining sound.

Was there any connection between the shortcomings of vocabulary and the consumption of alcohol? Radhika did not take long to react and gestured to Satish. It would not be cold, but beer flowed freely in the house. If only he would stop making the whiny sounds.

Satish briskly made his way inside.

"Nothing serious. Hm," said the man with a yawn, disappointed that he had been summoned for such trivia. "Nothing serious, everything is fine."

"Is that what the father is saying?"

"He says that it's okay," he summarized. "It's okay. Times have been hard, but everything is promising to work out well. The preparations for the marriage are on."

"Marriage? Who is getting married?"

"Ah, well. Wait. It's very complicated, very convoluted, the way he expresses himself. I've never seen anything like this. He's jumping in all directions. But ultimately what is he saying? Nothing much."

"You will have a beer and everything will be much better, isn't it. Stop making that noise," she added in a low voice.

"What?"

"I was saying that it's so noisy out on the street. Noisy. I'm talking about the noise."

"That's true," he conceded and resumed the whining again.

"We should have insisted on a written translation," she thought. Too late. He was taking the liberty of judging the words of the minister sahib. In spite of her curiosity, Mrs. Rao was ready to sacrifice the letter in order to get rid of him and his whining. In her opinion, he was more like a plumber picked up from a train station than a real translator. The beer arrived. He began drinking it in tiny sips, and continued making the unbearable sound after each swallowing.

"Much better," he said as he burped.

Satish was looking at him admiringly, with an enraptured smile. Linguistic knowledge and burping, what a marvelous combination! What a refreshing change from all those so called professional translators. It didn't take longer than a minute for a new series of low whines to reach Radhika's ears, but this time it wasn't coming from the man seated in front of her. It was coming from a different direction.

"Satish! Stop. Please, stop. You are driving me crazy."

The guest appeared surprised. Just then the phone rang and she rushed inside.

"Ammu darling!"

"Everything's okay?"

"No. Satish is imitating a drunkard. No, everything is not okay. He brought me a drunk fellow from the station who won't stop whining like a puppy. I am exhausted, Ammu. Exhausted."

"Where has the drunk fellow come from? Why did you let him enter?"

"He's a translator," revealed Mrs. Rao wondering for a

moment if she would even be believed.

Oh no, I shouldn't have told her that! She's going to guess.

"A translator? You need a translator for what? Why did Satish . . . "

"Let me explain it to you, my dear Ammu," interrupted Radhika, searching feverishly for a way to cover up. What could she invent? Lying on an empty stomach wasn't easy.

"I've decided to learn French," she improvised.

"You are saying Satish brought home a translator, because you asked him, I suppose? He . . . "

"He basically gives lessons, language, history, a little bit of everything, and naturally he translates also."

"But . . . Why Satish?" Ammu insisted. Pradeep could have found a tutor at the universi . . . "

"I wanted to surprise him!" Mrs Rao interrupted joyfully, as if the truth had finally come to the rescue of misunderstanding. "I want to be able to talk to him in French as soon as possible. Ammu dear, I bet you think it's an enviable idea, don't you? Unfortunately, he brought me a drunkard. I want to create the impression that I am interested in that great country which he loves so much, and which has such a bad reputation. An unfair reputation," she added, since she had been reading news articles assiduously with Brinda online.

"Of course," said Ammu who couldn't stop herself from feeling suspicious of this sudden about-turn in favor of France. "Too bad he's a drunk. I don't envy you."

"What can one do, one can't have everything one wants. It's just too bad, yes."

"You are not under any obligation to learn French from a drunkard. Sobriety is the first thing one expects from a teacher."

"It's . . . "

She looked out of the window and found Satish and the translator engaged in a mysterious discussion. She took leave of her *bahu* and returned to the shady patio.

She immediately had an intuition that they had reached some kind of an agreement behind her back. Neither was emitting the whining sounds. It was good news. She sat down. The lies she just told had done her a lot of good - the pain in her right leg had disappeared. Lying had relaxing effects, like a hot bath. She reflected. Instead of telling the truth, somewhat like everyone else, it would be better if she took recourse to lies preemptively more often, before being constrained to do so by embarrassing situations. One had to act preemptively. And choose ones lies systematically.

Lies felt good. All of them, not just the petty ones. They were all white lies besides, almost all of them. What were they if not a settling of scores in disguise? Freedom. Almost her whole life, she had told the truth. And at the end of the day, she had nothing to show for it in this big hostile world filled with pretence and falsity as represented, in this instance, by the fool in front of her.

"Can I have my translation?"

"Okay. It's coming," said the man without whining. He spat out a jet of saliva, red because of the betel *paan* that he had been chewing.

This was going to be a protracted affair, like the long wait at Malar Hospital that one had to undergo before Dr. Panayappan saw you.

"So, what is he telling us, this great man? You know it's very long. And the print is very small. I'll summarize it for you, all right? Otherwise all of us will be here till tomorrow:

"We are going to defend you . . . friends, we want to create a best society, French and Spanish are going to give rights to the humiliated because we are asking ourselves the question . . . hm mm he is not saying things clearly . . . How is it that you know such people?"

"Exactly!" exclaimed Radhika, forgetting how much his whining had crossed all limits.

"*The road of liberty needs the law. Society has the respect that it deserves . . . tradition is heavy . . . the minority, beautiful word, victory is victory . . . freedom is triumphant . . . What is it if it* isn't mumbo jumbo?"

"Pray continue, this is quite interesting," replied Mrs. Rao, steadfast thanks to her hope of discovering the hidden face of Philippe and his family.

"And tell me what wound does one do to the composition of marriage, to the thought of marriage, by subscribing that two people are going to marry . . . each his own sex? It is curious that the question gives to mockery, helpfulness, a worst crime, with our perfect laws which we will never be able to redo. Is it the law of the first of the strong?"

"That's really not very clear, no? He has such a poor style of expressing himself," she commented.

"We are doing no harm to marriage by marrying them. Everyone has rights and advantages. The idea of family demands refreshment . . . In the country people are not in agreement. Is our family code shifting? They believe it. Let's avoid pain for nothing . . . The society which takes care of the minority is going to cut the neck of the society in progress, without having the fear of publishing the forwardness of its freedom . . . "

"Enough!" thought Mrs. Rao. "Enough! Fortunately my stomach is empty."

"*With the law our country marches towards freedom and tolerance, she provokes, not us. Yesterday, the rights of women, today divorce. Do we remember that they did not have the same rights as the men? Pst, pst, pst . . . Today we have the extraordinary chance of inventing the freedom towards those who have need of it . . . Today I have loved to convince you that our spirit has opened its doors very big, with the invention of bridges and of the justice which will say no to suffering* . . . I have to stop for a bit, Mrs. Rao. It makes a normal man like me tired, this kind of language."

She sympathized by taking her eyes off him. Satish, highly attentive, chased off Kuchu who had approached the table.

"*We are all going to be equal with the law, marriage is for those who want, I lean on all those who with sacrifice, with suffering that their sexual direction has given, physical or moral, by the family dismissal* . . . "

"It's absolutely incomprehensible."

"There is nothing more to be gleaned from it. I read and reread it. The trash can is where it belongs, as I was telling you. Well, listen to the last sentence anyways:

"*Other countries, everybody will follow us, attracted by the forces of the irresistible: liberty and equality* . . . "

Mrs. Rao got up. The hour of deliverance had finally come.

"I have understood," boasted Satish before walking to the gate with his translator who took his leave with one last whimper.

16

Kerala Coincidences

The 6041 Chennai Alleppey Express departed for Ernakulam and Kochi on the dot early in the evening like a good old fashioned French train. Before night fell, it was traversing a zone filled with shanties that had corrugated roofs. The three travelers gazed out towards the slum colonies that lay beyond the broad windows of the train and then began settling in for the night. No sooner had Philippe laid his head on the pillow than he began thinking of his father.

He turned to the other side. It made no difference. Try as he might, thoughts of his father kept invading his mind. The narrowness of the berth did not help either. He tried to shake off the thoughts.

How could he have ceased to worry about the senator at a time when his entire career was in danger of going down the drain indirectly because of one of his sons? Glancing at the unbroken row of insalubrious homes enveloped in darkness - a strange metaphor for his father's life - he was hit in the face by the prospect of his father's famed public persona meeting an ignominious end in what Salman Rushdie eloquently called the "stink of the conscience of politicians." It was the stink of one human being amongst many. That he might be a father or a brother was just a minor detail. As soon as the lights in the compartment went off he got entangled in a web of dreams.

Mrs. Rao was speaking to him; she slapped him, and made

herself invisible like a sorceress. Satish, an angel, fluttered around her. She was rubbing elbows with the senator at a picnic; they were sitting on the grass. An improbable encounter of the two families on neutral territory somewhere in Russia, or maybe it was Poland? She took Philippe aside at the end of the feast and confessed to him that she had fallen in love with the extraordinary man who was his father. I love him, and I want to marry him. It's annoying, isn't it, that he is married to such a talkative woman, just look at her! She was counting on him to keep her secret. No jokes, Philippe, no leg pulling! He reassured her, he liked her too much to betray her, and if he ever betrayed her one day, it would be because of love. Betrayals for the sake of love, aren't you familiar with them? Ask your family. Aren't such betrayals the most powerful, the most genuine? One could live easily without them, don't you think? You are such an evil monster. Don't worry, Radhika, I will not say anything. Your secret is safe. It's such a surprise. Almost a shame. You, in love with my father. And I, Radhika, also want to confide a secret to you. And only to you. Sit down. It's something I won't tell even Dipu.

You bestow too much honor on me, Sahib.

You are the only one who can understand.

What is it? You elude me, Philippe. I don't know if I enjoy feeling intrigued, take note. It's a rare thing to be truly intrigued these days. No, you do not intrigue me. Nobody intrigues me, except my Sushil. He puzzled me so much that he died.

Well, exactly. I have a wish that is very dear to my heart . . .

You got married to my Dipu. What more do you want? Aren't you exaggerating a little bit?

It's not about Dipu, dear Mrs. Rao. It about the other realm. Ah!

The other side of life, beyond the biscuits that we like to share during evening time, after dinner - mm mm, they are tasty, aren't they – the transcendental connection that you will allow me to prolong with your son, won't you?

I'm not sure if he is going to end up with you forever, not that there's anything wrong with you. I'm not sure if he will end up eating all the biscuits with you. Maybe he will change his mind, maybe he will share them with someone else? Who knows!

That's not what I mean. I'm talking about the next life.

How many laddus do you consume every evening? Your next life? You must be dreaming. Breathe slowly, calm down.

About eight. Ever since I met you, Mrs. Rao, I have taken a vow, of not taking birth in France. I have made my decision. It's come from someplace distant. I married Dipu to escape from a country. You understand, I hope.

Understand what? How dare you say such things, Philippe? Do you want me to denounce you to your father first, and then to all the political and judicial authorities of your land of birth? Oh, I'm so happy to hear what I have just heard. You are absolutely right, isn't it marvelous, abandon your . . .

It's not that. You misunderstood me. I don't want to live in ANY country. NONE! Do you believe it's possible? I don't want to take on any nationality, none.

Hmmm. Not easy, I say.

Precisely! It's not easy. I don't want to sing the same song.

I don't know what to say.

I don't want to be clad in a nationality. That's my only dream in this world down here.

I have a suggestion. I suggest that you stay with us until further notice. You know, the History of men evolves at the same pace as kitchen recipes. Countries come into existence, recipes too. Stay with us while you wait for all this to change, whispered Mrs. Rao, glimpsing the possibility of keeping her son with her till the end of time. I have an idea, what if you just take birth in India? She offered the suggestion suddenly as if it were like placing an order for a delectable dish, served in gold-plated vessel.

Yes, but it's a country.

It's India, Philippe.

True. It transcends the notion of country, but even then.

I told you, it's a temporary solution. You could always revert if you wanted to.

Never!

Granted, Philippe.

In that case change the whole décor for me, begin by changing my conscience. Move a vacuum cleaner through me, cleanse me profoundly from inside, I won't ask you twice.

We will get Satish to take care of it. Satiiiiiiiiiiiiiiiish . . . You are fully capable of becoming an Indian, stressed Radhika in a somewhat raucous voice, without appearing convinced. After all, extraterrestrial life too was within reach. The foreign sahib was such a riot, a false tourist. Look at him, Bira, disguised in his dhoti, as if he were walking on the ramp at a fashion show. Well Sahib, this is not a fashion outfit. You are so ridiculous that we can't help adoring you!

Gosh, how can I say no!

But why, Philippe, why? Why don't you want to stay where you are? I must say that as far as I am concerned, she continued as she patted her bun, I would prefer to be reborn in Europe. Let's trade places. Let's make a pact.

With this last word he woke up with a start. Pact! Always this word! Why always a pact? The need for recognition without which one lived in the doldrums? Could life be lived without a pact?

He did not have the faintest idea what time it was, or what place they were in. Had they crossed the border into Kerala? It was too early. Their coach was enveloped in darkness. He made

240

sure that his backpack was still attached with the heavy chain that he had bought before their departure.

On the top berth he could make out Dipu's brother's silhouette. He was also dreaming, or so Philippe imagined. But of what? Who knew what people dreamt of? It was a burning question. What could Abhi be dreaming of? As a matter of fact, he could take him aside the next morning during breakfast (*dosa* and *aloo paratha* for everybody!) and question him, as if it had something pertaining to a serious geopolitical issue: What did you dream about last night? One never really dared asking such questions. Was he also poisoning his blood by thinking of a life without a country, without the new form of racism that French "cultural exception" stood for, as understood by his compatriots who seemed to be *teleguided* by their politicians still resentful of the loss of their colonial empire? No. The new rampant isolation that exception entailed was first and foremost a syndrome of fear. Abhi would have never called into question the fact that he was Indian. Only idiots like me, pathetic, stooping so low! Abhi was probably dreaming of his guru . . .

He fell sleep again.

The rivers are carrying away dozens of cadavers, the bomb exploded less than an hour ago, the heat from the radiation has reached 1000 degrees Celsius, I am in hell, oh mother, a hell on a little piece of land. Little Boy went off at 8:15, a small child is begging me to give him some water, he is dying in my arms, without giving me the time to do something. Just a little water, but where, where to find it?

He was awakened by a strong jolt. He fell into slumber again . . . *The Delcourt family is wandering in the ruins of the city devastated by the H bomb . . . Everything is decomposing in the brackish stagnant water which is attracting towards itself a sea of ghosts, and swallowing up those who are approaching it . . . Nuclear weapons, murmurs the desperate voice of the senator who has survived*

*the tragedy, nuclear weapons are dangerous, I beg of you, make no
more nuclear weapons. No more. We cannot coexist with them.*

Around seven o'clock they entered a restaurant in Ernakulam,
near the station.

"*Masala dosas* for everyone?" proposed Philippe.

A spectacular way of waking up. Dipu's answer was more of
a grunt than a yes. Abhi was in wholehearted agreement: a
graceful horizontal movement of the head.

"What did you dream of?"

Dipu's brother wasn't expecting it. Even his mother did not
ask these kinds of questions. They did not broach things this
intimate. Inquisitions under Mrs. Rao's government? Definitely
yes! But they did not trespass on dreams! Too close to lies! An
unusable raw material.

"I dreamt of Paris," he replied.

"You'd like to go there?"

"Yeah. I was visiting Dipu who dropped me off inside a
huge museum. He abandoned me there for two days."

"Two days! I'm so sorry."

"You came back to get me. 'You saw everything? Are you
sure? You didn't forget anything?' You took me to an Italian
restaurant for lunch and there you ordered a strange dish for
me which I pretended to like, but really felt like spitting out."

"We don't use spices and chillies like you," Philippe thought
it appropriate to explain.

"So you are speaking on behalf of Europeans now?" remarked
Dipu.

"It was a disgusting preparation. Not at all nice. After that
we went to a small island. Dipu handed me his cell phone and
I took his picture. Then something very strange happened. We
all leaned over and looked down at the screen and the image
that appeared wasn't yours!"

"Was it Radha?" Philippe joked. "Satish, maybe?"

"It wasn't Dipu who was on the screen, even though it was him whom I had photographed. The camera had captured somebody else's picture."

The gray cells of the three went into overdrive as they tucked into the *masala dosas* that had just arrived. How was the apparition to be explained? With the help of museums and Italian cuisine Abhi and Dipu had traded off their fraternity and veered into anonymity. The cell phone camera was a witness, it had denounced them. Abhi threw the question back at Philippe.

"And you?"

The sahib hardly ever remembered his dreams. He had woken up and had fallen asleep again. Only the last fleeting one made itself available to Memory. The older generation of dreams had preferred to disappear without leaving a trace.

"I dreamt of Jean Bé, one of my brothers. I accidently ran into him in front of a department store in Trivandrum. 'I didn't know you were in India,' I say to him. 'When did you arrive?' He doesn't reply. Just gives a smile. 'Why don't you want to tell me?' Well, me too, it's curious Abhi, because, because . . . "

Apart from a few details, it was the same dream, experienced during the same night. From one berth to the next, individual brains had picked up the same frequency, eminently star-crossed: impossible reunions. The sahib and Jean Bé had not managed to even keep up their pretense. Arctic coldness in the warmth of South India. The coincidence of the meeting had been immediately absorbed, as if everything could be quashed, even amazement. Space and time nullified, family and religion exposed. It was all a farce. Two dreams devoid of illusion, like a car colliding with a wall at high speed. Was this the river at the estuary about to join the deep open sea? A fissure in the earth's crust, slight but powerful . . .

Abhi and Dipu at one end, the West, Jean-Bernard and the

sahib at the other, the East. Was the separation between brothers as irremediable as that? Were dreams premonitory?

" . . . because . . . " he stammered.

The waiter came to his rescue just then. Who needed more *sambar*? A coffee?

"What should we do now? What's the plan?"

"We have made no plans," said Abhi, "except for seeing Amma on Saturday. Till then it's open . . . "

"Let's go to Trivandrum!" suggested Philippe, more excited than ever. "Let's be spontaneous. Let's go."

Dipu took his revenge. "To meet your brother? He's waiting for you in front of the department store?"

"Come on," he laughed. "Come on, I don't know much about Trivandrum. It's a nice opportunity. Hurrah for coincidences! It will be a tribute to coincidence."

Abhi burst out into laughter. When it came to celebrating a god or a coincidence, he was ever-ready. They came up with a program in five minutes. They would spend the day and night at Fort Cochin and they would arrive in Thiruvananthapuram the next day, in the evening. The weary army of waiters watched the enthusiastic trio make their way out onto the street.

If one has faith in travel guides and their tendency to push the same old fascinations with relish, the cliffy region of Varkala has beaten Kovalam in the game by becoming the most fashionable beach resort. Despite its nonchalant coves, its narrow streets bordered by small boutiques and coconut palms, Kovalam is the object of the regular ire of those who having loved it passionately in the past (to the extent that they even loved the sonority of its name) have not been able to get over its overwhelming success which started coming at the end of the sixties. It deprived them of their piece of a deserted beach. The rancor of the guides is tenacious. No question of a change of opinion in the next edition! One should never backtrack! Expressing even a few official words of approval for Varkala's rival is now out of fashion. Suddenly accused of all the ills, Kovalam is badmouthed by those who loved it: overrated, blighted, congested, too expensive! "Don't go there," is the new slogan of those who are cool. Invade Varkala instead. It's heaven, we assure you, it's like paradise! We will inform you, in our next edition, of the new pearl that the Indian government will dig up for us with bulldozers, you will be the first to be informed, as quickly as we can publish it!

Philippe had quickly understood the exercise: the company of a travel guide when one travels in India is indispensable only if one understands that the less one uses it the better off one is. There is no harm in seasoning the advice given with a dash of skepticism. It often pays to visit the places such guides disparage. Not choosing the recommended hotels often leads to pleasant serendipity. One can even avoid one's compatriots by opting for the sites that travel publications botch up in two paragraphs and ignoring the attractions that get their approbation. Excessive mistrust is not a requirement however. The journey itself makes choices for you.

Just before embarking on the trip to Kerala, Philippe had spent an afternoon in the company of travel writers convinced of what they were advancing, positive that they possessed the correct knowledge as they serenaded the reader with their masked patriotism. Treating tourists like children was part of the contract with the reader. It was the crafty Senator Delcourt who, before his departure, had alerted him to the traps laid in some of the guides. His advice was to consider only the facts and nothing else, to disregard the commentaries which smacked of typical prejudices, to know that travel guides were not novels and that it was important to unmask value judgments disguised as objective points of view. Read them, yes, Papa had advised, in order to avoid the places they extolled. And especially, he had advised, they needed to be read one against the other, even if it meant that one's backpack stayed heavy. Nourished by this paean to distrust, Philippe paid even less heed to the recommendations that Dipu was dismissive of. He smiled at the passages that the Frenchman brought to his attention; occasionally he even burst into laughter. The naïveté of the guide books transformed India into a "conquered land."

There was another thing that travel guides unfortunately did not have the power to describe, neither from close up nor from afar: coincidences. Their mission was more humble, they did not touch upon things mystical, things hidden. They essentially accomplished their task the way a school child fills up a school bag, unspoken assumptions of the colonizer thrown in for good measure.

Helda Schweitzer had not needed a guide to come to southern India. Martina, the old friend who was accompanying her, had convinced her to go in for ayurvedic treatment at a reputed center in Kovalam. They had been spared the trouble of looking elsewhere thanks to what they had heard about the place through word of mouth. Although it had an excellent reputation, the establishment (whose name was suggestive of an appeal to the West for funding: International Friendship) faced stiff competition. It was not the only place in town that promised the best possible *panchakarma*, an ayurvedic procedure thousands of years old involving the elimination of toxins that led to the pacification of the *doshas* and the rejuvenation of mind, body and spirit. The three *doshas* - *vata, pitta,* and *kapha*, each with their respective biological humors played an important role in the complex process of energy and well being. While *Kapha* happened to be more concentrated in the lungs and stomach, *vata* created movement even as *pitta* transformed food into energy.

Helda and Martina, aged 79 and 77 respectively, had undertaken the long journey to balanced *doshas* with great enthusiasm. Upon their arrival they discovered an unknown method: the daily application of a stream of hot oil on the forehead. It was among the five forms of therapy that *panchakarma* offered as part of their extended medical care. Doctor Joseph had designed a strict program for them. Informed of their arrival a month in advance, he had reserved a small, shady cottage for them, away from the sea, close to the center where they would take all their meals. They did not have the permission to go near the famous beach. As some sort of compensation, they fell under the spell of Joseph with his skinny physique and impeccably tailored long pearl-gray *kurta*. With his somewhat wan smile and his sophisticated mannerisms, he served them with extraordinary devotion which was not entirely devoid of pecuniary motives. The wealthy German *frauen* did not discourage him either.

After six weeks the success of the treatment was such that Helda, brimming with energy and gratitude, decided to prolong her stay by a month, till the 23rd of January. She laughingly declared that she had become addicted to the massages that the young Anil lavished upon her using a wheat and chick-pea flour based mixture. He ended his routines by rubbing her with a cream whose fragrance intoxicated her. She instructed him to purchase fifteen jars of her favorite *kumkumaadi lepam* for her. She would have gladly traveled all the way to India just for this cream, despite her age. Another aspect of the treatment required her to swallow several spoonfuls of ghee everyday, a laudable remedy for the imbalance of her principal *dosha*. It was something she did without batting an eyelid. Martina had to be back in Düsseldorf for Christmas, and Helda, her heart bruised at the thought of finding herself alone in the resort town, accompanied her to the airport in Trivandrum.

To drive away her blues, she decided to spend the day in the capital city of the state. After a short visit to the Napier Museum which soon caused her to feel tired in the legs, she asked the driver to drop her off on MG Road, in front of a big grocery store. There was nothing to be found in Kovalam, she reminded herself, except for what the tourists went for. Not the kinds of things that an old lady like her loved. Her tastes were more traditional. Good old Joseph! He had provided her with a list of some useful addresses in Thiruvananthapuram. In scorching heat, she crossed the threshold of the store knowing for once what she wanted. She made her way to the spice aisle on the left and soon found a stinky resin that had fallen out of use everywhere else except India. The Romans used to use it once upon a time, it was the extract of a plant related to wild fennel, asafetida, whose other name, even more evocative, was none other than devil's dung. In small quantities it gave a heavenly taste to lentil and vegetable curries and helped with digestion. Dr. Joseph had been very insistent. *You must get some!* In her craze for spices and aromatics, she was ready to squander all the benefits of her treatment by gadding about from one market to another in her quest for new flavors and fabulous healing ingredients. She finally clutched a precious packet with a very sober looking label: *Compounded Asafetida*. Finally! A mix of English and Latin, it was part of the phenomenon that her trip to India had become which included her magical and zany treatments and things big and small that took her back to a primordial source.

She closed her eyes for a few moments in order to compose herself. She arranged the four packets in a pile, certain that she had triumphed over all her stomach aches forever. They were going to have it, the monsters! She headed to the counter, made her purchase, and readied herself to join the driver who was waiting by the store entrance. The doorman opened the door for her, and she let out a cry.

"Philippe! How is this possible? What are you doing here? Heavens!"

"Helda! Helda!"

They fell into each other's arms. A young couple passed them with a smile and entered through the other door of the shop. They continued embracing each other, immobile, forgetting that they had blocked the passage.

"Incredible to see you here, it's just incredible!" repeated Helda. "I must be dreaming."

"Let me introduce you to my friends, please."

He turned to Dipu and Abhi who had chosen to stay a few feet away out of discretion.

"This is one of my mother's closest friends, Helda Schweitzer. Helda, meet Pradeep and Abhi Rao."

"Very nice to meet you!"

"The pleasure is all mine."

"Nice to meet you," echoed Abhi. "Namaste."

"Namaste. My God, how is it possible? I think this calls for a celebration. What do you say? Do you have plans? I was just thinking of having lunch at this restaurant that my doctor recommended. Would you like to come along?"

The three travelers smiled and glanced at each other. They certainly did not have any plans other than obeying the gods of coincidence. So why not over a meal? They dropped the idea of going to the zoo and piled into Helda's car.

"When was the last time we saw each other?"

"Let me think. I'm so happy. Just a short while ago I left a friend of mine who had to go back to Germany, and *voilà*, a few hours later I run into you. Talk about the world being a small place!"

Abhi and Dipu seemed even happier than Philippe. The chauffeur made a right turn into a small street that took them straight inside a residential neighborhood.

Yes, the two brothers were of the opinion that coincidences were a blessing to all, even the couple that had had to use the other door.

"Poor Domitille, she died in seventy-nine, wasn't it, and we saw each other for the last time one year later, do you remember? It was at Sartre's funeral, I saw you in the crowd at Alésia."

Philippe closed his eyes. Little by little he recollected the scene.

"Yes, you were in a van, and I caught a glimpse of you; you were in the front and waved to me, and then the van continued its way through the crowd. We did not see each other again at the cemetery."

He bit his upper lip. Nineteen seventy-nine. The car accident in Montreal. He used to live with her at that time.Domitille and Helda had met in the wake of the war. She had been sent to Bonn as a correspondent by her Quebecois newspaper, and she had met this young woman who was then working for a radio station. Helda made several documentaries, most of them committed, so to speak, including one on Simone de Beauvoir and Sartre as a couple. In the mid-fifties, Domitille was sent to Paris again by her newspaper where she met Senator Delcourt. The two women had remained very close till the accident.

Philippe had not wanted to keep in touch. He did not return her calls, because of the grief of mourning no doubt, or whatever they call it. He wanted to turn the page, forget and move on. It was an illusion fomented by his young age. But the gods of coincidence were not quite done with them. They had a surprise in store for them, and they took all their time. Almost twenty-four years. Twenty-four years is not that long. They had waited until the beginning of the winter of 2004. It had been orchestrated under the sunny skies of Thiruvananthapuram. Far away, the moment they saw each other again, the solemn burial of the author that Helda loved so much flashed before their eyes - the last episode of their meetings, behind a sheet of glass. So near and yet so far. The gods had taken the form of packets of asafetida, the ultimate remedy for distended tummies.

"It's here, I recognize the place, isn't it charming?"

She descended from the vehicle with a sprite step, refusing Abhi's help. Her silhouette had changed, she walked slower now. Long ash-blond hair, the hint of defiance deep in her eyes was still there. When she talked politics she was full of life. Even her advanced age did not obscure this essence. Her first two attempts to make conversation failed. Dipu and Abhi looked at her with a smile. An impressive succession of macrobiotic dishes ensued, as grand as a feast for a Mughal emperor. They leaned forward and examined each dish as they tried to identify the ingredients. Low-cal foods, vegetarianism, natural cures, enemas, fasting – all these came up for discussion. Helda shared her ayurvedic expertise with the three young men whose exquisite politeness she found delightful. The water inside a coconut, she informed them as she closed the subject, was an absolutely fantastic thing to have during long periods of fast, when one abstained from eating.

"How is your father?" she finally asked.

Knowing Philippe's complex family history, she had hesitated. But her old-maid curiosity got the better of her. Thanks to the magic of the coincidence that they were still under the spell of, one could take such liberties.

"He is ready to fight it out in the Referendum, I suppose?"

"Yes. He is getting ready. But it does not interest him as much as it did before, you know, even though he will not admit it."

The liquidation of his mother's estate had taken four years. The tax authorities had managed to discover the unspoken: a bank account in Switzerland that Olivier Delcourt had opened for his mistress. With the dark complicity of the people on the Swiss side, they had hushed things up.

"What do you mean?" the old militant enquired indignantly. "For people of our generation the constitutional treaty will mark the end of . . . "

He was listening only with one ear. It was almost like he had found his mother today, at the appointed place, instead of his half-brother from his premonitory dream. When Domitille had died, he had tried approaching one of his aunts who claimed to be close to him. He had knocked at her doorstep awkwardly, without advance notice, a week after the funeral. She had turned pale on seeing his strained face but she had received him like a perfect stranger. He and his grief disturbed her. She made it a point of honor not to even offer him a glass of water. For a long time he had wondered. Why? Was she settling some old scores? Was she afraid that he would ask for money, a smile? What were her obligations? Did she have any? Did the heart have to systematically close itself when fear knocked at the door? He understood that he had come to the wrong place. The reasons for rejection could have been myriad, ranging from cynical to liberatory. You are without your mother, could you be wanting another one? For ten years he had asked the same question: what did family relationships signify in times of sorrow? At what point did one end the hypocrisy? What script did one have and what role did one play?

Helda paid the bill and they all left the macrobiotic temple but not without buying precious packets of shampoo made out of herbs and crushed flowers.

"I'm sure Dr. Joseph can find you rooms at the village. You will see, he's an extraordinary man."

All of a sudden Dipu's attention was caught by a huge poster.

"Look, it's Amma!"

"Who is Amma?" asked Helda.

"Amritanandamayi. A saint," replied Abhi. "We are going to her ashram tomorrow."

Helda did not respond. Dr. Joseph's house was her ashram. And her favorite priest was Anil. She had no need for any other spiritual mumbo-jumbo.

"Here's one more," pointed out Dipu. "Slow down, please, slow down. Hey . . . she is here today! She is in Trivandrum right now," he announced.

This time the coincidence was not as mind-blowing. After all, Amma, the hugging mother as she was widely known, traveled across India and the world all the year round. There was nothing astounding about the fact that she was in town that particular day. Having barely recovered from his premonitory dream and his encounter with Helda, Philippe, squeezed against the door, felt new emotions stirring inside him.

"Okay, let's go. Is it far?"

"I don't think so. It's somewhere in the south part of town, according to the advertisement."

Helda had not given her assent.

"But . . . why do we need to go?" she finally said. She was more interested in going back to her doctor and introducing the three young men to him.

They explained to Helda who Amma was, the crowds that came to see her and followed her on her travels, camped out on the stairs of her house at the ashram. It was a lot of information that seemed to produce a somewhat negative effect on her.

"I'm very wary of these kinds of things," she explained with frankness. "Big crowds, hmm? No. How awful. In my youth I saw from very close quarters the influence Hitler had on the masses, and I know what that can lead to. I am not saying that your Amma . . . By the way, have you noticed something, how come there are so many copies of *Mein Kampf* all over the place here? It is banned in Europe."

"If there are that many copies of the book over here as you say there are, it is probably because they are all used copies that have no takers. But Helda, how can you say such a thing? Do you realize, how can you even compare the masses who follow Amma with those who followed Hitler?"

"I don't trust easily, that's all."

They insisted, and she ended up accepting. It was such a ridiculous exaggeration. Even if National Socialism could be interpreted as a religion, it was not even by a long shot based on the same principles as Hinduism. Curiosity began to get the better of her. She had seen the portraits of Sai Baba and Amma in the shops in Kovalam. These two personalities were big stars in South India. At the approach to the temple where the one known as the mother divine was giving *darshan* - a chance to be seen - to thousands, the crowd was so thick that the driver of their vehicle could not find a place to park. He dropped them off at the entrance and received the instruction to stay in the vicinity. They walked up a long narrow lane before reaching the immense hall. Philippe held Helda's hand tightly, the crowd was pressing forward so much that he felt afraid for her. He looked at her. The close contact with the devotees and merchants had transformed her look. She suddenly seemed interested, like at Sartre's funeral, more interested than she had been earlier in the day when they had looked at other things. Maybe she was remembering the crowds of her childhood, but what resemblance could she find? She seemed tired, moving ahead was a cumbersome and slow process, and the crowd was growing every minute. She did not succumb to panic and held onto Philippe's hand. As much as possible, people around them tried to make way for her without letting her get pushed.

They were now only a few meters from the entrance. Small video screens had been set up on tables which played images of Amma embracing the faithful a few dozen meters ahead.

Suddenly Helda stopped in her tracks, transfixed. They all saw the same thing: a woman threw herself into Amma arms, crying. Music and devotional chants filled the air. The alliance of the tears, sounds, incense, crowds, and the peace pervading the air had an effect: it pierced Helda's heart as if the meaning of things had suddenly been revealed to her in the act of the woman throwing herself into Amma's open arms.

Poignant, yes! A return to the source, a return to childhood. With humid eyes, Philippe slowly turned towards his mother's friend. She was not crying but seemed intensely moved, almost angry to be so. She seemed stupefied. Ravaged, penetrated by the pain of this woman who had come to share her sorrow and her disappointments - in the space of four seconds, enough for an embrace - with the one who would take away her burdens while nonchalantly conversing, in a rather comical way, with one of her devotee-companions. Helda was struck by Amma's simplicity. It felt familiar. She asked Abhi to help her get closer. They crossed, with some effort, the distance that separated them from the stage where the saint was seated. They had to step over numerous people who were sitting still, being nourished by the music and the devotion. Finally, they were only a few feet away and Helda observed Amma for a few minutes. They were long minutes.

"I like this woman," she said softly. "I like her."

17

Ashram

An unprecedented shortage of onions hit Chennai. Caused by floods in Maharashtra, a major onion producing state, the crisis compelled Satish to disturb Memsaab, who was resting in her room. He knocked and entered.

"I have not been able to find them anywhere for over a week. Everyone is after them."

"Good gracious! You did not stock up on onions? Surely, there must be some. You bought lots before the shortage began, no?"

"No."

"Not a single one?"

Not a single one! Mrs. Rao took the opportunity to get up. The monsoon had been severe. With his big ears and foolish demeanor the poor Satish could hardly be blamed for the shortage.

"Brinda is in the living room?"

"No."

"Where in the world has she disappeared?"

A shortage of onions . . . And the shortage of fiancées for her two sons, wasn't that a bigger concern? The disappearance of onions was not going to be permanent. But how were they going to cook the dishes that she loved the most?

She heard Suneet's voice. Ammu had not called the previous day. Her oldest child really disappointed her at times. He did not have a sense of sacrifice, not in the least. Apart from fasting, he did not seem to practice any form of austerity. He was not terribly useful. She did however agree with him on one point - it was not his job to find spouses for Abhi and Dipu. But two or three years down the road, it would be his duty, as the eldest, to find a good match for his sister. He would have to take action; she did not have any intention, this time, of taking a risk. Sacrificing himself, doing *tapasya* as it was called, was Suneet's duty. His spiritual elevation entailed ensuring Brinda's happiness. Mrs. Rao was convinced of that.

After a quick check of her hairdo, she greeted him and dove into her newspaper. It was her favorite day, the day they published the matrimonial ads. Four columns devoted to it. Enough material to intoxicate her. All these parties inviting alliances! Back in her time, all this did not exist, it was a different procedure. Apparently the internet was even worse; there were thousands of proposals to be found there, each more tempting than the other. When the time would come she would herself prepare a classified which would help attract the best possible match for Bira.

A rather long ad drew her attention: "I have studied the Bhagavad Gita. I love cricket and find intellectual discussions stimulating. I cannot go for a single day without eating curd-rice. I speak seven languages. I'm a vegetarian but do eat eggs. We speak Hindi, Tamil and English at home. Nobody in our family drinks. We are a family of Sai Baba devotees."

"Suneet, just look at this profile. Tell me what you think."

For the second time he regretfully abandoned the article about his brother that he was reading.

"For Bira? Are you already thinking . . . "

"Nooooo. No, of course not! Not yet. I'm just keeping myself informed, that's all, my dear," she stammered.

"He is forty years old!"

"Oh! I missed that," she lied. "Have you noticed, Bira does like older people. Has he given his time of birth?"

"No."

"Then let's not talk about it. He eats curd-rice everyday. That is really the only positive point. Along with Sai Baba, I suppose."

Brinda came out of her bedroom.

"What are you discussing?"

"I was reading a matrimonial ad."

"Ah. Don't tell me you have found another gem for Abhi! Or for Dipu, maybe?"

"I am thinking of preparing a matrimonial ad that I would like to place in *The Times of India*, on their website, I think. So, my dear, I was trying to find inspiration. Don't get all upset, I have no intention of occupying myself with you. First of all, I think that it is Suneet's role – he will take it seriously, I hope – when the day comes. I have more than I can handle with the other two. When they are both married, I will begin to look for a good match for you, with your brother's help. By placing an ad for Abhi we will get many responses, don't you think, and families will come to see him, every Sunday. They will see what we are offering them . . . "

Bira interrupted her.

"You can begin writing about me that I am a) a good cook, b) an expert in henna designs, c) a most talented housekeeper, d) a future college graduate, e) a girl who is modern and traditional at the same time . . . I can sleep in peace if you are counting on my brothers."

"You are mistaken, dear," replied Mrs. Rao patiently. "Though I'm sure you are already dreaming of that special day."

"That's what you think."

"I know that it's still too early for you, but you know, it so happens, now that I read the newspaper, I come across some ads that are really very very interesting, it's astonishing. You won't have to do anything. When the day comes, I will myself go, along with Satish, to all the good families that I will select. With your photo in my hand, I'm not worried. There will be plenty of choices. You are so fair."

"I'm a lesbian!"

"Darling, do not joke about these things."

"Maybe I will get married to a woman, why not?"

Radha did not yield to the provocation and did not stray from her trajectory.

"You heard her, Suneet, you heard her? Doesn't it make you want to find her a husband? You are very young. You have just begun your studies. I was just looking at the ads casually, just for fun. And also so that I can learn the proper technique of writing such ads. I will wait for the day when I will be inspired; it will be magnificent. I wanted to take advantage of the opportunity. Abhi is not here this weekend; I wanted to give him a surprise when he came back."

"He is going to appreciate your meticulous attention to detail, you can count on it. What are you making? What is all this wool for?"

"I'm knitting Philippe a sweater. He said that it was cold in his country. May he go back there and never return!"

"How cruel," said Brinda.

"That is not what we are discussing. I have an idea. We could prepare an ad for Abhi, all three of us. We could then take the best part from each resumé. And we could also have Satish write one! I have always said that he has more common sense than we realize."

"Especially when it comes to using washing machines! I categorically refuse to write a personal ad for my brother."

"You are heartless," admonished Mrs. Rao for whom the danger mark had been reached. At thirty-one, Abhi had entered the most favorable period from an astrological point of view. The most critical. A published ad would be just the thing to set the ball rolling. Entire families would flock to Adyar to see the marvel in person.

"And you, Suneet? Can I count on you?"

"Don't you think you would do it better?" he replied, shrugging off the responsibility that was being thrust on him, like a coward.

She reflected. They better not contest her strategic choices later. She would come up with a masterpiece. With an imperceptible movement of the head Satish indicated his assent. He was willing to play his part in the whole matrimony business.

"Don't tell me that you are thinking of helping me?"

"Yes," he replied, retreating.

Picking up the paper Suneet brandished a page and showed them a photograph depicting an innocent looking Pradeep below which was a brief new write-up.

"I have never seen this photo," observed Radhika.

"I'll read it to you; you will realize the mess he is in. They are quoting what Dipu reportedly said . . . "

"It starts well."

"Just listen to what it says: *I was looking for evidence that would confirm the existence of UFOs, which I was sure NASA was hiding . . .* "

"Good lord!"

"It's getting really serious," squealed Brinda. "Fantastic."

"Can I please finish? *I did not find any evidence, Pradeep Rao confirmed during a recent interrogation. I destroyed some files, purely by accident. I wasn't sleeping, I was tired and was just trying to kill time. I did not have any evil intentions. I was just fiddling with the keyboard, that's all. I'm not a spy. Now everyone knows, thanks to me, the shortcomings of the US military's IT network. I did not discover anything significant because I don't know what could have been of significance. I don't think that the top secret defense networks can be breached via Internet, although there are certain ways of penetrating them as well . . . "*

"Dipu just can't keep his mouth shut . . . " exclaimed Mrs. Rao.

"My brother is a genius," gloated Bira.

"Be quiet."

" . . . *There are serious ramifications. A high-up FBI official who requested anonymity believes that Rao's words are malicious and call for drastic measures. He assures that his government will seek the extradition of the young Indian for crimes committed against the United States' security interests. Behind the scenes however, it is believed that the Americans think of Rao as a complete idiot who believes in extra-terrestrials, a brilliant and harmless programmer whose skills they would readily make use of."*

"Tell that to Hollywood that there are no extra-terrestrials!" said Brinda sarcastically. "In any case, Dipu is out of danger now. He has moved on. They will have to close the chapter. We all know that the investigation will not be successful. Philippe explained to me that on both the French and the Indian side there is no interest. The whole thing is far behind us now," she insisted. "He has moved on now."

Mrs. Rao smelled a rat. They were hiding something from her.

"He has moved on where? Can someone please tell me? I personally think that he is still badly stuck, along with the rest of us."

Brinda looked her mother straight in the eye: "No need to pretend, you know very well that he wants to marry a Frenchman, that too an old one."

She had said it involuntarily, the truth wanted to come out. Mrs. Rao had never imagined that one day one of her own children, that too the youngest, would stab her in the heart.

Her first reaction was to close her eyes to better concentrate on the blow she had received. She felt like she had died. The morning of December 26th had started so badly. Brinda and Suneet looked on, fascinated by her expression.

"Don't pretend you don't know."

"I know," she sobbed suddenly. I knew it. I've always known."

"Good."

"Of course not," temporized Suneet. "Of course not. That's such an exaggeration. He isn't all that old."

"He IS old," insisted Radhika, choking under her sobs. "He is old just like his country."

"Like his country?"

"That's what I read."

"So what? A younger suitor would be more acceptable to you?"

She seemed to hesitate.

"No, no, no. I'm just saying it like that . . . like one would say 'as stupid as Satish.' I'm not talking about the heart of the matter which is something over which I will never compromise."

"Huh . . . "

"You have brought up a very serious matter, my children . . . "

"So what!"

"It's so serious that I am wondering . . . how we should discuss it."

"It's no big deal, Mummy."

The servant had missed the uncomplimentary remark concerning him. He peeped in from behind the door.

"Get back to your work! Don't keep standing there."

"Mummy," said Brinda with dramatic emphasis. "Are you homophobic?"

"Of course I am," she replied indignantly. "Of course, I mean, my dear, why wouldn't I be, although the fact is that I don't really care."

"That makes sense!"

"I am, without really being so, if you will. Or rather," she added for nuance, "I am not, even as I am vehemently so."

Even Satish, who knew his Memsaab well, appeared impressed.

"You have always been a simple soul," mocked Brinda.

"I believe in the protection of family values. Our Indian family values. I don't give a hoot what they do over there. Plus, I have not lost the sense of what is illegal, if that's what you are referring to," she declared with self-satisfaction as she threw the *pallu* of her sari back over her shoulder.

What was illegal in India was sinful in Europe. To each their own. Two civilizations, both similar – more similar than one realized - when it came to excluding others.

"So over there everybody is crazy, and we are the ones who have it all right, that's what you mean?" Bira tried to reason. "They also have families, they also have principles, and religion . . ."

There was a long silence.

"You cannot compare the light from a candle to the light from the sun; that is how our religion is, compared to others," burst out Mrs. Rao quite mystically.

"Do you really think we can be so boastful in the light of what Dipu has done? Don't you think it's enough . . . "

"Exactly!" she interrupted. "That proves it. Isn't it Satish? I would like to hear your opinion."

"Satishji, pray tell us what you think of Dipu's marriage plans," exclaimed Brinda, raising her pitch.

The servant was exhibiting a most woebegone expression. The day had gotten off to such a bad start as it is thanks to the news about the shortage of onions.

"I just heard the news on the radio."

"So? We are talking about Dipu right now."

"There has been a tsunami. There have been many casualties. People on Marina beach . . . "

It would have taken more than a tidal wave to draw Memsaab's attention away from a subject as dramatic as the one with which they were presently dealing.

"What are you blabbering? Tell us what you think about a union with the Sahib?"

"The coasts of Thailand and Indonesia were also destroyed."

"We are waiting for your opinion!"

"What union?"

"Don't be an idiot, Satish," threatened Mrs. Rao. "I'm already upset with you over of the onions . . . "

"The onion shortage?" asked Bira in astonishment. "That is one thing he is not responsible for at all, I dare say."

"They announced that thousands of people have died," he continued.

"And I am announcing that you are being very annoying. You don't even know what you are talking."

The servant gave up. He finally pronounced his verdict.

"The sahib comes from a good family."

"Would you give him your daughter if you had one? No. So just imagine if you had to give him your son!"

"Everything can be worked out," retorted Satish.

The furious Mrs. Rao pointed to the door, signaling him to get lost.

Helda Schweitzer hesitated. She had two choices: either a very unappetizing pizza with a three centimeter thick crust or a shriveled vegetarian quiche that looked as if it had been vegetating in the heat. For a moment she felt nostalgic for the refined cuisine of her favorite doctor and the tiny dining room that she had left behind in Kovalam.

"What would you like?" asked the young volunteer behind the counter. Hundreds of people were waiting in line for their turn. She decided to fast. It was actually an ideal time for it. It made sense to fast rather than pick the tired looking quiche or the doughy pizza. The doctor would definitely approve. She joined the others who were sitting around a table that had been set up in the ashram garden.

"You aren't eating anything?" asked Philippe in surprise.

"I'm not hungry. I have a reserve of energy," she laughed.

"You didn't find anything you like?" prodded Dipu, who was stuffing himself like a pig. "This is the best pizza I've had in a long time."

"Not now, tomorrow," she replied, making a mental note of going to the village the following day to get her supply of coconuts.

She would manage to survive till then without touching those indigestible poisons that were not even seasoned with asafetida. My *vata* needs *hing*, she reminded herself. The next day, Sunday, she would be back at the Center. The International Friendship would serve her dinner that would be ten times more macrobiotic than all these dishes which were cooked with devotion, for sure, but by incompetent Western disciples who lacked Dr. Joseph's flair and his brilliant culinary guidance.

She had been in the company of her three young friends for over twenty-four hours now; she had been sticking to them like a shadow. After having approached the stage where Amma was giving *darshan*, Helda had requested Abhi to take her back to the car. As much as she would have loved to be embraced by the saint, she did not have a ticket. A ticket was needed to go up to her, like when one travels in the metro. Madame Schweitzer - whose principal mode of spirituality was her coquetry, her prim and proper elegance - would have absolutely refused to turn her age into an advantage. It would be very unfair if she allowed herself to cut in ahead of all these people who had been waiting for hours in the midst of all the chanting, fervor and fatigue.

She held on to Abhi's arm firmly and he immediately assumed the role of the perfect *chevalier*. Philippe and Dipu followed in tow. It was easier going back, despite the crowd. Helda seemed to have acclimated herself. The space that she needed and the multitude were no longer at odds, as if her mind had figured out new ways of evaluating distances. A big crowd, especially one such as this, was something she could take in her stride.

Her sheltered sojourn in Kovalam had totally distanced her from India, she thought to herself. As soon as she was in the car and had heaved a sigh of relief, she began thinking of the ashram. The furtive contacts with strangers that she had just experienced were worth more than pseudo family-relations. Why not go and see from close quarters what went on there? It wasn't spiritual tourism, ah no! The evening with the doctor and the trio was dull. They talked about Paris, the seventies. Insipid. The image of the Indian woman throwing herself into Amma's arms kept appearing before her eyes. Try as she might, she could not get rid of it. It was burnt in her memory. It filled her with trauma. And happiness. Both. Around eleven o'clock that night, with a vexed look, she asked her guests what time they were planning to leave the next day.

"Very early. As early as possible."

"It will take us about three hours to reach there."

"Do you have a driver?" she turned to Dipu.

"We will travel by train till Kollam, and then . . . "

Helda shifted in her armchair.

"I have an idea," she interrupted him in an unsteady voice. "A bus till Trivandrum, a train, and then a taxi . . . You won't get there before noon, that too if you're lucky. If you want we could all go together with my driver. It will be very quick. Less than three hours, I think. I'll spend Saturday night at the ashram and I'll come back on Sunday - what date will that be? - I always have to know the dates. It's the twenty-sixth, I'm sure; what do you say?"

Philippe was not able to conceal his lack of enthusiasm.

"You don't think you will feel tired?"

"Tired!" she exclaimed as if the word had been banned from her dictionary. "Tired . . . I am in form. Heavens! I saw your Amma today, so why not see her tomorrow? You are giving me the opportunity. After all, don't Indians go from one temple to another, throughout the year? I have not done anything else apart from this treatment, isn't that limiting oneself? It's not like me to be like this. I need to expand my horizons. Now that Martina has left, I am free, like air. I want to see Amma again," she concluded.

"Would you like some water?" Dipu asked her.

"Thank you, yes."

There was a lot of activity going on at the ashram. It was because Amma was scheduled to give a special kind of *darshan* that evening, more solemn than the others, known as *Devi Bhava*, during which her aspect as "divine mother" would come to life. Even the wide arm chair where she would receive in her arms those who came to her was going to be special. Thousands of devotees were expected. Whether she wanted it or not, Helda ended up receiving a lot of special attention because of her age.

The ashram was situated on a lagoon, on a narrow strip of land between the sea and the backwaters beyond which were the canals lined with homes and plots filled with coconut palms. It was visible from a distance thanks to its three brightly colored fifteen floor high towers. It felt like a Parisian suburb that had made itself at home in India by the shore of the Arabian sea.

Visitors often arrived by boat; there was a service that linked Alappuzha to Kollam. The travel guides often featured the ashram as just one more curiosity, to be added to the itinerary like a tiger reserve or a tea plantation. The "Hugging Mother," depending on whether the publications were Anglo-Saxon or French, received a treatment that was several paragraphs long. The tourists who came spent anywhere from a few hours to several days before they took the boat back to return to civilization in the beach resort of Varkala.

"Why do Westerners nod their heads up and down to mean yes?"

The thought-provoking question was posed by an elderly Indian gentleman who was conversing with Abhi with a cup of tea in his hand.

"I don't know."

Helda heard the question. She would find out from Dr. Joseph at the earliest opportunity. Yes. Why? Why do we nod that way?

"Well," said the Indian. "It basically reflects an aggressive approach to the world, a desire to conquer it. Rejecting doubt by saying yes through body language, the individual affirms his power. You must have noticed that a dog also moves its head up and down while barking as if it were saying yes in its own violent way. They have imitated the animal."

"Oh!" exclaimed Helda in surprise. "But does it have any other choice? And what about your way of saying yes? How do you explain that?"

"Indians sway their heads in such a way that it almost seems they are saying no - according to your criteria - because they let themselves get carried along more by life, like a wave moving towards the shore; they do not seek obstacles for the sake of finding obstacles. Acceptance does not bring about such body language."

"Hmmm, very interesting. Thank you."

Madame Schweitzer was enchanted. Why had she cloistered herself in the ayurvedic center in that dull little village for so long instead of exploring the thousand and one facets of this country that she was discovering for the very first time at the age of eighty?

The *darshan*, the *Devi Bhava* actually, was about to start. It would undoubtedly last fifteen or so hours. Amma would hug and hug without pausing and receive the never-ending constantly moving line of people with open arms. Philippe got the impression that a new journey, within his own, was about to begin. They entered the immense prayer hall. Helda felt a shiver, like she had the previous evening in Trivandrum. For many years, she had regularly attended the festival at Bayreuth. It was something that she could never miss being the big Wagner fan that she was. This festival with Amma was of a different kind, though really not different in essence.

Philippe sat down on a rug on the floor next to Dipu. He had been hesitant to take a ticket but Abhi had insisted. "Since you are here, don't miss the experience. Get a hug from Amma!" The ticket had a reference number:

5601-5700

Indians and Westerners lived almost segregated at the ashram. Clearly, the pizzas on the one hand, and the *thalis* served on banana leaves on the other did not work very well for unity. The assignment of rooms was also based on the difference of nationality. The color of the *darshan* tickets also differed depending on whether one was Indian or an international visitor. It was like in the trains: there was a quota reserved for people like the foreign sahib. Everything was strange and familiar at the same time. The feeling was constant. Whether one understood it or not did not matter.

At about nine o'clock Philippe decided to call it quits and go to bed. He was not going to sit around and wait for a hug from Amma; he was sleepy! Dipu did some calculating and informed him that his turn would arrive between 4:00 and 5:00 AM. Couldn't he for once wait and remain awake, for Amma's sake? Couldn't he sacrifice one night like all those people around them?

"No!"

He made it clear that he would not sacrifice a night and refused to even set the alarm. Helda decided that she would "hold out" till midnight, maybe one or two more hours beyond that as well, thanks to rest she had accumulated at Dr. Joseph's . . . The idea of going the extra mile and keeping vigil the whole night was tempting. Didn't the beloved Amma sacrifice her own nights for the sake of people who came to see her from far and wide? Helda felt a sense of pride in being part of this crowd like a child who is allowed to stay up till very late on New Year's Eve.

He fell asleep very quickly. He was in her arms and asking her: "Amma. Amma. What do you feel when you are in Toulon or in Oklahoma City? Do you also perceive a difference between India and the rest of the world like us?" She placed her two hands on his head and replied with a smile: "The barrier created by the body and the mind is what separates us from each other. Amma does not feel these differences. For her, there is no difference. A flower is made up of many petals, but it is one. The human body is made up of many elements, but it is one. The world is made up of different countries, cultures, languages, races, people, but for Amma there is just one world, just one."

When he woke up it was already seven o'clock. He had missed

his turn. He got ready quickly, donned a pair of pants and a pale yellow *kurta*, applied his *tilak* (three red lines on his forehead!) and headed for the temple. This part of the ashram felt timeless to him. It was Sunday, the 26th of December. The tragedy brought by the ocean had already begun further south. At the ashram, the night had ended and the day had begun without any disturbance in the atmosphere. The projectors were still beaming Amma and her goddess-armchair onto the monitors. The chanting was also still going on.

Om Namah Shivaya . . . Om Namah Shivaya . . .

There was no fatigue discernable on any face. The *darshan* was not over and would continue till the last ticket was presented.

Although his turn had passed, he was led to the stage where her devotees, those who loved her the most, had surrounded her. He was not sure if he would get a hug even if he wanted one. The previous year, while on a tour of Europe, she had stopped in Toulon. Like in Trivandrum the previous day, he had learnt of her presence at the very last minute and had gone to the huge sports arena that she had been occupying like a rock star and where she had been dispensing her hugs for three days. He had observed Amma's fans. Some left her arms crying, others appeared as if they had been relieved of something heavy, some showed no emotion at all. More strange, he remembered having noticed a young hooligan kind of fellow who had the A of the anarchists tattooed on his hand:

Even they, he thought, even him at any rate, felt a need to see her. He had reached there too late that evening to even get a ticket. The only participant who could have convinced him to embrace Amma was... an anarchist! He also remembered that alongside the long single line of people waiting to enter the *puja* and *darshan* hall, members of the organization had joyfully walked up and down with a bunch of brochures asking everyone, "Have you met Amma? Is this the first time? Have you been hugged by her? Does everyone know Amma? Has everyone already received a hug?" - like intrepid and merry hawkers at a fair advertising their spiritual goods. Come and see the Mother, come.

"Those who have not yet met her, let me know please."

Philippe looked all around. An underprivileged young girl named Sudhamani born into a family of fishermen in a small Kerala village had managed to create a spiritual family all around herself which was defined neither by ties of blood, nor race, nor nationality. "Finally!" He thought to himself. "Finally, here's some good news!"

It must have been a little after eight o'clock, and he decided to go and look for Dipu and also the dear old Helda. How many hours had she slept?Had she liked the view of the Arabian Sea?

"Where are you going?" someone asked him. It was one of the devotees in charge of managing the *darshan*.

"I don't have a ticket; I'm trying to find my friends."

"Wait. Come, follow me."

They were not going to let him leave like that, with his nice yellow silk outfit. Stepping over bodies, he found himself on his knees, at last, only a few feet from Amma who was joyfully chatting with one of her female attendants. He was asked to state his nationality.

"French."

"It's your turn next."

A strong fragrance of rose filled the air all around the saint as if millions of flowers had pressed against her.

All you need is love . . . Hmmm, but first he would have to wait his turn.

All you need is love . . .

Could love wait? They pushed Philippe towards Her - the end of the journey! He stopped moving. He was in her arms. She murmured: "My dear son, my dear son, my, my, my . . . " Two seconds elapsed. The syllables whispered, it was time to move. They thrust a sweet and a tiny envelope containing ash that had been blessed by the Mother into his hands.

"Hey, did you sleep well?" asked Dipu. "No regrets?"

"I just received a hug from her. Where's Helda? Where did she go?"

He had not left Amma's arms crying like other people. Why? What was the reason? Why did there have to be any reason? Did it need to be an experience like when one goes to the theatre or to the stadium to see a football match? Was it an act of love? And if yes, why had he not felt anything? Why had he wanted to have breakfast as quickly as possible and then do something else? Amma had not awakened the small child inside him. Not that morning, December 26. Was there that much dryness in his heart? It was time for some soul-searching . . .

"How was it?" asked Dipu. He had been embraced shortly before 4:00 AM.

"I don't know."

"What did you feel?" he insisted.

"Nothing great."

"Damn!"

"You can say that."

"Tough luck, I guess."

He still had not told him where Helda was.

"No regrets though, I hope."

"No. On the contrary. It's just that I don't know if I felt anything, that's all."

They continued their discussion as the morning advanced and the big hall started getting empty. *Darshan* was over - the special observation of the saint had come to an end.

Why not him, he wondered. Why had Amma's embrace seemed almost strange, almost alien? A new injustice. Could only those who had been lovingly held after birth feel Amma's love fully? Twenty, thirty, forty or fifty years later they embarked on a fresh quest for it and the saint offered them her welcoming arms and her plenitude. What nostalgia did he suffer from? His mother had never taken him in her arms. Amma's open arms thus had to be a little incomprehensible, a closed path.

In the cafeteria next to the temple he started crying in front of Dipu.

Shouts from the outside suddenly reached their ears. "The sea! The sea!" they heard.

The first tidal wave from the tsunami that had hit the shores of Indonesia and Thailand a few hours earlier suddenly surged over the peaceful peninsula where Amma had come into this world.

18
Tsunami

"I cannot pronounce the word or hear it spoken by anyone else without producing one myself," Bira explained apologetically.

"Is it a riddle?" stammered Satish.

Mrs. Rao expressed her impatience.

"This means you did not hear it, my poor Satish! And I'm supposed to be the one who does not have sharp ears!"

"Hear what?"

"I AM SORRY, okay!" squealed Bira.

"So, if I understand it correctly this means that each time we are out of gas in the kitchen and I tell Satish to order a cylinder from the gas agency, I have to make sure that you are not around!"

"That seems to be the case. It would be safer not to say the word around me. It's like yawning. Besides, I have seen . . . No, nothing . . . There are people, as soon as they hear the word *yawn* they start opening their jaws wide . . . "

"It is indeed true," confirmed Satish.

"Oh really?" replied Mrs. Rao.

"It's the same with me," continued Bira. "But it's not a yawn. It comes from further down . . . "

"Okay, all right, all right," interrupted her mother. "We understand, dear. You are a nice girl. You are not going to be that stubborn however, correct? Needless to say, I would prefer if you yawned instead."

"Words have power, they are evocative," warned Bira solemnly.

"You are right. So, have you finished now? Can we talk about something else? Oh, Bira! Again! Nobody said the word this time! You see! Your way of reasoning is completely illogical."

Dipu's sister had a bagful of arguments.

"It is very logical. When I told you words have evocative power, I shouldn't have said so. It came by itself."

"She is right," butted in Satish. Nobody had solicited his opinion. He had been striving to get into Mademoiselle Rao's good books. She still had not forgiven him for putting her kitten in the washing machine. "We have to be very careful with some words. If someone says yawn, we will yawn, and if . . . "

"And if I tell you to shut up, you will shut up!" barked Madame Rao, disconcerted by the apparent rapprochement between the two. "Aren't you ashamed Satish, and you too, Bira? An extraordinary calamity has taken place - they are talking about tens of thousands of people who have perished - and you are going on and on about . . . Satish, I repeat, there is no more . . . in the kitchen. Get it?"

This time Bira didn't need to apologize. A big smile flashed across her youthful face.

"You see! Nothing happened this time, because you did not pronounce it."

"But I thought of it! According to your logic, that should have been enough to influence you. Anyway, I don't care . . . "

"You did not pronounce it," she insisted. "You should not even say that you didn't pronounce the WORD. Because then, there is still a risk."

Confronted with such insanity in the wake of a gross lack of foresight on Satish's part— his failure to stocking up on onions and cylinders of G— Mrs. Rao, feeling distressed, picked up her knitting work. She was no longer in a hurry to finish the sweater that she was knitting for the sahib. Superstitious that she was, the news of the tsunami had shaken her. Her two sons had been in the company of the French sahib at the time of the disaster. There were two possibilities: either he had protected them, or he was the one responsible. He had insisted on going for the trip that weekend. Figuring out how much he was to blame was not an easy task. It did appear that he had a role in all of it. Her instinct caused her to slow down her knitting. She had been trying to finish the sweater while he was having a close encounter with death . . . She shivered at the thought. It would be better if she waited till they returned. Here was proof, yet again, that he brought bad luck, this old sahib that her Dipu was amorous of. All those fishermen's boats destroyed in the sea, south of Madras . . . She suddenly felt rage against him.

"Seriously Bira, listen to me. Don't you think your brother should see a psychologist?"

"Why should he?"

"You know very well. Plus, all this hacking business, it's overwhelming, don't you think?"

"If you even utter the word *psychologist*, I'm going to do *it* again, I'm warning you. You think you're a doctor now?"

"I know, I know it very well that I mean nothing to him now," said Mrs. Rao, in a hurt voice. She was as determined to move the masses to tears by her plight as the late Princess Diana when she had publicly revealed her loneliness in front of the Taj Mahal.

"Aren't you exaggerating just a little?"

"I don't mean anything to you all any more," she repeated, hoping her words would have the same devastating effect as the famous photograph of the princess which had caused a great number of anguished earthlings, from Islamabad to Buenos Aires, to exclaim, "Where is Charles?" as if the monument had been especially constructed so that, lost in Agra, she could influence public opinion. Dipu had shamefully deserted his mother.

"Aren't you exaggerating a little? I'm sure you don't mean

it?" Bira needled her mother using a musical tone.

"I'm exaggerating? To have principles is to exaggerate?

"Can't it be?" replied Bira. "Can't it be, in some cases?"

"I won't let him get married."

"How dramatic!" protested the daughter. "You are such a drama queen, I have to say. That's what you are. You won't let him! You must be dreaming, Mummy! There is nothing you can do to stop this marriage except for taking the Europeans to court for allowing such things."

"I'll do whatever is necessary, just wait and see," she retorted without going into details. "I don't have to take anybody to court. He will obey me in the end. As long as I'm alive, he will not marry the sahib."

"You are so exasperating. I'm going to get a newspaper."

The telephone rang.

"Ammu!"

She waited till Bira had left before asking Ammu the same pressing question.

"Don't you think your brother-in-law should see a psychologist?"

"I'm not the best person to ask for such advice."

"Hmmm. It's always the same. Everyone is so evasive. That's how I see things. It makes me wonder who knows what to do and who does not. What drives me crazy, Ammu, is what he said to his sister before going to Amma's ashram."

"What did he say?"

"He says it's high time we stopped the lying. And that he needs our support during this enquiry, and that the truth, the whole truth, should be told. He told her that he has come out of the closet; do you understand what that means? Brinda is making such a big fuss as if it's my fault, as if I'm preventing him from breathing. Ammu, have you heard this expression before that these English sahibs use – 'coming out'?"

278

"Yes, I have."

"Poor Satish, even he knew about it by listening behind the door. I am the only one who did not know. I am not familiar with the notion and would have preferred it that way. Anyway, he wants to come out of the closet. It means I will have to take measures, like they do in all the families where such things take place. Because, alas, I'm sure we are not the only ones. All this would not have happened if he had not gone to France. By the way, I have a very good story to tell you . . . why am I rambling? I have lost too much time. I did not watch over him like I should have. His poor father did the right thing by leaving us before seeing this day. I have decided:he will go to see a psychologist. And you must have heard about the tsunami..." she continued.

"What has the tsunami got to do with all this?"

"I am so annoyed."

"Hmm," sympathized Ammu.

"He will end up listening. I want him to get medical help. Another thing that he dared to tell his sister: people like him, in India, are dormant volcanoes, because of all the social and family repression."

"And what do you think?"

Mrs. Rao remained silent.

"True. But that's not the issue. There's a cure for everything, right, Ammu dear?"

"It all depends on what one thinks."

"Oh, another thing, everyday I read such astonishing things about the city where Philippe comes from. Can you imagine, in Paris they have a pastry shop for dogs, yes, yes, for dogs . . . "

"For dogs?" exclaimed Satish, pricking up his ears.

"That's what I said. They have all kinds of biscuits for dogs – chicken biscuits, vegetable biscuits, pumpkin biscuits. What kind of country has my son chosen to live in?" she wondered.

"It all makes sense."

"Can we get some of those biscuits?" enquired the servant.

"Shut up, will you! No, not you, I was talking to Satish."

Their conversation became protracted. Mrs. Rao needed to get the weight off her chest. She had done her research. On the legal front, the English, while the sun was setting on their empire, had taken the correct steps. A law passed in 1861 criminalized these kinds of relations. As much as ten years in prison, at least on paper! For hacking, on the other hand, one paid a higher price - about sixty years! It was better not be a hacker in the twenty-first century while illegal relations were almost encouraged!

"What did you say, Ammu, I didn't hear you? Because of Satish. You should not talk when I am on the phone - it's not polite. Those biscuits are not available over here. Our Indian dogs eat chapatis, not chicken flavored biscuits. What, Ammu? I'm treating him like a criminal? Why do you say that? I'm not treating him like a criminal. What purpose would that serve?"

She opened the previous day's paper. On the fourth page she located a brief article: "*In Austria, Croatia and Estonia, unlike in other more advanced countries, there is no civil union between partners of the same sex. A law passed in 2000 enables employees to sue employers for discrimination based on sexual orientation. Guidelines on such issues issued by the European Union are becoming more frequent and are making their impact felt on member states. These three countries stand out as the black sheep within the European Union . . . "*

What a nasty bunch!

"I found this letter on the floor," announced Satish, positioning himself across from Memsaab.

"Show. What is it?"

"I have not read it."

"Then give it to me."

"It looks like Dipu's handwriting."

"Let me see."

He handed over the sheet. "Dear Bira . . . " *I cannot read this*, she thought to herself. "Well, I'll just read the last portion, then you just put it back where you found it, okay? She will be back soon."

"It was lying on the floor, outside her room."

"Let me just read the last few lines. *When I understood that I was letting myself go astray in Paris with my hacking, Bira, I gave myself one year for things to change, for someone to come into my life. If Philippe had not walked into my life, I would have returned to India and become a sanyasi, I had made up my mind...*"

It's not too late, she thought. Let him become a *sanyasi* and follow the teachings of the guru - that would be much better than the disgraceful thing he is planning. I know what I need to do, I will encourage it. He can go to Varanasi, to an ashram, or . . .

"There, put it back. No, just wait, I'll read the whole thing and give it back myself to her. One should not let letters lying around on the floor if one does not want other people to read them."

The loud gate creaked, and all the dogs that were not allowed inside the house began barking in joyful unison. Tommy also joined them. The siren of an ambulance passing through Greenways had been heard earlier but Adyar had quickly regained its calm.

"I have changed my mind, quick, put the letter back."

Mrs. Rao did not allow her daughter to show her the newspaper page where the media was still obsessing over Dipu's doings.

"Come, sit here, my dear, I want to tell you something. Make yourself comfortable. There . . . You know we used to live in Bandra, we were there for a long time. Well, I became pregnant around the same time as one of our neighbors; she was like a sister to me. You know what pact we made?"

"That you would both deliver your babies on the same day?"

"We promised each other that if we were lucky enough to give birth to a boy and a girl, they would have to marry each other. And that is what happened, Dipu was born fifteen days before Diya. Unfortunately we lost contact with each other. She must already be married and well settled by now."

"Maybe not. Would you like me to hire a detective to dig her up?"

"What I'm trying to say is that out of all my children Dipu is the one who, in a sense, got engaged right from birth."

"I don't see how that has anything to do with the situation at hand."

"What I'm trying to say is that I have always loved him a lot."

Bira did not argue. By entangling everyone, by saying this and that, by rigging her emotions to suit her beliefs, her mother really knew how to be exasperating. Even Satish had no waited for Memsaab's monologue to finish.

"You are keeping up with the news, I hope."

"Just read it to me, if you don't mind. I'm feeling faint; this tsunami has completely devastated me."

"I'm warning you, it's becoming more and more confusing. This whole thing has become very hard to understand. *According to sources, Rao's father-in-law is none other than a former minister in the French government who currently holds a very important post. The question being asked is if he was aware of his son-in-law's activities. This time, on the eve of Christmas celebrations, the French press is asking itself . . . "*

"Son-in-law? But for Dipu to be his son-in-law he would have to be married to his daughter. I have never met her, I just know he has a daughter," protested Mrs Rao, succumbing feverishly to another denial attack.

"Would you like me to continue? *Officials in New Delhi have refused to comment. A former director of the Intelligence Bureau, India's intelligence agency, has unofficially stated that the whole affair has been blown out of proportion. The IB has other concerns which are more to the north, he specified. It is believed that Rao got married less than a year ago and is reported to have said that he did not wish to involve his family in his wedding . . .*"

"Outrageous! Such lies! What marriage? There has been no marriage, and that is the real problem. Anyway Bira, if it can save him, they might as well lay the blame on the minister sahib's door. It's actually good for us. Dipu must have known that he is going to cover up for him."

At the Azhikkal beach, two kilometers from the ashram, the sun was going down. It was a perfect picture postcard sunset with crimson streaks across the sky. The villagers lit the pyre. The corpses were coming in. Two days earlier, the tidal wave had claimed around forty people in the village. Most of the houses on the shore had been destroyed when the sea had surged in just before one o'clock. After the first onslaught, which had not killed anybody, the Arabian Sea had retreated. The water had receded hundreds of meters from the shore, and nobody had understood why the majestic sea had pulled back so far. The lull had lasted almost a half hour - enough time for everyone to forget the first wave that had completely submerged the white sands.

The fishermen had resumed their activities during that time. Far from the shore, the sea was getting ready, preparing itself for a major attack. The second wave was a killer, a giant wave. It came like a huge wall and crushed the entire village and the huts of the fishermen erected on sand. When the water retreated several hours later, it left behind toys, shoes, and kitchen utensils scattered all over the land near the beach. The village had slowly taken stock of its dead. By the end of the day, the Arabian Sea had become calm, as if nothing had happened.

The following day, a camp for those who had lost their homes and loved ones was rapidly set up. The villagers brought logs and firewood. Assistance flowed in from other villages. The bodies were first transported to a tent and then to the cremation site. The sudden arrival of the body of a young child caused at least five women to react the same way: they all ran up to the corpse, each one thinking it was her child. There was chanting of verses from the eighth chapter of the *Bhagavad Gita*. It was accompanied by the sound of crickets. The fire crackled. After the cremation, Philippe, Abhi and Dipu, their palms joined in prayer, sat facing the lagoon. A harmonium, as well as a microphone and an amplifier arrived from the ashram, and everyone - villagers, visitors, devotees – participated in the chanting. *Lokah samastah sukhino bhavantu,* may all beings in all the worlds be happy . . . Families kept vigil the whole night around the burning pyres on the beach.

The chaos had struck Kerala last, several hours after Chennai and the Tamil Nadu coast. After the first wave had come sweeping in around 12:20, the ashram authorities had made announcements on loud speakers, in many languages, asking residents to evacuate to the fifteen storey building. The two old elephants of the ashram, Ram and Lakshmi, were made to go up the temple steps. Then it was the turn of the cows. They were led up to the big hall inside the sacred building. The water had come up till the kitchen where a huge vessel containing a hundred kilos of cooked rice suddenly transformed itself into a boat out of a children's fairy tale and began to float. Half an hour later, water rushed in from the sea with a thundering noise and submerged the ashram.From the roof of the temple, where they had taken refuge, Philippe and Dipu, squeezed next to each other, contemplated the unbelievable scene: the wave, which had started out from the north of Indonesia and had traversed thousands of miles in a few hours, was lashing out violently for the last time.Having lost some of its force along the way, it had encountered the resistance of the high towers against which it seemed powerless. "She has built a Noah's Ark for us," said a young woman next to them, referring to Amma - an observation that was not false given the fate of the fishermen barely a few hundred meters away.

Abhi had seen Helda only once during the morning hours. In just a few hours, the old lady had woven a network of relations that comprised a wide range of people, from the ashramites to pure Western products of spiritual tourism. She had not felt bored at all. Once they descended from the roof, they began to feel anxious. Where was she?

She had left a short while ago, they were told. She had been among the first to be evacuated; Amma had placed her in the care of her close associates. They took a ride in a ferry to cross over to the other side. They were finally all together again, on the campus of a university belonging to the ashram which had been converted into a shelter.

Her calm seemed almost frightening to them. Madame Schweitzer was pale, her look empty. She lit up when she saw them.

"Helda, Helda, where were you?"

"With everyone else. I wasn't afraid," she told Philippe embracing him, as if she were trying to convince herself. "I didn't even have the time to be afraid, you know. There was no time to even blink an eye. I thought of nothing, not even that my hour had come. It was so powerful, my god, I was downstairs, I saw the wave come; they pushed me up the stairs . . . ." She paused and closed her eyes.

"I will never forget the noise," Philippe confessed, holding her hands firmly.

A few days after the cremations of December 28th, they left the ashram to take Helda back to Kovalam. They took the same road, but in the other direction, towards Thiruvananthapuram. It did not run parallel to the shore, and there were no signs indicating what had happened. Gradually, they learnt how the tsunami had wreaked death and destruction in many countries almost simultaneously and what had happened elsewhere. Tragedy had taken place in other places too, not just where they had been.Chennai had also been affected. In the car, they talked about the wave as if it had been a person who, in an outburst of rage, had picked up a machine gun (no, that didn't describe it well enough) and wreaked devastation all long the coast. The onslaught had lasted just a few minutes - it had virtually been a war, one against which everybody had been defenseless. They tried to find out how everything had started, at what time, how long it had taken. The most incredible stories were already in circulation. A dog, and also a cobra had saved a little child. The dog had returned to get the forgotten child from a hut and had taken it up a hill. When had the sea returned to a state of calm? What did *they* owe their lives to? On the fourth day, they got a chance to listen to eyewitness accounts on television; they watched the amateur videos. Helda turned her eyes away. The same wave that had struck the ashram had also buffeted Peru, Canada, and France. Satellites had tracked the wave's itinerary. It had moved in a pattern which had surprised the experts. Guided by underwater craters it had been unpredictable, complex, and had circled the earth several times before losing strength and bidding its victims adieu. Ocean-floor sensors had detected it even twenty-four hours after the earthquake. It had been higher in Peru, which was about twenty thousand kilometers from the earthquake's epicenter in the Indian Ocean, than in Cocos Islands, situated more or less a thousand five hundred kilometers south of the zone where the initial rupture had occurred. Why had the Wave been higher in Peru than in Sumatra? The explanation was given by a scientist they met in a refugee camp. The east-west orientation of the energy of the tidal wave and the action of the craters that had concentrated it had determined the power of the Wave. It had made its way wherever it could in order to diminish its force. It had measured 45.2 centimeters in the Falklands, 26.4 centimeters in Alaska and 8.1 centimeters in Brest.

They discussed the refusal of the government to accept assistance from other countries. India, so proud of its new image as an emerging power, could afford to decline aid for its fifteen thousand victims! It made Philippe and Helda angry. Dipu and Abhi remained silent.

"Why are they refusing international help?"

"They will not refuse it for long," predicted Dipu. "They have not gauged the magnitude of the disaster."

In Kovalam, Dr. Joseph came out on the verandah to receive them. He gave them news from the other villages. Further south, in Kanyakumari where Philippe had spent a couple of days a few weeks earlier, the toll had been particularly heavy.

"The worst affected," he added, "was the district of Nagapattinam. More than five thousand dead. The second wave was the one that caused so much death."

"Is it far from here?"

"Not too far," replied Abhi. "It's on the way to Chennai."

"Can we stop there? We'll do whatever we can, to help."

They took leave of their friends. Though Dr. Joseph was not very keen on her departure, Helda decided she would go back to Germany earlier than planned. She immediately left for the village to get her ticket changed.

Mixed with the sea breeze and the sour smell of the lime-scented antiseptic powder covering the roads and by-roads, was the odor of death that permeated the air. It had been a week since the tidal wave had struck. The Rao brothers and Philippe stopped in the village of Nagapattinam. The stench was suffocating; it felt stuck in the back of their throats. They left the beach and made their way back towards the road. The stench seemed to follow them. They encountered Chandra, a young municipal employee, a *dalit* by caste.

"How long have you been wearing that mask?"

"On the first day, we had no masks, no gloves, no shoes even, we worked with our bare hands," explained the "untouchable" whose job consisted of collecting garbage and removing and dismembering dead cows. After the tsunami, he and his colleagues had been summoned. In normal times, he worked in another village. Hundreds of *dalits* had been brought in as reinforcement to sweat out the tropical heat and rid the village of Nagapattinam of its thousands of corpses. Inhabitants belonging to other castes, terrified by the risk of disease and as discouraged as the two brothers and Philippe Delcourt because of the terrible smell, balked at the work all the more so since they knew very well what awaited them: in the sand and in the debris they would only discover the bodies of dead friends and neighbors. The *dalits* of the region would do the work. Although a week had passed since the catastrophe and although the zone of destruction was limited to a narrow band of land next to the sea, each day brought with it the discovery of new corpses, discovered because of the stink and the swarms of flies.

"It's better now, we have all the necessities. It's our job, in any case. Who will do it if we don't? Whether it's a cow, a dog, or a human, it is we who clean up."

Not far from there, another pyre was lit with an old tire and palm leaves. The body of a young woman that had just been discovered under the debris was thrown into the fire.

"This is nothing. The worst was when I reached the first day, one hour after the second wave. On the beach there were stray dogs that were tearing up and eating the bodies of a woman and a child. The police came and shot them."

"And what about aid? Did the *dalits* who lost everything receive assistance?"

Chandra looked at the Frenchman with surprise.

"We received help, but after the others, in the end. They first helped the fishermen and the others. We were provided aid later. The farmers also did not get as much help as the fishermen, although some of them also lost everything. With all the salt in the fields, they will not be able to grow rice anytime soon. It's a catastrophe."

Philippe asked his question again. Chandra confirmed what he had said. The *dalits* had not received the same treatment. How could an earthquake measuring 9 on the Richter scale and a tsunami killing 250,000 people in a few hours have breached the walls of caste and creed? That was not their role.

"And over there, in Nambiar Nagar," he continued, "I know at least a dozen families who were not allowed to come inside the refugee camp, so they are living out in the open, on the street, they have not been helped like others. They don't even let them approach the facilities set up by the United Nations."

Abhi seemed to be ill-at-ease as he translated Chandra's account for Philippe.

"So, finally, two days ago, they built separate amenities especially for *dalits* so that there wouldn't be any friction. We don't need that kind of trouble after all that has happened. Everyone has faced their share of suffering. They give them the leftovers, like dogs, I saw it, they don't have the right to use the same toilets, they don't have the right to drink the water given by the UN. The fishermen stop them. I am lucky to still have my house and my job. But they lost everything. They are denied even the biscuits and the milk powder. 'It's not for you,' they tell them. They took away all the bags of rice, the clothes. They did not let them enter Neelayadatchi temple when the rice and the money were being distributed. A family went to a school where the homeless had taken shelter and they were told that there was no more place inside. I know it isn't true. The truth is that they did not want any *dalits* inside their beautiful buildings."

Philippe looked at Chandra. He seemed as exhausted by the injustice as by the back-breaking task of extracting corpses.

"That's not what I read," corrected Abhi, addressing Philippe. "Everyone received aid. What he is saying isn't true. He is exaggerating, lying. If the fishermen are blocking aid it's not the authorities' fault."

"It cannot be possible that he is not telling the truth!" exploded Philippe. "I believe him. I don't want to stay here anymore. It's disgusting. They excluded these people during the worst possible calamity. Such discrimination is not tolerable. It's unacceptable," he repeated on the brink of tears.

"Don't preach like that. Stop accusing us of discrimination," said Abhi hotly. "I think India has treated you very well."

"Me? Definitely! India has treated me very well. Foreign sahibs like me are a privileged caste here. But what about them?"

"Another family went to see the District Collector," continued Chandra. "He told them not to worry, that they would be given shelter, and then he left. Afterwards they never saw him again. And even the *dalit* fishermen in the refugee camps, they are kept at bay. They cannot come close when the trucks arrive with the food. They sleep outside, on the verandah. Everyone else has been given rooms. Some aid organizations did not have a choice; they have started preparing meals for *dalits* in separate kitchens. If necessary, they will have to set up special refugee camps for *dalits* in the end. It is important to avoid any further friction."

Another tragedy had superimposed itself on the first, at least in the eyes of the French sahib. Abhi and Dipu seemed resigned, as if they didn't have a right to take sides. Philippe gave Chandra some money instructing him to distribute it among the people he knew, *dalit* or not, according to his discretion. The Rao brothers remained silent. They departed from the village.

"Government aid has not been confiscated," Dipu said in defense, a few moments later. "It's just not possible. Everyone has received it."

"And the separate camps for the *dalits*, what about that? Do they exist or don't?"

"Discrimination exists," Abhi sighed, with regret in his voice.

"So the response to the tsunami in Nagapattinam is proof that castes are a catastrophe for this country," retorted Philippe.

"Stop all this moralizing!" Dipu warned him, feeling annoyed.

"I'm not moralizing."

Dipu did not respond. They were all tired. Only the driver of their Ambassador gave Philippe a smile in the rearview mirror.

Upon their arrival in Chennai, an email from his father immersed him in the hacking incident again. "Things aren't going too badly here. Christmas and the tsunami have been a blessing. Imagine, this is what we are getting to read these days: *It is believed that individuals closely related to Senator Delcourt were involved in hacking of certain American military sites. The incident risks causing a scandal and could end up becoming an embarrassment for the senator in the run up to the Referendum campaign in which he has already put a lot at stake. In a live interview yesterday morning on a public channel he declined to comment on the affair. His refusal, which was accompanied by a nervous fit of laughter, was reminiscent of Giscard's attitude during the Diamond affair.* Do you realize, my son? It has now reached a state where anything goes. Giscard and the diamonds! Who benefits by spreading such stupid ideas?

Who is orchestrating the leaks? Actually, I'm not writing this email to talk to you about these things. I wanted to thank you for yours; I know there were no Westerners among the victims in India, but it was reassuring to hear from you so soon. Contrary to what they are saying, this affair will not escalate into something big. I'll make a public statement after the festivities and I will announce that you are both engaged to each other. I will announce your imminent marriage. Since they are asking for a scandal, they can have one. I suppose there will be a scandal in India too, tsunami or no tsunami. It will be the second tsunami, perhaps? Prepare Dipu's family. The media will have a field day. I am assuming the family is already aware. The speech of the Spanish Prime Minister is nothing compared to what I will dish out. They have been creating scandals over nothing, they are about to get what they didn't bargain for. There is nothing to fear, it will quiet down. There is a big difference between those who concentrate on politics and all these sheep who are loyal only to their own party interests. I belong to the first category, and I am proud of it (and a minority). A member of the National Front demanded that I be put on trial for my "deliberate insult to French identity." Always the same old story. If that is the line of reasoning they start following in all the other countries of the Union, we will never reach anywhere. They are obsessed with national identity, and I am not! They are obsessed with our former colonial power, and me, I combat this erstwhile power that infiltrates into our public life in other ways.Long live globalization, if it puts countries back in their correct place, and if it enables us to throw our masks away. I will write at greater length to you again tomorrow. Wishing you a happy return to Madras."

Looking very elegant in her new dark-red sari, Mrs. Rao welcomed them back. She was knitting furiously, trying to finish Philippe's sweater. She still had a long way to go before it would be ready. Her upper lip trembled when she heard what they had experienced on the morning of December 26th, but she did not show any other emotion or say anything. She only had one comment:

"And during that time, your sister . . . Bira . . . was busy . . . ." Afraid of what she was going to say, she checked herself.

"Busy with what? What did she do?"

"She was busy yawning!" she suddenly remembered.

The episode involving the LPG cylinder that she had asked Satish to replace in the kitchen came to her mind. It must have taken place at the exact same hour when the second wave had swept across the ashram.

"How interesting!" said Philippe wryly. "While people were dying, Brinda was yawning, is it? Mind you, in the final analysis, it's all good . . . "

"I'm sorry. Of course not, that's not what I was trying to say. Satish will serve you dinner."

And the truth? When would it ever be possible to tell the truth, all the truths, even the inconvenient ones? The right of life to contradict itself had not come into this world with her. *It is me Radha, Radhika Rao, who precipitated my husband's death by giving him his medicines in bigger doses in the end. And now I am here to stop my son from getting married. It is not Dr. Panayappan who should spend his final days in prison like my Sushil had predicted. I only gave him more pills than he should have taken that day.*

No. Never. Some truths are never meant to come to light. Not even when one is very old.

ACKNOWLEDGEMENT

How can one say thank you to a country? It's hardly possible. Particularly in my case. For several reasons, I never developed the habit of saying thank you to mine . . . . So I will just say thank you to my Indian friends. They helped me with so much precious information and advice. I doubt whether I could have written this story without them. The material is theirs. I pay tribute to Kyamas Anklesaria, Shagoon Satpathy, Joydeep Ghosh, Govind Kumar, Niladri Chatterjee, Balaji Kesavan, Jai Prakash Shukla, Radhika Koppikar, and Manish Garg. They all shed light on aspects of Indian family life unknown to me. And as a stranger, how do I say thank you to all the people I met, sometimes so briefly? People who have no names in my memory. Their invisible support has been powerful just like the support I received from my beloved *amie,* Sheila Moore. Many thanks also to Martina Zimmermann who encouraged my Indian adventures, and to Shonu Nangia who translated my novel into English. Our discussions about the cultural and textual intricacies were simply fantastic. I am especially indebted to my agent, Sherna Khambatta. It has been a joy working with her. Internet email servers have probably crashed due to the high number of emails we exchanged! Many thanks also to Uddipana Goswami. May the god of coincidences, if such a god exists, bless them all. *Merci beaucoup*!

I dedicate this novel to my late parents whom I miss so much.

MINI NAIR

THE FOURTH PASSENGER

'An inspirational story . . . a terrific read' *Publisher's Weekly*

'A lovely novel . . . affecting and inspiring' Shashi Tharoor

'A feel-good read' *The Bookseller*

Set in Mumbai during the Hindu-Muslim conflict of the early 1990s, *The Fourth Passenger* is the story of four women raised with traditional Indian values, whose partnership give them the temerity to stand up against the religious extremism. Having reached their thirties and disillusioned with their lives and husbands, their decision to open an urban food stand is mingled with their memories of a distant past when two of them loved the same man. But, in order to establish their fledgling business, they must contend with individual temperament, extortionists, ruthless competitors, and most importantly, the prevailing religious intolerance.

Mini Nair has had two of her books published in India. A post graduate in chemistry, Mini Nair lives with her family and twin daughters in Mumbai where she was also born and brought up. *The Fourth Passenger* is her first novel.

Hardcover | £14.99 | $24.95
ISBN 978-93-80905-06-8
Available at your nearest bookstore

www.romanbooks.co.in

FIONA McCLEAN

FROM UNDER THE BED

'Compelling . . . fulfilling read' *The Bookseller*

'More than a journey . . . an experience' Mary Wood

Alice loves to paint pictures of fish. Her only problem is her addiction to cakes and pastries. To feed this obsession, she steals . . . and to rid herself of her spoils, she makes herself sick. Stick thin, Alice puts her fragile mind into the care of a psychiatrist, Professor Lucas, and tries to learn the rules people should live by. But her recovery soon brings a new and dangerous addiction—Brendan. As Alice struggles to cope with Brendan's violent outbursts, her dying father and poverty, she takes solace in her job at a massage parlour where she finds comfort with motherly Helen. But these are just temporary respites as her life with Brendan spirals downwards becoming a nightmarish maze.

Fiona McClean was born in Dusseldorf, Germany as the daughter of an army family. After studying Fine Arts at the University of Wales, Newport, she now lives the life of an accomplished painter in South France. Fiona loves to spend her time writing and painting, walking and horse riding. *From Under the Bed* is her debut novel.

Hardcover | £14.99 | $24.95
ISBN 978-93-80905-05-1
Available at your nearest bookstore

www.romanbooks.co.in